WINTER QUARTERS

Also by the same author and available from NEL :

THE CUNNING OF THE DOVE
THREE'S COMPANY
FAMILY FAVOURITES
KNIGHT WITH ARMOUR
THE LADY FOR RANSOM
COUNT BOHEMOND
FOUNDING FATHERS
ELEPHANTS AND CASTLES
THE LITTLE EMPERORS

Winter Quarters

Alfred Duggan

NEW ENGLISH LIBRARY
TIMES MIRROR

First published in 1956 by Peter Davies Ltd., this edition 1972
© Alfred Duggan 1956

*

FIRST NEL PAPERBACK EDITION APRIL 1974
Reprinted March 1975

*

NEL Books are published by
New English Library Limited from Barnard's Inn, Holborn, London, E.C.1.
Made and printed in Great Britain by Hunt Barnard Printing Ltd., Aylesbury, Bucks.

45001775 3

CONTENTS

Prologue

We came back two days ago from the last patrol of the year,
and now we face four months of stagnation in winter quarters.
I enjoy patrolling the Sea of Grass, though we hardly ever
meet the Red Riders; even though our horses go unshod, and
we muffle their bits with pieces of rag, the raiders nearly
always hear us coming and avoid us. They are not interested
in honourable fighting; all they want is to snap up unprotected
travellers and pillage outlying farms. Sometimes we stumble
on their waggons, and then a few knocks yield us good
plunder.

The best thing about a patrol is that it gets us out of Margu,
an unpleasant place. The district is densely inhabited, but no
one lives here of his own free will. The farmers are serfs; and
the garrison is made up of people like me, slaves or fugitives
from the outer world, who must ride for the Great King or be
drafted to toil in his copper-mines. Even the Parthian nobles
who command us are exiles, posted to this edge of the Empire
in honourable disgrace. We have all drifted here because this
is the extreme limit of the world.

What is odd is that Margu lies on the limit of more than one
world. During that last patrol we were reminded of this once
again. We had been riding all night, slithering over the frozen
tussocks of the Sea of Grass; our horses could hardly keep their
feet, and we all knew that henceforth we must keep them
stabled until the spring thaw. As the sun rose over the limit-
less plain, climbing above a clear-cut horizon that really does

7

look like the open sea, our Parthian commnader halted us with a wave of his hand, calling: 'Now we return to Margu.'

I suppose he saw the boredom on our faces. We had all hoped for one brush with the Red Riders before we settled down for the winter. He tried to encourage us with a well-worn catchphrase: 'Yes, back to Margu. Where is Margu? You tell me.'

This was our cue to bellow in unison: 'Margu is the navel of the universe.' It is the refrain of a long poem the peasants chant as they follow the plough, a poem which tells of Margu as the most ancient city in the world and the best. Certainly it is a very old place. Here Alexander founded a city, naming it Antiocheia Margiana after one of his generals; but after they had founded the city Alexander and his general Antiochus got away as quick as they could.

I looked out over the Sea of Grass, and thought what a queer setting it is for the navel of the universe. The Sea of Grass looks its best at sunrise, or rather it then looks least repellent. The horizontal light picks out little hollows, and for a few moments there is the illusion of hills and shade; the sky is bright blue before the midday haze has turned it yellow; birds sing, and you may see a gazelle, surprised by daylight, scuttling off to the lair in the long grass where he will lie hidden until nightfall. Perhaps it is not such a bad landscape in itself; it is the knowledge that if you rode for a month to the north, east, or west you would see the same scene repeated, and that the dusty, waterless plain stretches far beyond the knowledge of man, that weighs on the soul.

Our chorus, that Margu is the navel of the universe, had been introduced into the regiment to stop arguments as to where it lay. For though we had all come a long way to get here, we had come from different directions. I lead a section of a dozen troopers, and naturally I know something of their earlier lives (though I never ask indiscreet questions). Of this dozen one is a Black Cloak Scythian from the far north, who thinks Margu the hottest place in the world (as it is, in summer); three are fugitives from the wrath of an Indian king, and they think Margu the coldest and most northerly city in the world (in winter one might agree with them); six, including myself, come from the lands which obey Rome, and we of course think of Margu as lying almost east of the sunrise; and two are beardless Huns. These two tell a most fascinating story; and they stick to it, drunk or sober, until they have persuaded me that it is the truth.

They say that a very long way to the east, six months' riding for Huns (which means about a year for other men), there is a boundary to the Sea of Grass. A great wall girdles the whole earth, and on the other side of it lies the Land of Silk, with cultivated fields and stone cities, and all the works of civilised men that we know by the Mediterranean. When the Huns have finished fighting their cousins they plan to storm this wall, and sack the cities on the other side.

Thus you might truly say that Margu is the navel of the universe. The Sea of Grass divides the worlds of men: the Land of Silk to the east, India to the south, the true and important world to the west; and Margu lies in the midst, a fertile plain guarded by men who have travelled incredibly far from every direction to reach it.

When the sun was fully up our commander called a halt, for no one hopes to catch Red Riders by daylight. We dismounted, loosening our girths and giving the horses a mouthful of water from canvas bags we carried on the saddle. Then we drank a very little ourselves, while our commander watched us.

We stood by our horses, stretching our legs and munching biscuit. Presently the Black Cloak drew his sword and stuck it in the ground; he stood before it with his head bowed, and the Huns came up to stand beside him. I knew they were praying, to the North Wind and the naked sword. These are the only gods worshipped by true Scythians, though Huns also reverence demons. Ten years ago I myself would have prayed at sunrise, to Lugh of the sky and Epona of the horses; but the gods of my kin are far away and it seems useless to call on them. A man feels lonely without helpers, and I decided that when we got back I would ask the Black Cloak to teach me his prayer; though of course he was not seeking help, he was begging his gods to spare him until next time. If the North Wind does not get a Scythian the sword will.

The Indians did not pray, for their gods cannot be worshipped away from home. One of the Romans began muttering a hymn to Isis, and I drew away. I dislike goddesses, or rather I dislike the Goddess. She can go anywhere, but so far she has not troubled us in Margu, and I hope this lonely worshipper does not call her down to him.

Soon the sun went in and a north wind, with flurries of snow, set us hastening southward to the farmlands. I rode alone at the head of my section. The only troopers I could chat with easily were my fellow-captives from the Roman army; but the Parthians are understandably suspicious if we seem to cling together, and it would be bad policy for me to ride with them in the presence of a Parthian officer.

In the afternoon we began to skirt the swamp which is the end of the River of Margu. The hot sun drinks up this river, and it never reaches the sea; that is one reason why unguided strangers cannot cross the Sea of Grass. We emptied our waterbags and at once filled them again, and as dusk was falling came to the first cultivated fields.

In very hot weather the woods and hedges of Margu, and the glint of water from the irrigation ditches, have a certain charm. At the end of autumn, when ice is beginning to seal the swamp, the whole place looks desolate and dreary. The fields lay fallow, sere and frost-bitten; the shaggy cattle cowered back to wind, and the handsome horses were all indoors for the winter. There were few peasants about, and they, muffled in thick felt, looked pinched and miserable; they are a people who can endure fierce heat, but they have never learned how to cope with the biting cold that plagues them every winter.

The horrid little village where we halted was as uninviting as ever. The only houses are one-storey cabins of mud, and they lie scattered among the fields, not concentrated in a community. Someone once laid out a village green, but the only buildings facing it are our barracks and a big rambling inn, with much more accommodation for animals than for men. There is, of course, a city of Margu, where if you look hard you can see traces of the Greek columns of Antiochus; but it lies forty miles south of this margin of the cultivated land, and we seldom have the leisure and the energy to visit it. No trooper can leave his quarters for more than half a day unless he arranges that a comrade will look after his horse.

The whole place is as flat as the palm of your hand; there is nothing to be seen but scattered groves of trees, and the irrigation ditches make it impossible to ride off the main road. When I first came here, more than eight years ago, I had a good look at the whole settlement; since then I have never bothered to travel more than a mile from my parade-ground, except on duty.

We were dismissed at our barracks, and told that we might rest for three days as a reward for our arduous patrol; though of course there would be the usual morning and evening stables, to make sure we looked after our horses. When I had rubbed down and bedded my horse I walked over to my own cabin. As a section-leader I draw double pay, and our commander lets me sleep out so long as he knows where I am. I have a little cabin behind the barracks, with a woman to keep house for me.

Alitta is a good girl. She is careful with money, and cooks no worse than her neighbours; though I must still summon up my courage to face her suppers, even after eight years in Margu. I picked her up two years ago, when we caught some waggons of the Red Riders; but she was born in another Scythian tribe. They had stolen her to sell, which was why they had left her a virgin. Now we have a boy nearly a year old, and another child on the way. I can't understand very much of her language, but we get along well enough.

One thing about her pleases me; she has no special female religion of her own, or if she has I have never noticed it. When she met me at the door of the cabin she bowed to my sword, and whenever it blows she bows to the North Wind; I have never caught her worshipping the Goddess.

Of course, since she is a true Scythian of the Sea of Grass, she had known for hours that the patrol was coming home. Scythians know where every horse in the world is at every moment of the day. There was a hot stew waiting for me, and in

11

our bed a copper warming-pan. But when I had eaten and was getting ready for sleep she made me understand that there were interesting travellers at the inn. A man from the sunset, who could talk my native language, was what she said; though of course there is no one within a thousand miles who talks my native language, and Alitta has never heard me speak it.

I put on my best trousers and a white felt cloak, to walk over to the inn. The ostler told me that a merchant from the Tigris, some kind of half-Greek, was buying cotton in the district. He had meant to return that night to Margu City, but the weather had made him change his mind and he was stopping until to-morrow. At present he was eating, but he had promised that in half an hour he would tell his news in the main room.

That is the custom of Margu, as it is the custom of my home-land. We exiles hunger for news of the outer world; a traveller would have no peace if he allowed every chance comer to question him, so it has been laid down that travellers must be left unmolested if they promise to tell all they know at a definite time.

The main room was full of Romans, sitting frugally before untasted cups of wine; but the other troopers were not interested in a traveller from the Tigris, and the place was not too crowded. I joined another section-leader, Marcus Sempronius, a genuine citizen of Rome who had once been a legionary. He was the only full citizen in our barracks, and a very lonely man; but he was always glad to see me because my Latin, though incorrect, is fluent. Together we bought a jug of wine to reward the teller of news, and that gave us the right to sit by him and ask questions.

The traveller, when he appeared, was a seedy little man, fat and pompous and evidently saddle-sore. But he knew the customs of Parthian travel, and that the sooner he told all the sooner he would get to bed. I was disappointed to find I could not understand his Greek, which he pronounced oddly; but Sempronius, who was more or less bilingual, translated swiftly into Latin.

First the traveller spoke a rolling period about the peace and prosperity of Parthia; that was for the benefit of the police spies listening in a corner, and we were too tactful to ask questions about the civil war between rival sons of the Great King which is said to be raging in the mountains of the south. Then he boasted that he had left the Tigris only three months ago, and that a friend in Syria had sent him a message just before he set out. 'There is still war between Parthia and Rome.' Sempronius translated, 'but this winter there will be no campaign. The Roman army on the edge of the desert has dispersed. The Romans are about to fight among themselves, because their king has been murdered in full council, stabbed in the back by his leading councillors. Do you hear that, Camillus? Whom do you think this bag of lard would call the King of Rome?'

A few questions settled the point. It was Caesar himself who had been murdered, last March, in the Senate House. Sempronius and I did not wait for more. We went out to walk together on the moonlit parade-ground, where we could not be overheard.

'What shall we do now, my Gallic barbarian?' asked Sempronius softly. 'You advised us to accept our fate, serving our new masters loyally; because Caesar would come to rescue us in the end. Now Caesar has gone the way of his colleagues. In Rome they will be too busy to remember a few prisoners on the rim of the world. Will you come with me if I take a chance on the hospitality of the Red Riders?'

'You have seen what the Red Riders do to their prisoners,' I answered. 'Last month you helped me to clear up that mess by their camp-fire. Is there anyone else who can defeat the Parthians and force them to release us? I know there is no other Roman who could lead an army from the Euphrates to Margu.'

'If Crassus couldn't beat the Parthians no one can. But you were always a staunch Caesarian. Very well, the Romans won't fight to free us until they have finished this round of the civil war. Either we escape unaided, or we stay here for the rest of our lives.'

'My dear Marcus, we have argued this before. Unless we go due west by the guarded road we must plunge into the Sea of

Grass. We have horses and arms, and if we choose our time we may not be missed for a day or two. But in the Sea of Grass we will die of thirst unless the Red Riders catch us; and no one can travel the guarded road without a pass. You know as well as I do that we are here, armed, in Margu, because this un-walled district is the strongest prison in Parthia. Perhaps we might persuade our comrades to mutiny all together, and so cut a way by force through the Red Riders.'

'We might, if we could agree on where to go. Can you see Huns and Indians riding west? Or would you yourself like to ride east to the Land of Silk? Anyway, some trooper would betray us for the price of a pot of wine. Then we would end in the copper-mines.'

'What do you suggest?' I said in exasperation. I was still shaken by the news of my old leader's death.

'Don't talk to me. I must think,' answered Sempronius, and walked on in silence.

Then he turned to me with a resolute air. 'Camillus, my old comrade, didn't you once pass for a citizen? Come and meet my wife.'

'In Rome I was known as Licinius Camillus, but that was quite irregular, as I have told you before. I am a Gaul, not a Roman. As for your girl, I've seen her often enough. Do you want me to take her off your hands?'

He frowned in silence, then caught my arm and hurried me to his cabin.

His girl came out to greet us, surprised that he should have brought home a guest. In this exile one of our few amusements is to steal one another's concubines, and a wise man does not introduce his comrades to the woman of his house. She was a mountaineer from the south, with eyes as blue as a German's and a fairly pleasing complexion, ruined by rancid butter which she smeared on her cheeks to protect them from the wind.

Marcus faced me, and spoke formally in Latin. 'I, Marcus Sempronius Capito, of the Scaptian tribe, a citizen, hereby take to wife Gaia, daughter of a citizen of unknown gens and tribe, in the presence of Marcus Licinius Camillus, citizen.' Then he relaxed, smiling.

'There,' he said cheerfully, 'you don't often get so many legal fictions in one sentence. Her name isn't Gaia, her father is no citizen, and you are not a citizen either. But it's the best I can do. Perhaps my children will be legitimate.'

At last I understood. 'Then you are staying for the rest of your life? You won't try to escape? Then why bother about the status of your sons, if you have any?'

'Because Rome never forgets. With Caesar dead we shan't be rescued for years, probably not before I have died of old age. But rescued we shall be, in the end. My sons will grow up Parthian soldiers, and their native tongue will be Margian. Yet if they want to go back to civilisation when the time comes, perhaps they may claim citizenship.'

He wrote a few words on a scrap of sheepskin, and asked me to seal it by pressing my finger-ring on a blob of clay. He wrote so easily and quickly that it gave me an idea.

'I also shall stay here,' I said, 'and my girl has already borne me a son. He cannot be a citizen, but one day he might return to his father's people, if rescue comes. Yet if I am dead he will know nothing of his rightful inheritance far in the west. Marcus, will you write down my story as I tell it? Then if my son ever gets free any Roman can read it to him.'

I had made up my mind on the instant. I would live and die in Margu. I had intended, one day, to run away and join the Red Riders; that was why I had taken a Scythian concubine, who could teach me the language. The Red Riders are treacherous and cruel, but strangers who can ride and fight are sometimes permitted to enter their tribe.

Now that I am staying, I see that there is something to be said for Margu. You get enough to eat here, and the horses are magnificent. But the best thing about it is the absence of the Goddess. Since even his mother worships only the North Wind and the naked sword my little Acco will grow up a true warrior, never pestered by the things of the women. He is named for my best friend, whom the Goddess and the things of the women hunted right across the world; it will be my revenge on her and them to see him a man all through, bowing only to men's gods.

15

'That will be one way of getting through the winter,' answered Marcus. 'You may dictate to me here in the evenings. Say what you like about the men of my City, who have left me here to rot. I shall write out fairly exactly what you tell me.'

As I walked home the frozen mud and straggly trees looked more friendly. This was now my home, and the North Wind was now my protector; the naked sword has been my protector for many years.

Here follows my story.

CHAPTER I

The Hills of Pyrene

My true name is long and complicated, and if strangers know it they will be able to cast spells on me. I shall only say that I am a Gallic noble, born thirty-one years ago, and that my friends call me Camul. My father's name is not important either, but his position in our nation must be mentioned: he had inherited the office of horse-master to all the cavalry of the Elusates.

My people live among the northern foothills of the great range which separates the Gauls from the Spaniards. These mountains are the domain of the nymph Pyrene; but our valley, and the slopes which enclose it, are especially her home. West of us, among the high crags, live the Basques. No stranger can learn their tongue, their idea of fighting is to throw stones from a distance, and each of their tiny hamlets is a sovereign state bound by no ties to its neighbours. We were not always at war with these queer people, but we did not often visit their land.

On the south we have no neighbours, until you cross the range and come down among the Spaniards; to the east and north live other Gallic tribes, our cousins, rivals, and friends. Farther to the east the Roman strangers hold sway, though their own land is a long way off. They held the country only because through it runs their great road to Spain, which they rule; so they did not bother their neighbours to the west. We heard a great deal about them, especially about their invincible power in war; and we took great pains to keep on good terms with them. This was easy, for as they marched up and down their great road they were always buying food and military supplies. We sent them grain and cattle, and the iron ore of our mountains; they were glad to get it, and paid honestly in coined silver, every piece of the same weight and fineness. We were free to use their great road, in small numbers; but these trips were not very enjoyable, for their soldiers despise all foreigners.

Our own land is a fertile grassy valley, hemmed in on three sides by mountains; though we also rule narrower valleys to east and west. Most of our land is stony and steep, and too rough for horses. But Gallic nobles must fight on horseback, so in the main valley we keep a herd of mares and a few stallions; these are national property, supported by the grain of every landowner. My father managed this herd, as his father had done before him; and when he died the post would come to me, his only son. So you see that only twelve years ago I, Camul of the Elusates, held a considerable position in the world. My father knew all the lore of horses, and by the fire at evening he taught me his wisdom, as was proper.

That was the first winter which I spent on my own. My father had recently brought home a second wife, a pretty young girl; and of course I regarded this as a slight on my mother. Perhaps my father also feared that I might get on too well with my new stepmother, for in those days I was considered handsome and gallant. For whatever reason, he announced that I was old enough to set up my own household, and too old to hang round his cook-hut teasing the maids. He gave me three servants of my own, and a little knob of land on the upper slopes where I might build a cabin. Before the snow came I was living there, alone except for the servants and a friend of my own age.

My friend was named Acco. His family was poorer than mine, almost disgracefully poor; but his blood was very noble. He was then what we call an Ovate, a student learning how to be a Druid; in the summer he went away to some centre of learning in the far north-west, and I never knew what he did there because it was all done under an oath of secrecy. But he came back to his own people for the winter. He and I had been born in the same year, and we had been close friends since we

18

were old enough to walk. He was so poor that his parents had been unable to betroth him; but he used to meet a girl in secret, and they were very much in love. He had no hope of marriage until he became a full Druid, and the tests are so stiff that most Ovates never get any further. That was one reason why he studied very hard. Though I never said so, I thought privately that dear Acco was wasting his time; for he was not very clever. But perhaps the Druids who would presently examine him in magic and divination would be influenced by his noble descent and honourable character.

The autumn, when frost has hardened the ground but snow has not yet hidden the paths, is the best time for hunting in the high mountains. Acco and I went out every day before sunrise after ibex or deer. Near my cabin was a cave where ice lingered all summer, and meat stored there kept sweet; if we were lucky we would eat fresh game at midwinter, while our parents down in the valley made do with salt beef. When we climbed high we went always together, for my father had taught me that a man should never journey alone among the peaks. But on the wooded ridges we did better alone, for a companion tempts the hunter to talk when he should be silent. That is Acco's saying; he was fond of such sententious scraps of wisdom. But I guessed that he really wanted to hunt alone so that he might stumble by accident on Grane, the girl he was courting. She was a little slip of a thing, perhaps pretty but not beautiful. Acco loved her, I think, because she was poor and neglected, so poor that she had to herd cows every day. Acco must always have someone weak to protect.

So far I have not mentioned my gods. That is because until I was nineteen religion had not bothered me. The Druids and their magic are a thing apart, which spreads from the western isles and is not really a Gallic business; though Acco was interested I was not. For the rest, the Elusates as a nation honour the Wargod and Skyfather, under names which I do not propose to make public; and my family knew certain rites which give pleasure to Epona, Lady of the Mares. (Her name is known to every Gaul, and her image can be recognised because men see her as a woman with the head of a horse; so

I reveal no secret.) In spring and autumn there were public sacrifices, to please the Great Gods; and every day I, and the members of my family, remembered Epona. But no public ceremonies appeased the nymph Pyrene, though everyone who ventured among the hills kept her in his thoughts.

We did not worship Pyrene becase we did not know how to go about it. We are newcomers. It is only five generations since we conquered the Basques who used to live in this valley. Their warriors did their duty, and were killed; but our lower classes intermarried with the widows, and we kept some of the children as slaves. That is how we know that Pyrene rules here. But the women would not tell us what we must do to please her, and in consequence she is not pleased with us. However, we have the Wargod and Skyfather on our side; and so far we have dwelt in her valley in spite of anything the nymph can do to us.

So on the day when our adventures began Acco and I performed no particular rites. When the dog-boy called us Acco threw aside his furs and stood facing west while he whispered a poem; that was part of his duty as an Ovate, though at the time it seemed to me rather like showing off. To keep level I in my turn went apart and muttered a prayer to Epona; my father had told me to do this every day, but if Acco had not spurred me I might have forgotten it. Then we sat down together on the threshold of the hut, watching dawn tinge the sky and discussing how we should pass the day.

We might work a ridge with the hounds, driving the deer to open ground where we could use our bows. That was what we had intended the night before. But Acco, who fancied himself as a weather-prophet, said the day would be very hot, and better spent on the high peaks. He suggested that we take our slings after ibex among the rocks. He often suggested that, partly because his Druid teachers recommended frequent meditation far from the haunts of men; I found it excessively dull when he stood staring at the sky and trying to work himself into a trance, so I answered that I did not feel like scrambling. I would hunt downhill with the hounds, after whatever I might find; and if he wanted to stay on the heights he might take his javelins after hares on a grass slope I knew; it was steep but smooth and open, and should be safe for a man alone. As we talked the cook brought our porridge; she interrupted to say that this was a most unlucky day for hunting on the heights, and that Acco had better come with me. That confirmed our plans. The cook was my old nurse, who thought anything I wanted to do must be dangerous and inadvisable; and an Ovate studying magic does not like old women to tell him which days are unlucky. She went back to the cooking-hut, muttering that Pyrene did not like Gauls on her mountain; and I shouted after her that the Elusates had driven the servants of Pyrene from all this countryside, and that if the nymph did not like it she could argue with the Wargod.

Soon after breakfast I went downhill alone, and Acco, with a couple of javelins, climbed a shoulder westward to look for hares. I grinned as I watched him go, for I recalled that yesterday I had seen the spoor of a stray cow heading in that direction; he might run into Grane as she searched for it.

Acco was right about the weather. The day was unpleasantly hot, and my hounds would not draw cover properly because they were always stopping to drink. Pushing through dense thickets in the windless valley was more like work than pleasure, and by midday I had had enough. I reflected that no one had ordered me to hunt deer in this heat; I was not a serf, to work every day. I coupled my hounds and climbed back. When I had left the hounds with the dog-boy the sun was still high, and there was nothing for me to do alone in the cabin. I decided to see how Acco was getting on with his hare-hunt.

It was a stiff climb to begin with, along a narrow path. The path wound among high rocks, and I heard the clatter of some-one scrambling down at speed before I could see who it was. Then round a corner I came face to face with Acco, blundering from boulder to boulder so fast he could hardly stop.

At first glance I took him for a demon of the hills. He was covered in blood, which had dried and stiffened all down his sheepskin tunic; as far as I could see he had no wound, but he had wiped a bloody hand over his face. Worst of all was the look in his eyes, staring, the pupils dilated. He carried no

21

weapons, and his shoes had been scored by the rocks. He staggered to a halt, staring at me without a word.

'Gently does it,' I said quietly, to calm him. 'If you want to raise the alarm I can get home quicker than you. If someone is after you I have arrows and a hunting-knife.'

'You can see me, then?' he gasped. 'I feared I might be a ghost, already dead. Someone is after me, but your bow will not check her; she will hunt my trace over any ground. You must come back with me to the high meadow, and help me carry down poor Grane.'

'Is Grane hurt?'

'No, she's dead. Pyrene killed her. But I think I have killed Pyrene.'

'Then let us carry down Grane for burial. You and I can do that without the servants. If you have started a blood-feud you need a free man to help you, not unarmed slaves. Here, take my knife, in case we meet your enemies.'

He was in no state to be trusted with a bow; his arrows would have gone all over the place.

As we scrambled up the path I went first, my bow bent and an arrow on the string. We had no breath for talking; I imagined, naturally, that Basque raiders had caught Grane, and cut her throat after all of them had raped her. It is one of their customs.

When we reached the open meadow I could see no enemies. The ground was covered with long grass, in which an army could be hidden. But Acco had just come down alone, and where he had been I must go. I set my teeth and followed his trail, plain in the trampled hay.

Suddenly I reached a place where the grass lay flat. First I saw the carcass of a cow, her neck broken; then beside her the body of poor Grane, her whole head and shoulders a mess of blood and flies, so that I recognised her only by her bracelet. Once before I had seen such wounds, and I knew no man had dealt them. But I had always thought Grane a poor snivelling creature, and though she was of my own people I felt no particular grief.

'What a death, and for one wretched cow!' I exclaimed. 'But

we can take our time about carrying her down. The danger is past, for a fat autumn-fed bear will never attack two men together.'

'Don't worry about the bear. It's dead. I killed it. But this place is deadly to Gauls, and to all male creatures. Take her feet, and let us get away as quick as we can.'

'What? You killed the bear? You had two javelins and no sword, for I saw you set out. You must tell me the whole story. But why are you afraid, after such a deed of arms? Lurking Basques will not attack a man who has killed a bear single-handed. I suppose you really killed it?'

His tale was so unlikely that I wondered for a moment whether grief had driven him crazy.

'Follow the track. You will see,' answered Acco wearily. 'The bear is dead, and so is Grane. And I am under the curse. All these hills are subject to the Goddess. I must get down to the plain as quick as I can.'

Through long hay I followed the track. The ground was too hard for footprints, but a creature bigger than a man had galloped across the meadow. Then I saw something else.

'Here's blood on the trail,' I called.

'Yes, that's where I caught it with a javelin-cast behind the shoulder. It missed the heart, and I could only follow.'

'H'm. You had two javelins. You threw one, stoutly enough to pierce the hide of a bear. Then you followed up, with a solitary javelin and no sword. Acco, you have lost your sweetheart, but the bards will sing of your hunting.'

'Who cares? Grane is dead. But since you still don't understand let us follow the trail to the end.'

We went on, at an easy trot. The trampled track led straight to a rock-face bounding the meadow on the south. When we were close I saw a crack in the rock, just wide enough for one man at a time. But the blood-spoor led through it, and I followed.

I crept gingerly through the narrow passage, my bow bent. After less than a hundred yards the cleft suddenly widened into a grass-floored clearing, walled by sheer cliff. I had never seen it before, but I recognised what had made this secret hiding-place. The roof of a great cave had long ago fallen in, and grass had spread to cover the floor. It was a strange and secret place, and even the smell of the air was hostile.

In plain view lay a great she-bear, with a javelin in her side and another in her breast. I saw she was a female, for she lay flat on her back, an enormous parody of a woman.

'You see,' muttered Acco, still in the same weary unemphatic voice. 'Here was her lair, and there is no other way out. When I followed and she could flee no further she turned to rear on her hind legs. Then I came close and stabbed with my javelin, as though it were a spear.'

'And that's the deed of a great warrior. You will be famous while you live and remembered after death. You must tell me all about it, every detail; for there was no one here to see your exploit.'

'It was seen,' he answered slowly, as though to utter each word was an effort. 'When I had stabbed her I jumped clear so fast I fell down. As I picked myself up I heard someone speak behind me. "Young man, you have killed the she-bear. The Goddess will be angry!"'

'You mean someone lives in this bear's den?'

'Perhaps no one lives here always, but your cook told us that this is a special day in the mountains. I turned and saw what I think was an old woman. But she wore a queer headdress, a tall pointed hat coming right down over her face, like a basket upside-down; and her body was covered by a long gown girt at the waist. The skirt was one flounce over another. So I could not make out the shape of her figure.'

'I recognise what you mean. She looked like the painting we saw in that cave over in the south?'

'Yes, and like the painting on the rock behind you.'

I turned, and saw for the first time that the cliff-face was painted with many figures. They were mostly deer, and other horned creatures of a kind I have never seen; but in front of them, painted over them as though to mark them as her property, was the black shape of a woman. She was depicted side-face in solid black, so that no detail showed; but she was unmistakably an old woman, for the artist had emphasised her

24

pendulous breasts. As I looked I remembered that goddesses are always drawn young and beautiful. This was not the Goddess herself, but her priestess.

I understood why Acco had been frightened. But half the business of priests is to terrify the faithful by wearing strange clothing. After all, the Wargod is a Gaul like the rest of us, and I suppose he wears Gallic war-dress and carries Gallic arms; but his priests dress like nothing on earth. I tried to soothe my comrade.

'Come, come. You are an Ovate, training to be a Druid. During your training, have you never seen ordinary men wearing strange masks and walking on stilts? If you didn't, half the funny stories about Druids must have been invented. You met an old woman, deliberately dressed up to look frightening. She was doing what she could to make her mistress appear as terrible as possible. But if Pyrene were more powerful than our Wargod we should never have conquered the valley where we dwell.'

'I have met men born of women wearing the garb of the Immortals. It is not done to frighten students, but to illustrate truths which cannot be put into words, and I don't like funny stories about it. I was not frightened by the old woman's clothes; I was trying to explain why I knew her for a servant of the Goddess.'

'Well, what happened then? She spoke, and you were not afraid. But when I met you on the path it seemed to me that you feared something.'

I was extremely unsympathetic, partly because I myself felt frightened, and therefore angry with the man who had brought fear on me; partly because I thought the best way to get Acco back to normal would be to make him angry.

'She did not speak further to me. First she hid under her skirt a basket she was carrying. Of course I looked away, for priestesses often carry holy baskets and men should not look on them. Then she came past me and spoke to the bear. She spoke gently, in an ordinary voice, not as though reciting a ritual but as though saying goodbye to a friend. I could not hear her words. Then she dodged among the rocks, and I did not see how she left this narrow place. Then . . . I don't know what happened and I can't describe it. I went forward to pick up my javelins, and as I bent over the bear I felt the anger of the Goddess. The peaks and the rocks and the grass under my feet seemed to be shouting silent curses at me. I heard the rustling of skirts and the shuffling of little feet, as though a crowd of women hovered near. I saw no one, but there were many who saw me. And I began to feel sorry for the bear. That's odd, isn't it? The bear who killed my Grane and tried to kill me. . . . But perhaps she was doing her duty. She may have been appointed to perform that work and nothing else. . . '.

His voice trailed off into a vague muttering.

A most unpleasant idea had entered my mind. Grane's cow had strayed unusually high among the peaks, far higher than our cattle usually strayed; it was also unusual that a single girl should be sent to seek her so far afield. When Grane set off, that unimportant plain little girl, there may have been women in our valley who knew she would never return.

I looked swiftly round the little hole in the rocks which was the sanctuary of the Goddess. I saw one cliff was spotted with pictures, but I did not peer closer; those pictures must have power to enchant, otherwise why were they made?

The base of the cliff was hidden by a litter of boulders. People might be hiding there; or if not people, other beings. I could feel in every hair of my head that we were not alone.

I wrenched the javelins from the dead beast, and seized Acco by the arm. As I strode away he followed willingly, but as though he hardly knew what he was doing. In silence we squeezed through the narrow cleft, and still in silence crossed the grassy meadow to stand by the body of poor Grane.

When I made him do things with his hands Acco at last came to life. I dulled the edge of my hunting-knife cutting boughs from the nearest trees, and soon we had the corpse hanging in a bundle between two poles. We carried it down the steep path to the cabin, and ordered our servants to bear it on the to village. I expected them to be afraid of touching the body; but they handled it eagerly, as though it held good luck. They also had seen Grane as a foredoomed sacrifice.

Acco made a package of his weapons and clothing, and the rest of his personal possessions. When I saw that he was determined to leave the cabin for ever I followed his example. I had no idea what would come next, but I felt that we would never climb that mountain again.

When we reached the village it was long after dark, but we found everyone awake. First we delivered Grane at her father's house. They laid her on the best bed, and women came to wash her and lay her out. That rid us of the idlers, for sightseers would rather gaze at a woman who has been killed by violence than at any other spectacle. I did not tell anyone that Acco had killed the bear, and he did not speak at all; so I suppose they thought we had come across the body by chance. Then we went to my father's house, beside the stalls of the brood-mares.

My father was entitled to marry as many wives as he could support, provided that when he brought home the second he made it clear that she could not be the first. But polygamy cannot work unless you keep your women shut up where no one can hear them grumble, as they do in Asia; my father found domestic life so stormy that he had built two little cabins for his two wives, in distant corners of the courtyard. In his main house he spent the day alone with his servants.

Our house is the finest in the village; only timber and clay, of course, but a party-wall divides it into two rooms. I went straight through the common hall, still leading Acco, and sat down with him on a bench in the inner room. After one startled glance at us my father followed, pulling shut the door-curtain.

I told my father the whole story, while Acco sat silent and numb. Then I went on to say that I would never return to my cabin, and that I would be happier if I never again climbed among the high hills; but I would hear my father's advice on what to do next.

I was glad to see that my father was not frightened. But he was worried, as though menaced by dangerous but human enemies. For a while he thought in silence, as was his custom; he disliked aimless excited chatter. At last he straightened himself on his stool and spoke.

27

'I forbid you to flee secretly, as though you were guilty of some crime,' said he. 'The nymph will be your foe, but your kin will defend you. Yet your wisest course is to go abroad for a while; though you must go at leisure, after telling your story to the family council. Your friend Acco seeks our protection, or so I suppose. We shall willingly defend him, unless he prefers to go with you.'

'Very well, father. I shall go abroad when I have decided where to go. But first I should like to consult my mother, if she is at home.'

He looked embarrassed, as always when his married life was mentioned. He paid dear for that second wife of his, and I think she was unhappy also. Now he waved me to the door, bidding me go where I wished.

I left Acco sitting on the bench, and walked alone across the court.

My mother met me on the threshold of her house. I saw at once that she had already heard the news, and her first words confirmed it. 'Come in, my son,' she said quietly, 'but come alone. Your friend is polluted by blood, very terrible blood. He may not enter a clean house until his guilt has been removed.'

Before I heard any more nonsense I determined to put things on a sensible footing. 'At present Acco is not well enough to visit ladies, but he is neither polluted nor guilty of a crime. He killed a man-eating bear, most bravely, with no weapon but a hunting javelin. Tomorrow we shall fetch the skin, which will be preserved as a memorial of his heroic deed. Besides, he is in our house now, so he can't pollute us more than he has already.'

'It's not a house he is in, Camul,' said my mother with a bitter laugh. 'Your father and his companions drink in that shelter, but what makes a house is its hearth. There are, alas, two hearths in this court. But both are clean, and not to be defiled.'

'Very well, mother, I shall sit by your hearth alone. I wish to hear your advice. You can also tell me how Acco is to be cleansed from his pollution. He can't stay here for ever.'

I could tell our story quite well by now, and it did not take me long. Then it occurred to me that I must repeat it yet again.

I asked my mother whether I ought to call on Grane's family that very night.

'That is unnecessary. Tomorrow they will hold the usual funeral, and you may attend the burning as a mark of respect. Tonight is the women's affair, and there are things to be done in private.'

'You mean there is nothing I can tell them? Did Grane's mother know this morning what would happen this afternoon? Is that why the girl was sent on the mountain alone?'

'Don't ask me questions which I may not answer. Women have their mysteries, hidden from men. I can tell you that the slaying of the bear was unexpected. Nothing like it has ever happened before. It brings ghastly pollution, and no one among the whole nation of the Elusates knows how it can be removed.'

In my country, as in others, from time to time we sacrifice men and women to the gods. It is not a thing we like doing, but the gods demand; sometimes the victim, if he knows his fate in advance, is less concerned than his relatives and the priest. But there was a flaw in the theory my mother was hinting at.

'I have always understood that the nymph's day comes round once a year,' I argued. 'Of course I don't pry into the things of the women, but that's what we men believe. Yet since I can remember until today, only one girl has been killed by a bear.'

A slave-girl giggled, looking up from her pots. My mother frowned, and spoke reluctantly. 'All these mountains are the domain of Pyrene. I am glad to hear from your own lips that you think it wrong to pry into the things of the women.'

That was enough. I should have guessed earlier that the whole nasty business was Basque business. It was horrible to know that my mother did not object to it. I said a polite good-night and returned to my father's hall.

Acco and I slept side by side on the floor, and by the morning he seemed to be getting over his shock. He ate a huge breakfast, and was more aware of his surroundings. At dawn my father went out for his usual inspection of the horses; but he came home early, and could not settle down to ordinary work. I recognised the symptoms. He was going to make an important decision, a prospect that always made him nervous.

I did not talk much with Acco. I was still very tired, and I wanted time to think. At the family council I would have to explain my plans, and there seemed no point in going over them with Acco before I made them public. In his present mood he would agree with anything I might suggest; but then I was always the planner in our partnership, for I have never feared responsibility.

We had dinner earlier than usual. Then my father turned all the servants out of the house, and dragged two benches from the wall. Acco and I sat on the floor, with a few cinders strewn beside us to symbolise a layer of ashes. That was in case we were genuinely polluted; for ashes keep off evil spirits, and unless they came very close to us our kin would still be clean.

My father was careful of formalities. When the advisers filed in and took their places I saw that he had summoned everyone in my compensation-group. (If I were murdered my kin would share the compensation in due proportion; if I committed murder they would be bound to contribute in the same proportion to the fine I must pay. Other races have much the same institution; I describe it as it exists among the Gauls.)

My father began the proceedings by telling all over again the story of Grane and the bear. His audience knew it already, but it was a good story, and he told it well. Besides, this opening gave the others time to compose their own speeches. We Gauls take speech-making seriously.

When he had finished he called on Acco to speak first, since he was the youngest present. To begin with the youngest and finish with the eldest is the best way of getting a genuine opinion out of everyone at such a council; but it takes a very long time. I foresaw a tedious afternoon. However, Acco spoke only one sentence, to say that he was in great trouble through no fault of his own and would value the advice of his elders; though he would not promise in advance that he would follow it. Then he sat down and it was my turn.

I had worked out exactly what I wanted to say, and I put it clearly and as shortly as I could. If the whole war-band of the Elusates would follow me we could march west and stamp out the cult of the Goddess among the beastly Basques who were our neighbours. If the whole kin would promise to protect us day and night we might stay at home, defying the Goddess to do her worst. But since we were young and untried warriors this was really too much to expect of our kinsmen. Therefore our best course would be to go abroad for some years, until the devotees of the Goddess were in a better mood.

My kinsmen praised my unselfishness in few words, one after the other, until it was my father's turn to speak. He rose and, resting his hands on his hips, settled down to a long oration; which was his right, though if his mind was made up he was wasting time by assembling this council.

He assumed that we would be going abroad, and that the only question was where we should go. In central Gaul the Arverni and the Aedui, who had been at feud for generations, were both raising armies; either would welcome two noble recruits. If we rode west instead of north we would come to the Ocean, where pirate ships were always short-handed. If we crossed the mountains there were brigands on the hills of Spain; though the Romans had suppressed true warfare, and among the Spaniards only these brigands were free. If we went east the Romans would pay us a regular wage to fight for them; though perhaps it was not fitting that nobles should work for a wage. He made it clear that in his opinion we ought to join either the Aedui or the Arverni.

That opened a wide field for discussion. Every speaker told at length of all the foreign wars he had seen, which in most cases meant that he related the history of his adult life. I ceased to listen. I was to leave this narrow valley, with the goodwill of my kin; so much was already settled. Now my uncles and cousins were enjoying themselves, making long speeches to an audience which must sit to the end. A Gaul of noble birth knows only one higher pleasure: reciting poetry of his own composition. For we are a quick-witted people, with a love of the beautiful and intricate; but since we do not build in stone, or carve statues, or paint, oratory and poetry are the only arts we may cultivate.

At last the council closed with a speech from my senior

great-uncle, the oldest noble present. He spoke chiefly of the
exploits of his youth, and seemed to hanker for a campaign
against the Basques; but none the less the sense of the meeting
was that we ought to go abroad until the death of the bear had
been forgotten. In a graceful summing-up my father at last
made clear the function of this council which had advised me
to do what I could very well have done without their advice.
Since my kin were sending me away it was only reasonable that
they should all contribute to an outfit worthy of my noble birth.
It was a roundabout way of raising a family purse, and it had
wasted a great deal of time; but then all the speakers had
enjoyed themselves.

For the next few days Acco and I remained in my father's
hall, not exactly in hiding, and certainly not under any legal
ban; we just thought it more tactful to keep out of sight. During
that time several eminent men dropped in to talk to us, until
we knew pretty well how the Elusates as a whole regarded our
exploit.

Two of our more interesting visitors came principally to see
Acco. The first was his mother, who sent word that she wished
to talk with both of us; but we must meet her in the open air,
with no fire nearby, and we must excuse her ragged attire; for
before she re-entered her house all the clothes she wore must
be burned. Since my mother also held that we were polluted
we did not object to these conditions. We received her seated
on the bare ground, at the back of my father's pigsties.

Acco had come out of his stupor. While he lived with men in
my father's hall he was not reminded of the enmity of the
Goddess; on the contrary, all the talk was of his valour as a
hunter. His grief for Grane was genuine and deep, but again
so long as he did not see other girls she sank to the back of his
thoughts. I feared that the interview might upset him, especially if his mother talked of nothing but bad luck and pollution;
so we decided that we would ask her to tell us as much about
the Goddess as might lawfully be known to men. Acco, an
Ovate, was interested in theology; the subject would keep his
mind from cowering before shapeless supernatural terrors.

His mother was very reasonable. She had known for years

32

that her son must go out into the world to seek his fortune, since there was no inheritance waiting for him at home. She held that he had been more unfortunate than impious. After a few observations about his health and the need to change out of wet trousers even on campaign, she asked me to do my best for him; since I was the elder, and he had incurred his misfortune while he was my guest. From that she drifted into talking more to me than to her son, and answered my questions civilly.

But no Gaul can stick to answering questions. Whenever we talk we must make speeches. As we squatted in the mud, hardly able to see one another through the dusk, she wandered into a long discourse on the power and attributes of the Goddess.

'These mountains, from the Ocean to the Middle Sea, are the peculiar domain of Pyrene; that is the name the Goddess happens to bear in these parts. But the whole earth belongs to the Goddess; because the whole earth, in a sense, is her body. And the Goddess is not always a nymph. You imagine a nymph as a maiden, with the maiden's hatred of the male who will hurt her; but a nymph is really any woman who is desired by men. So the Goddess is a nymph. But she is also a mother, and a child. Even the men know that, if they stop to think. You, my dear son, killed the servant of the Goddess. But the death of her servants does not always displease her. Her votaries in these mountains are angry with you; perhaps in others parts they will see that you were only the instrument of fate. You do well to go away. The Goddess does not desire the worship of men, and the best way a man can please her is by leaving her mysteries alone. Avoid her. She has few dealings with men; and I hope my son will never be chosen as the man she uses.'

She stopped short. There was evidently more in her head, but she had suddenly realised that she was speaking of things that usually are told only to women. We sat silent in the darkness, until Acco stumbled to his feet.

'Then it is goodbye, mother. I may not touch you, even for a last embrace. Yet do you think I am under a lifelong curse? Far from here, if I avoid the Goddess, can I live as an ordinary man among men?'

'Yes, my dear son. You have displeased the Goddess, but

she is seldom pleased with the deeds of men. All the same, men prosper. Far away you may live happily. But you may never return to these mountains.'

That was the end of the interview, which had been less harrowing than it might have been. Afterwards Acco felt better, and discussed our future reasonably. He had thought of trying his luck as a hired soldier of the Aeduans, while I had different plans; the next visitor who came specially to see him brought him round to my way of thinking.

This next visitor was our chief Druid, or rather, since Druids are wanderers, the most eminent Druid who was then in the neighbourhood. He was by birth one of our nobles; after travelling all the way to Ireland in search of wisdom he had recently come back to visit his kin.

He was not afraid of pollution, though he did not offer to cleanse us. But at least he met us in my father's inner room where a brazier burned and there were jars of mead. It was a more cheerful affair than the old lady's solemn warning.

Acco would have liked to talk with him in private, I suppose to discuss things that are known only to Druids and Ovates. But the Druid made a point of asking me to be there, so that Acco would control himself in the presence of a third party. For the purpose of the interview was to tell Acco that he must abandon his hope of a Druidical career.

'My poor boy, you have been unlucky, nothing more; and no one can blame you for a very gallant deed of arms,' he began, with a friendly smile that was obviously a mask for bad news. 'But one thing every Druid must have is luck. I betray no secrets when I say that we are not servants of the Goddess, though in all we do we are aware of her. Neither are we servants of the Wargod, or of Skyfather. In case Camul feels puzzled I shall tell him that we do not, in our capacity as Druids, serve any god in particular; though as men we worship in the usual manner of our nations. We explore certain supernatural forces, and by our wisdom strive to control them. That is all there is in the mystery of the Druids. Of course, the exploration is arduous,' with a twinkling eye and a bow to me, the outsider.

34

'But one of the strongest supernatural forces in the world,' he continued, 'is Luck. Now the luck of individuals seems to be curiously constant. There is no rational explanation, but if you observe you will notice that some men are all their lives lucky, and others unlucky. You, my dear Acco, have been very unlucky at the outset of your career. Of course you did right to attack a bear which had killed a member of our nation; of course you were very brave to attack her single-handed, armed only with a javelin. You did nothing wrong. But Luck stepped in, and now you must leave home. The Druids, who use Luck as a force in the service of man, have no room in their ranks for the preternaturally unlucky. You must never return to the college in Carnutia; and, unless you wish to make another group of powerful enemies, you will forget the lore you learned as an Ovate.'

'Must I be a hired soldier all my life?' Acco asked in dismay.

'Who knows? You may prosper in some other calling. You will never be a Druid. However, just to show there is no ill-feeling, I myself will contribute to your outfit, though I am not of your kin; and here is a little gift from the order of Druids as a whole. Never mind how we knew that it would be needed. It is only a brown stone set in a copper finger-ring, but it has one remarkable property; the man who wears it will never feel thirst so long as he lives. In Gaul thirst is not a dangerous foe to the warrior, but there are parts of the world where this stone will be very useful. I wish I could offer you something more powerful, something that guards against steel, for example. But if we could distribute charms of such potency the Romans would not be marching through our country.'

The Druid, a tactful man, bowed himself out while Acco was still thanking him.

Thus it was agreed on all sides that we should set out to-gether, to seek service as hired soldiers. The only question still undecided was which chief we should serve. Acco, who would never return to Pyrene, wished to find some gallant nobleman with whom we could exchange the oath of comradeship; then we would be members of his war-band, sharing his wealth while he lived – and sharing his death when the time came for him to fall in battle. But I thought that after a few years my offence would be forgotten, and I had no wish for an oath that endures to the death. I wanted to serve in an army for a definite term.

Our nations often hire extra soldiers. But as a rule, unless they are oath-bound companions, they are hired by the month and turned adrift in the winter. It is the best service for a young warrior seeking to win a reputation, but he is not expected to earn a steady living; between campaigns he should go home. Since we had no home this would not suit us.

We could join a gang of brigands or pirates. No one would think the worse of us, so long as we did not rob our own people. But I had met several brigands (when they were off duty). They came down during the winter to sell their plunder in our handy valley, near the Roman market but beyond the reach of Roman law; and often they would buy our horses. They were swaggering, stupid, boastful men, and I thought their lives, spent in damp caves or on windy hilltops, must be very boring. There is no glory in the career of a brigand, and we were too young to be eager for riches. Neither of us was attracted.

I have left until the last the alternative I really wanted. I pointed out to Acco that the Romans were always eager to hire good horsemen. They engage Gauls by the year, and pay them winter and summer; and they will usually re-engage the same soldiers for another year. You could stay in the Roman army as long as you pleased, or leave it in any spring, when their year changes. Romans keep their promises and pay their debts, and their troops are fed regularly.

On the other hand, Romans make their soldiers obey orders, and think nothing of flogging free men for trifling faults. Some Gauls cannot stand the constant nagging. Gauls in Roman service had more than once visited our valley, and while some were content others counted the days until spring would bring freedom and self-respect.

Nevertheless, I was determined to live among the Romans; and since I knew no trade but war I must live among them as a soldier.

So far I have not spoken much of the Romans, but even in

36

those days they were constantly in my thoughts; indeed our whole valley thought about them constantly. They were already on their road when the Elusates won the valley from the Basques, which was five generations ago. We knew, of course, that they had not held their road for very long before our ancestors moved south, and that their true home was a long way away; but in our eyes they were not intruders. Since they had come before us, they were part of the landscape.

Recently they had begun to march about the whole country, in a most disturbing way. Some of our nobles said we ought to form an alliance to keep them away from the hills of Pyrene; but that meant an alliance with the Basques, which was abhorrent, so the council had done nothing.

Meanwhile the Romans had intervened in the ancestral feud between Aedui and Arverni. They had marched as far north as the land of the Belgians, though the Belgians boasted they had defeated them. Last summer they had been bickering with the Veneti of the west coast, and there were rumours of a great sea-battle. A Roman commander at the head of a force of Gallic cavalry had ridden through the south-west, between the mountains and the river, taking tribute and giving orders right and left; though he paid for his provisions and left the villages unburned behind him, so he could not really be trying to conquer the land. Our nobles said it was about time these Romans went back to guarding their road.

Every winter my father visited the Roman road. In the old days the horse-master had gone only to buy foreign stallions, but now it was a great expedition; he took waggons loaded with our spare grain. Romans buy grain wherever they find it for sale, and never seem to have enough of it. They pay in coined silver which can be exchanged for most interesting things.

My father talked a great deal about these odd people. He could make himself understood in their tongue, which is easier to learn than Basque; and as I was one day to succeed to his office he had two years ago brought back a cheap slave, an old man with a stiff knee, who spoke it fluently and taught me when he had time.

If we took service with the Romans we would see all the land of Gaul. I was tired of our hidden valley, and of the pine-clad mountains that wall us in. I was tired of visiting other Gallic nations, as I had done thrice; they were just like us, and it was not worth the bother of leaving home. Of course no decent man would wish to visit the beastly Basques.

Another point that came into my mind, though it was not the kind of thing I could say openly, was that the Romans seemed to be better at war even than the Gauls, the favourite sons of the Wargod. When I was born there were old men alive who could remember the Allobroges as a most warlike nation; now the whole land of the Allobroges is under Roman rule. Roman armies marched anywhere, without asking anyone's leave. And though the road in the east has been there since the beginnning of time, for it is the main way between Gaul and Spain, it was said that the Romans were making other roads like it all over Gaul. Altogether the Roman army should be worth a visit.

After some argument I got my father to agree with me, because I could leave the Roman army whenever I wished and yet they would pay me through the winter. He advised me to stay away for at least five years, until memories had grown dim; and then come home to take over the horses when he would be beginning to find unbroken colts a burden to his elderly thighs. Acco still had very little will of his own, and on our joint expeditions I had always been the leader. When the leaves fell we rode east in search of the Romans and their road.

CHAPTER II

The Army of Gaul

In one way our misfortune worked to our advantage; for ten days Acco and I had been the most famous young men in the village, and as a result our kinsfolk gave us more splendid equipment than if we had merely been going on a foreign campaign to win experience.

I rode a fine black stallion, six years old, named Starlight from the blaze on his forehead. I had handled him for three years, and he would come to my whistle; he was speedy and a stayer, and with me on his back would face any obstacle. I wore a blue woollen tunic over a linen shirt, and thick blue trousers. My shoes were supple goatskin, gathered at the ankle with a gay red lace. My short cloak was red, with a blue fringe; it was fastened by a bronze brooch, ornamented with scarlet enamel. My belt was of scarlet leather; from it hung on the right hip a steel knife, bone-hilted, in a red leather sheath, and on the left a purse of white embroidered kidskin. My baldric was woven from narrow strips of dyed leather, to form an intricate pattern of lozenges. It supported a long horseman's sword, a spatha of the best Spanish steel, pointed and double-edged; the bone hilt was carved into an image of horse-headed Epona; the wooden scabbard, covered with interlaced serpents, ended in great bronze chape on which a dragon crawled. This sword, called the Mare from the shape of its hilt, had been made for my great-uncle; it had killed seven Basques and two Gauls.

My round shield was of linden-wood. I carried it slung from my saddle in a linen cover; but when I strapped it on my arm

39

it showed the scowling face of the Wargod, with the bronze shield-boss for his nose.

On my head I wore a little red woollen cap, with an eagle's feather rising from a bronze brooch; but slung from my saddle was the stout leather helmet, with bronze cheek-guards, which I would wear in battle.

Acco also was dressed in blue and red, which are the colours our nation prefers to wear in battle. His sword, named the Raven, was far older and more famous than mine, for it had been carried at the conquest of our valley. But it was the only remaining relic of his family's past grandeur; the rest of his equipment was plain and serviceable.

He rode a good stallion, chosen by my father from the tribal herd; quiet in danger, fast and enduring. But though Poplar was a very good horse to ride on a journey, or to take to the races at some festival, as a warhorse he had one fault: in colour he was a light grey, and it is well known that grey horses attract more than their share of arrows.

Perhaps we were rather too well-dressed for novice warriors on our first campaign. But we were nobles of one of the noblest nations in Gaul. As yet we might not be important, but in a few years we ought to be famous.

To keep up our position until we drew our first pay we had been given a good weight of silver, some of it in coined money.

The money-bag was lighter by the time we reached Narbo, the Roman base-headquarters; for Roman territory began only a few hours' ride from our valley, and in Roman territory the innkeepers charge fantastic prices. It was odd to ride through a normal Gallic countryside, with Gauls working in the fields and Gauls travelling the roads, and yet to see everyone un-armed, and the villages unfortified. You could tell at a glance that the Romans kept good peace.

Until we reached Narbo we saw nothing warlike. But Narbo was so strongly fortified that it made up for the undefended country. The whole town was surrounded by a wall of sheer stone, square blocks piled one on another. Acco, very excited, wanted to examine it closely. I restrained him, pointing out that if strangers peered at the palisade round our village we should take them for spies; we must get into the Roman army before we could walk round their walls.

This impressive sight, the sheer walls whose stones had been smoothed by tools sharper than we could imagine, was all we saw of Narbo. The road led to an archway in the wall, but an armed sentry refused to let us enter with our swords. This sentry spoke the common Gallic of the lower classes, and it seemed odd that such a man should wear a sword. Many provincials are the sons of Gallic women from the dregs of the people; they pick up their mothers' way of talking, and insult our nobles by addressing them in the speech of kitchen-serfs. But they have learned Latin from their fathers, and the Romans treat them as free men and warriors.

The sentry was civil, in his fashion. He agreed that it would be unseemly for nobles to walk unarmed in a strange town, as though they were ploughmen. But we might join the army without entering the town, for the camp of the Gallic cavalry lay outside the walls. At this camp we were stopped by another sentry, and indeed spent most of the afternoon being passed from one sentry to the next. It was my first taste of army life, and I felt a little exasperated; but everyone we met seemed anxious to help, though too busy to help at that particular moment.

What impressed me most was the enormous multitude of people gathered in one spot. Here were more able-bodied men than the whole levy of the Elusates, though they were many miles from any fighting and had nothing to do but groom their horses and keep the wooden buildings in repair; for we were told that the active squadrons had gone forth with the Roman foot. Acco was less impressed. He had lost his heart to the stone walls of the city, and complained that the buildings in this camp were just like the houses at home; what was the use of travelling if you could not look at new things? I reminded him that this was a camp built in Gaul, for Gauls to live in; we would see plenty of new things if they took us into their army.

At last we were told that an officer could see us. We left our horses with a sentry, and were taken to a big square wooden building in the centre of the camp. In a small room at the end of a long passage we found a Roman officer, sitting at a desk and reading written papers. To our surprise, he greeted us in gentleman's Gallic, recognised who we were when we recited our pedigrees, and introduced himself as Cornelius Piso, a noble of the Aquitanians. He explained that for three generations his family had been in Roman service.

Immediately he got down to business. His first question was whether we were fugitives from justice, and if so what crime had we committed? I explained that though we had good reasons for leaving home we were not criminals. Then he asked about previous military experience, and examined our arms. When he had seen us ride across the parade-ground he told us we were accepted, as recruits to the fourth Gallic squadron of auxiliary horse.

'You will stay here a month, to learn tactics and the words of command, which you must obey the moment you hear them. That's what makes a Roman soldier, obedience. When you reach the main army you will be astonished at the number of grey-headed veterans you see in the ranks; Roman soldiers live for ever. And they live for ever because they obey orders. Keep that in mind and you will draw your long-service pensions; forget it and you will be flogged. It's hard at first, especially for young nobles who have always had their own way in everything. But presently you will see that obedience has made us the finest army in the world. I have served the Romans for more than ten years. Now I should hate to return to a Gallic war-band, where anyone may ride off by himself if he disagrees with his chief. I think that's all. But before you dismiss I must congratulate you on your horses. If they are killed in action you deserve special compensation. Oh, by the way, I suppose neither of you speaks Latin?'

I told him I understood it, and could make myself understood with a little patience on both sides. Piso marked this down on his writing-tablets. 'Your squadron is composed of Gallic nobles,' he explained, 'and of course all commands are given in Gallic. But we need interpreters to carry messages to Roman officers, and no one can be promoted until he understands Latin. If you learn to write it you may rise to high rank.'

But no young man on his first campaign will sit down to learn his letters. Though my Latin grew fluent, since I heard it spoken all around me, I never learned to read or write.

The days were lengthening when we rode north with a draft of reinforcements for the field army. After two months at Narbo we considered ourselves complete Roman soldiers. We could feed and strap our own horses and clean our own weapons, without grooms or servants; we could stand on sentry-go until relieved, even if the relief was late; we could dig industriously if we were ordered to throw up a rampart; even more important, we could spot the officer who was looking for a digging-party and dodge him without technically going absent; we could drink a skinful on pay-day and pass muster at lights-out; we could submit to abuse on parade and yet swagger in the evening; all because we were members of the mighty, invincible Army of Gaul.

In the last two years this army had done great things. They had destroyed the ships of the Veneti and the war-bands of the Nervii, one in the extreme west, the other far to the north. In fact this army, which for more than a century had sat quiet guarding the road to Spain, was now undertaking the conquest of the whole of Gaul. That was because we had a new commander, Caesar, a middle-aged politician of noble birth who had never commanded troops until two years ago – and was now proving himself to be a very great general. Everyone was surprised, for this Caesar had been appointed to the Army of Gaul especially because it had no enemies to fight. He was an orator, popular with the lower orders; and the mob had voted him to his great position.

Since his arrival he had picked quarrels with all the leading nations of Gaul, until his army now lay in the valley of the Meuse, hundreds of miles farther north than Roman troops had ever marched before.

Piso, who conducted this draft to the main army, told us every evening about Roman politics, which seemed just as complicated and violent as the politics of Gaul. He explained that, for the first time, the Army of Gaul had become the fashionable field of service. 'Under Caesar,' he said, 'are men

43

from the greatest houses of Rome. He himself is descended from the gods, though he leads the common people against his fellow-nobles. One of his subordinate commanders is Cicero, brother of the greatest orator in their council; and the commander of his horse is young Publius Crassus, son of the richest noble in Rome who is also one of their two rulers for this year. But young Crassus is more than the son of his father; he is a fine judge of horseflesh, a gallant cavalier, and a leader with a quick eye on the battlefield. He gets on with his Gauls; he can't speak our language, but he has taken trouble to learn our etiquette, and he remembers our social rank. You will see, when we reach the army, that I am treated as one of my birth should be treated; I am offered a seat while junior Roman officers stand at attention. You don't often find among Romans such natural good manners.'

That was true. The Romans are easy people to get on with, being downright, blunt, and uncomplicated. They are ruled by obvious motives, love of country, love of money, love of power; and they seldom bother to dissimulate. But their manners are amazingly uncouth.

This childish bluntness runs through all the Roman army. Men who do extra work or perform brave actions are rewarded, like children, with wine or small sums of money; those who fail to carry out their tasks are punished like children, by beating or some other physical humiliation. Their leaders seldom persuade them by flattery, or appeal to their pride. It struck me as odd that all ranks and all classes speak the same tongue in practically the same way; there are none of the elaborate honorific turns of speech that a Gallic serf must use when talking to a noble. The veterans at Narbo never boasted of the foes they had killed in action; if they boasted at all it was of their skill in finding well-paid jobs so far from the field of battle.

We knew Caesar's army was brave and resolute, for it had destroyed the terrible German host of Ariovistus. But it seemed to us that Romans can be brave to order, for a little pay and a daily dinner; and that they do not take pleasure in fighting.

All the same, the Roman army is a fascinating institution.

Acco never ceased to wonder at it and to praise it. He was delighted by the formalities of guard-mounting, the rigorous precautions against surprise which were never relaxed even in the depths of the Province, the division of labour by which armourers and farriers carried on their appointed work, sure that cooks would feed them, quartermasters pay them, and legionaries defend them, even in hostile country. He said that to watch a body of Roman troops at drill was as interesting as to watch a jeweller fusing a complicated pattern in enamel.

The religion of this army also reassured us, though as Gallic auxiliaries we had no share in it. In the camp at Narbo they kept a bronze image of an eagle, mounted on a pole. This was worshipped every morning, as the emblem of Skyfather; and we were told that the legions carried similar images into battle. Sacrifices were also offered to Mars, the Roman war-god, and we were told that the commander-in-chief discovered from the stomachs of sacrificial victims whether the gods were pleased or angry. But we saw no trace of the Goddess, nor heard her mentioned.

As regards pay and food the Romans deal fairly, and they are as rude to one another as they were to us. Once we had become used to their lack of courtesy they seldom made us angry. It was galling to obey orders shouted with unnecessary fierceness, but once or twice we saw Piso stand stiffly at attention while a senior officer was very fierce to him. Rudeness was the rule for all, and even the highest had to put up with it. Romans are just in their dealings with free men, though merciless to criminals and very callous in their treatment of slaves. Acco thought it odd that such intelligent men should show so little consideration for the feelings of others; he saw it as evidence of limited imagination. I did not care. They were brave warriors, in an ignoble way. I had come to the right school to learn the trade of war.

The Romans are more than soldiers; for wonderful things came from Italy into Narbo. The empty wine-jars they threw away would have been treasures in a Gallic house; common soldiers wore several kinds of cloth; their metalwork, even their

45

wooden tools, were made with a skill that in Gaul would be reserved for the ornaments of nobles. For all that they looked very ugly, thes e things were astonishingly cheap.

On the long journey north through blustery winter weather Acco and I rode together, though more than once Piso nearly separated us. He had discovered that I knew more about horse-management than the shifty little Italian who drew pay as our veterinary officer, and he was always making me inspect sore backs and puffy legs; and I could bargain with the Roman traders who sold us forage or lodged us in their warehouses. Thus I spent many evenings, after the day's march, in the company of the senior officers; while Acco was left by the bivouac fire. I explained that Acco knew nearly as much about horses as I did (which was true), and that when we reached the main army his very noble birth would be respected by all auxiliaries; if I were taken out of the ranks then my friend should come with me. I had my way; for Piso, in spite of his Roman training, still kept a decent Gallic reverence for noble birth. By the time we reached the army both Acco and I dined more often with the officers than with our comrades, though we still rode in the ranks.

The Army of Gaul, when we reached it, was encamped by the headwaters of the Meuse, a great river which flows north-ward to the extreme boundary of Gaul. That is some measure of the distance we had ridden. In my home all the rivers flow west, and of course by Narbo they flow south. The people round us were still Gauls, though of the Belgic race; Belgians are tougher and more uncouth than southerners, their dialect is full of German words, and they are organised into much bigger nations. I felt that we were almost in a foreign country.

Caesar's army was even more of a foreign country. When we first saw the camp, in the gloom of a late winter evening, I thought we had come on another city like Narbo. Close-set houses, with lights in the windows, stretched for nearly a mile; and the whole was surrounded by a palisade which looked stronger and more permanent than the defences of many Gallic towns. Piso set me right, boasting that Romans build a palisade of equal strength whenever they bivouac, even for one

46

night, and that for winter quarters they always make themselves these long straight-sided houses. Roman soldiers work with their hands after every day's march, and it is astonishing what these vast numbers of men can do in an evening.

We did not enter the palisade, for the cavalry were encamped to the south of it. The cavalry quarters alone made a town bigger than anything I had seen at home; there were more than five thousand horsemen, all Gallic, and a number of followers. Piso handed over his command and went off to the Roman lines, and as soon as we were among true Gauls we were carefully divided in accordance with our social standing; which meant that Acco and I were together in a squadron of young nobles. I was getting used to the fact that among Romans I was more important than he, but that among Gauls his birth gave him precedence. That kept us good friends.

In this camp we Gauls lived a busy but comfortable and interesting life. Every day we exercised, mounted and armed, under the direction of Roman officers; though our immediate commanders were Gauls. On parade we came under the iron Roman discipline, but in our quarters we lived after our own customs. Luckily the Romans saw that we were the better horse-masters, in that winter climate; nobody interfered when I took over the doctoring of all the horses in my squadron. They were good horses, carrying some of the proudest nobles in Gaul; and I kept them fit.

Among the Romans I made no friends, unless Piso be counted as a Roman. It seemed to me that the legionaries led very dull lives. They felt the cold intensely, and even more the early dusk of winter; when it grew dark they huddled in their huts, to shiver until dawn. All day they were hard at work, repairing the camp or that enormous palisade, drilling, even setting out on long marches which brought them back to the same camp at nightfall; this seemed an intolerable pastime which no Gaul would endure, but their officers commanded it to ensure that they would be fit when the campaigning season opened. It was hard to remember that men so bullied by their commanders were free warriors and full members of their nation, or rather City.

We got into the habit of talking of that City as though it was the only thing of its kind in the world, though every coast of the Middle Sea is fringed with cities, some of them more famous and more beautiful; at least, so I was told by certain auxiliaries, archers and slingers from Asia. But the City is certainly something to be proud of; I was proud to be one of her soldiers.

We were all proud of that service, and the Romans were proud of the Army of Gaul. They could look back on three years of outstanding victory, in which they had beaten not only Gauls and Belgians, but even Germans. I had known from my childhood that Germans are very terrible people, who drove our ancestors from our original home beyond the Rhine. Of course, a Gallic war-band will fight Germans, if there is no alternative except shameful surrender; but we do not expect to beat them, and we avoid battle if we can.

Sometimes, as our squadron wheeled on the open plain, we would be halted to make way for legionaries on the march. We were splendidly mounted and gaily clad, our bridles jingling with silver bells and our swords gleaming with enamel; they were short, dark and grubby, wearing coarse tunics stained with mud and sweat, their backs bent under the load of armour and baggage they carried in bundles on their shoulders; even their swords were in these bundles, so that they looked more like porters than warriors. It seemed unfitting that nobles should rein in gallant horses to let these labourers go by. Then I recalled that these little men had stood firm against the great horde of King Ariovistus, and he had driven his horrible Germans right across the Rhine. The Romans are professionals, who see no more romance in war than in ploughing; but any warrior in the world may yield the road to the legionaries of Caesar.

Caesar himself was in his own country. Piso told me he had gone there every winter since he came to Gaul, for though he was no longer one of the ruling magistrates he was still so powerful that no rulers could be chosen without his consent. He always came back in the early spring, and when he returned he would lead us against the enemy; though as yet our enemy for next summer had not been chosen.

However, when the grass began to grow and Caesar had returned we heard disturbing news, which told every true Gaul which foe should next be attacked. Two powerful German nations, the Usipetes and the Tencteri, had been driven from their lands by the terrible Suevi, the most ferocious of Germans, they had fought their way across the Rhine into the land of the Gallic Menapii, and their horsemen were riding out to plunder.

When our ancestors came west to conquer the lands we now live in it seemed that the gods themselves had fixed a barrier between the men who follow decent customs and those terrible warriors. Germans belong east of the Rhine, and from the Rhine to the Ocean is Gaul. When Germans cross the Rhine they must be fought. But without the Romans to help us it would have been a doubtful struggle.

Luckily Caesar announced that he would lead his army against the invaders. I heard him say it, for I made one of the guard of honour who escorted him to the parade-ground. He was a little man, like most Romans; reasonably good-looking, slim, and with the graceful movements of youth. But at close quarters his face showed every one of his forty-five years, for his cheeks were lined and his hair scanty.

With him was young Publius Licinius Crassus, who commanded all the Gallic horse. He also had been in Italy, to see his father installed as Consul. This was carefully explained to the auxiliaries, so that we might understand that this youth was a great noble, worthy to lead Gallic nobles. Young Publius was a good horseman, as we could see at first glance; and he carried plain Roman arms as though he could use them. At that time I knew no more of him, for he did not speak to us except to give a few orders from the Roman drill-book.

After a fortnight spent in collecting supplies Caesar's army broke camp for the summer campaign. It was a dark spring morning as we mounted before sunrise, for my squadron led the advance. We climbed a ridge overlooking the camp while it was still so dark that the cooking-fires showed as twinkling lights. Then, as the sun rose, the fires were extinguished all together, and a grey river of men poured out of the camp. There was complete silence, no accoutrements gleamed, but the column flowed inexorably, as fast as an active man can walk, without a single straggler or a man out of line. As we in our turn moved off I looked behind me to see the camp empty and fifty thousand men, obedient to a single will, marching in silence on one rutted track. Presently, above the noise of our own horses, we could hear marching songs and the shuffle of innumerable leather-clad feet; and so it continued for seven hours, by which time we had covered twenty miles. Yet a scout half a mile to the flank would have seen nothing of this great army; for they had been commanded to keep to the track, and not one of them strayed.

In the evening we halted where we were bid, and busied ourselves with watering and picketing the horses. When I was free to get my supper I looked back to see behind us a great palisaded entrenchment. The Romans had dug it on an open hilltop within the hour.

After a few days we hardly noticed the ground we rode over; wherever we went we felt at home, for we were part of the moving city that is a Roman army. We knew that our rear and flanks were secure, so that we need only guard our front; we knew that the same camp, with headquarters in the centre and the same gridiron of streets, would spring up behind us every evening; we knew where the supply-train marched, and that our suppers would reach us on time. Our advance into the hostile north was no more strange than one of those circular marches which brought the legionaries back at evening to the camp they had left in the morning.

It was wonderful to know myself a part of Caesar's Army of Gaul, the best army in the world.

Acco was not quite so happy. He agreed that we were serving in a very fine army; but he did not like the few Romans he had met, and he loathed the grey, smelly, undersized legionaries. 'They don't pillage, I grant you,' he said. 'But that is only because they have orders to behave peaceably. In their hearts they do not reckon Gauls as human beings. They are kind to us now, as a farmer is kind to his stock. If they thought it convenient they would kill us all without a qualm. I can't speak their tongue, so I can't explain how I know this. By the look on their stony faces, I suppose. They have no pity, and that's bad enough. But I really hate them because they are ugly, and because they take pride in their ugliness.'

There was something in his last point. I had admired Roman mercy, though I knew it was based on contempt; but I had to admit that most of their possessions were horribly ugly. And they had such a wealth of possessions that all Gaul was being flooded with plain iron swords, bulging clay cups covered in pictures of fat boys, and stinking hobnailed boots. All the same, I told Acco that we served masters who could protect us, and that when plunder had made our fortune we might settle down in some more beautiful part of the world. I had heard tell of Greece, where the friends of Rome might live undisturbed. I clinched the argument by reminding him that in this army we were safe from the Goddess. In our camp she had no altars, and no Romans served her.

After less than a week of marching we got in touch with the German invaders; and then all the Gallic horses were united in friendship with the Romans, thinking only of turning these horrid people out of our land. The first signs of their presence were burnt-out Menapian farmsteads, with corpses stinking where they had fallen; but at midday our forward patrols reported a small force of Germans advancing to meet us.

Without orders, five thousand Gauls closed on the centre and drew their swords, ready for the charge. Here was a chance of revenge; and if we outnumbered the enemy, well, Germans do not deserve fair odds. But Piso sent messengers down our ranks to tell us that the Germans were an embassy offering submission; we must let them pass unhindered to Caesar's headquarters.

Sullenly we drew off the track to watch the envoys. They were elderly men, unarmed and obviously worried. But there was no harm in making our own feelings clear, so we shook our fists and cursed them as they rode by. I saw them reach the Roman foot. The legionaries received them with impassive faces; to them all barbarians were the same, and Germans no worse than others.

That evening rumours flew about that the Germans had

agreed to withdraw without fighting, and that tomorrow our army would march west. But next day we continued north-wards, though orders came through that the Germans were still negotiating, and that we were not to attack their scouts. As a matter of fact I saw no scouts; but this was my first campaign, and others claimed to have spotted them lurking in the undergrowth.

On the second day we entered a region of wide marshes and boggy plains; there was nowhere to hide an army, and we rode in comfortable certainty that we could not be surprised. Never-theless, we were informed that the whole encampment of the Usipetes and Tencteri, with their women and children and waggons, lay only two days' march ahead. The German envoys were expected to return tomorrow; but no agreement had as yet been reached and we must be on our guard against attack.

We were now in the land of the Treveri, Gauls who had not yet made up their minds whether German invaders were worse than a Roman army. Though the peasants had withdrawn to fortified villages, they were not at open war with the Germans and a few of their warriors came out to talk to us. They were frank about the policy of their nation. They said that the Ger-mans were not genuinely seeking peace, but spinning out negotiations because most of their horse had ridden away on a raid to the westward. When these German cavalry returned there would be a battle, and the prudent Treveri would rush to the assistance of the victors. We passed this information back to headquarters. But perhaps Caesar did not believe it; for we received no order to attack.

Next morning we advanced very cautiously, knowing that the German camp was nearby. We had passed a disturbed night, seeking water for our horses. That may seem odd, since we were in the middle of a marsh; but the bog water was so foul that animals would not touch it, and the only clear spring had a meagre flow. I was lucky to get Starlight watered by midnight; some of my comrades waited their turn until it was time for the morning parade.

When we had advanced about five miles the German em-bassy made contact, and the whole army halted. That looked like peace at the eleventh hour, for it seemed unlikely that they would negotiate so near their camp unless they intended to submit. We dismounted to look to our horses. So long as the Germans went back to their proper place, east of the Rhine, perhaps it was a good thing that they should go without fighting. Of course we hated all Germans, and wanted them dead; but they are terrible warriors, and no Gaul looks forward to meeting their charge.

Then Piso summoned our squadron leaders to a conference, and our new orders were carefully explained to every man. Our leader told us that agreement had been reached in principle. The Germans had promised to cross the Rhine, to the land of the Unii, as soon as their cavalry rejoined the main body. So we were not to attack. None the less, we were to advance as far as a spring a few miles on, where there was clean water for our horses. Since this would bring us very close to the German camp we must be ready for instant action. The Roman foot would encamp several miles back, for their transport must be protected from German raids.

Those were all our orders. But Piso knew we would feel nervous at camping, only five thousand horse, so close to an enormous German army; especially with our Roman supports several miles in the rear. To comfort us he added unofficially that most of the German cavalry were still absent, so that the whole mounted force present with the enemy made up only eight hundred horsemen. Though they would be disturbed to see us camp so close to their women and children they were unlikely to offer battle at those odds. Of course, if the German foot moved against us we could fall back on the Roman army faster than they could follow.

Acco was vexed at this reiterated suggestion that all Gauls, were afraid of Germans, and did right to be afraid. But Piso was only facing facts. After all, Germans are bigger than Gaul and they pass all their days in warfare. Our advance for the next three miles, until we arrived at the spring, was one of the slowest movements ever performed by cavalry.

The spring gushed from the foot of a little hill, the only hill in the marshy plain. While most of our men dismounted to crowd round the water my own squadron was stationed as guard on the hilltop. Through the haze we could see a great smear of smoke, which was the German camp, only three miles away; and since the wind blew from them we could smell the crowded huts and unburied offal of a German town. It seemed rash to unsaddle so close to the enemy; but unless we were to stand to until our horses were exhausted there was nothing else to be done.

Suddenly Acco peered forward, shouting: 'Look, it's a battle after all. Here comes the German army.'

Over the plain advanced a black something; it was too small to be the German army, but soon we could make it out as German horse (no dust rose from the wet ground). Our squadron let out a yell of mingled defiance and alarm. Piso appeared from nowhere to put himself at our head, for we were the only squadron mounted and ready. While our comrades saddled in haste we rode down to check the attack.

'Bloody savages, charging us while their chiefs discuss terms,' I muttered to Acco. For riding into my first battle I felt too nervous to keep silent.

'German manners,' he answered with a grin. 'Do you realise that these are the eight hundred horse in their camp, offering battle to five thousand? I hope Caesar lets some of them get away; for, treacherous or no, this is a gallant deed of arms.'

Then everything happened very quickly, as two parties of horse closed at the gallop. We were four hundred strong, so the Germans outnumbered us; but we knew that in a few minutes they would be heavily outnumbered in their turn, once our other squadrons were armed and mounted. We met their charge with resolution.

I caught a quick impression of yelling Germans, huge men who waved heavy swords. They rode ugly little ponies, usually bareback; their arms did not gleam, for they keep them greased; and their coarse sheepskin coats stank with the smoke of many camp-fires. They did not seem gallant warriors; but they certainly looked dangerous.

At the last moment our line checked, as we shrank from riding into that wall of swords. I reined Starlight, to keep in my correct place; but Acco squeezed grey Poplar, gaining a clear length. Then a hairy great German swung at my head, and I caught the blow on my shield; I was too busy to look about me, though I took no harm and (I think) did no damage to the foe. Suddenly the crowd vanished; there were Germans all around, but not very close. I wrenched at the reins and set Starlight galloping to the rear. I was a paid soldier, not a sworn champion. If my comrades thought fit to run away it was not for a recruit to challenge the judgement of veterans.

I was relieved when Acco overtook me, swinging a bloody sword. He was drunk with the glory of his first charge, but he still had enough sense not to fight eight hundred Germans single-handed.

The enemy halted to order their ranks, and we retired unmolested on our other squadrons, who were now formed in the plain. Piso cursed us in very foul language, but I felt no shame. It seemed unnecessary for one squadron to fight to the last, against superior numbers, when nine others were coming up to help.

Then, to our amazement, the Germans charged a second time. Although we were formed in line we were not really ready to receive them; some of our men were bareheaded, with flapping girths. For whatever reason, and it may have been plain cowardice, our ranks broke before the German charge.

We stopped them, of course, by sheer weight of numbers. Soon a crowd of excited troopers were pressing their mounts against their adversaries, and banging about with swords. Since neither side had the impetus of the gallop we began to push them back. Then the Germans adopted a strange tactic. Many of them leapt to the ground, crouching to stab our horses in the belly. Their ponies stood motionless, firm as rocks in the swirling mêlée. If I had not seen it with my own eyes I would never have believed that horses could be trained to such a pitch of obedience. No wonder the Germans value these ugly ponies, never giving high prices for foreign chargers as we do. Ponies which will stand riderless in a hot action are worth their weight in gold.

A number of our men were unhorsed, to be stabbed as they struggled to their feet. I was nowhere near a German, for the press of horses kept me back; but when our line recoiled Starlight was borne along by the crowd. Piso waved his sword, shouting: 'You scum! You natural-born slaves to the Germans! Thank the gods I am a Roman. If you won't stand with odds of ten to one in your favour then I must fight alone!'

No insult would make me stand now I saw that the veterans beside me thought only of their own safety. As we fell back a gap appeared between the armies, while the Germans ran to their patient ponies. Within the hostile ranks we could see a flurry of waving swords and tossing manes, where a few of our men had been engulfed after standing too long. Acco caught my rein.

'We must rescue those men,' he called. 'One charge will do it.'

I shrugged, pointing to two Aeduan nobles who spurred from the fight. 'The Romans don't pay us to be heroes. If those men are earning their money we can run too.'

As I turned my horse Piso again came into view, this time in company with Crassus, our Roman commander. It seemed foolish to play the coward under the eyes of our leaders; so I merely backed Starlight, facing the foe from a safe distance.

Piso, quite mad with rage, was shouting at his superior in Latin. 'You must lead another charge, or be broken for cowardice in the field! I tell you my brother is in there! If no one will follow I shall charge alone!'

Crassus answered calmly: 'If we retreat at once I can rally them on the infantry. Another repulse and they will scatter all over Gaul. I forbid you to ruin all our horse in the rescue of one man!'

Piso charged all the same. He set off alone, and the German line opened to receive him. Crassus followed, three lengths behind; and three lengths behind Crassus came Acco and myself.

You will understand that this was a much more reasonable enterprise than the single-handed heroism Acco had earlier proposed. His charge would not even have earned us fame after death, since no bard would have seen our gallantry. This was legitimate advertisement, and if we lived the Roman commander would lie under an obligation to us.

For about five minutes things were very confused, though I believe I killed three Germans. Acco fought magnificently, like a true son of the Wargod; and I suppose Crassus and Piso also did well, though I was too busy to watch them. Then Acco and I were hustling two other horsemen to the rear, Crassus and Piso's brother; Piso himself lay beside his dead horse, but one down out of five was a light rate of loss for such a desperate attack.

Piso's brother had been dazed by a knock on the head. He came because he would do what anyone told him, as will most men in that condition. Crassus was as eager to be saved as we were to save him; he had come to his senses and remembered that Roman commanders are not supposed to charge single-handed, even if their men run away. On the whole we had less trouble than I had expected. Our little counter-attack had shaken the Germans immediately opposed to us, and they did not follow closely. Our only disappointment came when we rejoined our fleeing squadrons; Piso's brother at last understood what had happened, and turned back to avenge the family bereavement. After all our pains we had not rescued him.

But we had saved the commander of all the Roman cavalry, which must count as a very useful achievement.

Meanwhile our comrades ran like rabbits, though they held together in one body. After a fast gallop of five miles we reached the Roman infantry, and when at last we drew rein there was not a German in sight.

The foot halted at once, and those tireless legionaries set about digging their trenches. The horse were ordered to make camp in rear of the infantry, as far from the Germans as possible. Our comrades were bitterly ashamed of their flight, and in consequence very angry with the enemy; Acco and I felt in better spirits, for Crassus must reward us when he had leisure for such things. That evening he merely wrote down our names, and then rode off to explain himself to Caesar.

Of course we of the cavalry had no supper, and no breakfast next day; for our supplies were now in German hands. But the Romans generously sent us forage, to keep the horses fit for duty. At first light came orders to stand to arms, with horses saddled; but no one was yet to move. This was because the Usipetes and Tencteri, with true German inconsequence, had sent a deputation of all their leading men to continue negotiations. Apparently in German eyes yesterday's fight, which had disgraced us and cost us nearly a hundred dead, was merely a casual brawl, not an act of war.

Caesar was stricter in his views. All the German envoys were arrested as truce-breakers, and orders came for the whole army to march against the German camp. The cavalry were placed at the tail of the column, ostensibly because the storming of fortifications is a task for foot. We were in no condition to claim that the post was beneath our dignity.

The Romans, in full armour, advanced at a quick trot; as they covered the eight miles to the German camp they split into three columns, and then, without a check, went straight at the hostile entrenchments.

The Germans were taken by surprise. They supposed they had just concluded a peace, and all their leaders were chained in our camp. Many warriors were unarmed, and the others resisted individually, without ever getting into formation. The legions swarmed over the ditch as hounds disappear into cover.

We were halted on a flank, well to the rear. Presently we saw a stream of Germans, mostly women and children, fleeing from the camp in the general direction of the Rhine. Crassus rode up, and I overheard him shout to his interpreter: 'Order the rascals to cut down those German women. It's all they are fit for, if they are fit even for that. But they may as well make themselves useful if they can.'

That is not the form in which the order reached us.

Whooping, we set off after the fugitives. Here was a chance to get rid of a whole nation of Germans, or rather two nations. An occasional hefty young woman or spry old man put up enough fight to remind us that this was war, so that we saw

58

them as German enemies, not helpless non-combatants. The Roman infantry were storming through the camp, where the baggage of two populous communities would be their plunder; but we, remembering our shame of yesterday, desired revenge more than booty.

The remnants of the German army, fleeing from their captured camp, mingled with the throng of fugitives. Most had flung away their arms to run faster, and the rest were too frightened to stand and fight. From midday to sunset we slew and slew, until our arms were too heavy to lift the sword. The abject terror of the Germans inflamed us; such nasty, dirty, frightened people, whimpering as they dodged before our horses, deserved to be wiped from the face of the earth. Towards the end we began to know uneasily that it would be better for the honour of Gaul if there were no survivors to tell of this massacre.

There were few survivors. The fugitives headed south-east, and we made no effort to cut them off because it was easier to run them through from behind. Presently they reached the left bank of the Rhine, but they had no boats and were too exhausted to swim. They could flee no further, for here the river Moselle joined the main stream. They stood wailing on the bank, or jumped into the water to drown. When darkness fell our trumpets blew the recall, and our scattered bands assembled. By then there were no Germans still on their feet, and most of us had dismounted to plunder the slain.

I had found three Gallic brooches, probably spoil recently taken from the Menapii; and a long string of amber beads which I could sell at a good price to any Roman dealer. Romans like the stuff, thinking it tinged with magic; whereas they do not appreciate even the best Gallic enamel. That was not bad booty for such an easy day's work. Best of all, our supplies had been recovered in the captured camp, and we shared also the Germans' beef and beer. Tonight we would feast gloriously, after our glorious victory.

Not a man of ours had been hurt, and even the Roman foot, who had stormed the entrenchments of the camp against disorganised but determined resistance, had lost only a score of wounded and no one killed. There should have been nothing to mar our pleasure.

But Acco, sitting beside me, took the bloom off my rejoicing. He had been killing to the end, and thus had missed his chance of robbing corpses. So one of our neighbours, very kindly as I thought, offered him a mixed handful of German ornaments; this man, a petty noble of the Arvernians, had begun to plunder early and had taken more than he could conveniently carry.

Unfortunately the collection contained several of the little bead bracelets with which Germans deck their babies to keep off the Evil Eye; the strings were so short that only tiny infants could have worn them. Acco burst out that he was not in the habit of making war on babies, whatever might be the custom of Auvergne, and that he did not desire such spoil as a trophy. He went on to ask the man, who was only trying to be friendly, whether he had a juicy baby in his stewpot; for he supposed such a murderer of little children would be a cannibal also. There was very nearly a brawl, but everyone else was too happy to quarrel.

As soon as I could I took Acco aside. We were both desperately tired, but we walked out of earshot of that gay camp and sat on the ground. Acco at once began his complaint.

'I joined this army because Caesar was supposed to have the most gallant war-band in Gaul. I thought Romans were brave; a little unpolished perhaps, but worthy comrades in battle. Now I wish I had chosen a band of Germans. Germans kill infants in arms, just like Romans. But they don't attack while the enemy is negotiating, or imprison envoys who visit them during truce. How soon can we get away from this disgusting Caesar, to seek an army which honours the usages of war?'

I tried to bring him to his senses. I pointed out that it was the Germans who had attacked under cover of negotiations, which was why they had surprised us and forced us to retreat. Today's massacre was fit punishment for such treachery. As for the envoys, they had been detained to save their lives; we had heard that Caesar would release them tomorrow. Perhaps our attack had not been very glorious; but it had been most useful. For the next few years there should be room for all surviving Germans on their own side of the Rhine. Caesar had promised the Gauls protection in return for tribute: his strength really did protect our villages.

'It may have been the right thing to do,' answered Acco, 'but I wish I had not taken a part in it. Perhaps our ancestors wiped out whole families of Basques to win our valley. Yet this is something bigger. Do you know how many Germans woke in that camp this morning? The Romans found out by questioning the envoys. The total was publicly announced this evening, I suppose because it is the kind of news Romans enjoy; anyway, a man who spoke Gallic passed it on to me. There were 430,000 of the Usipetes and Tencteri; tonight there are none. Isn't it nice to think that one day we can tell our children that we had a share in the slaughter of more men, women and children than would fill the greatest city in the world? Four hundred and thirty thousand . . . how far would they stretch if they stood in a single line? Is there any other living man, even another Roman, who would kill 430,000 terrified fugitives in an afternoon and then go happily to supper, as Caesar now sits happily at supper? How many were we in our valley, ten thousand, twenty thousand? If the Romans wiped out the Elusates, and twenty neighbouring valleys besides, I suppose they would regard it as an ordinary day's work. I don't know the gods who rule this part of the country, but tonight they must be besieged by ghosts, hungry for blood. How many of us must die before they are appeased?'

'If the gods round here don't like us we can go somewhere else. You and I have angered the Goddess, but since we left home she has done us no harm, and she is unknown in these parts.'

But I had been tactless to remind him of our private troubles. He began to complain of another worry. 'No one round here has heard of Pyrene, but that does not mean that the Goddess is unknown. Down by the river I stumbled on a little cave with the images of three women in it. The Goddess sometimes appears in triple form, or so I have been told.'

'Only to women. She is the Goddess of the women, who cannot harm warriors. But it's odd no one here told me of her.

61

I inquired from the Treveri, and they say they worship only Skyfather and the Wargod, like the rest of us.'

'That's what they tell a stranger. If a stranger inquired the Elusates would say the same. But the Goddess is there in the background. Perhaps Skyfather will protect us, but wherever we travel we shall still be in the realm of the Goddess.'

'Very well, the Goddess remains our foe. I can't see that so far she has done us much harm. Yesterday we both came through a dangerous charge without a scratch; today we have been completely victorious. The Treveri may keep images of her in a cave, but she does not rule this land.'

However, there was no pleasing Acco. When he went to sleep he was still grumbling at the savagery of the Roman army; and complaining that the Goddess would be waiting for him, in every land he should happen to visit. Considering that this was one of the greatest victories Gauls had ever won over Germans, and that our comrades intended to celebrate it as long as the captured beer lasted, he was being a tiresome spoilsport.

Next day was a holiday, because the Gallic contingent was too drunk to go on parade, and even the legionaries in no state for marching. I was in fairly good shape, since Acco had dragged me so early from the feasting. He and I spent the morning looking after our own horses – and most of the other horses in the squadron as well; if we had not fed and watered them the beasts would have starved while their masters slept off the feast of victory. In the afternoon I got hold of a stray Treveran, a local farmer who had come in to buy German spoil; he was quite willing to talk of the three images in the cave.

They were really German goddesses, but the people on both side of the Rhine were always stealing each other's women, and German slave-girls had brought them to the western bank. They must have had names of their own, but to the men of the Treveri they were the Three Ladies or the Three Mothers. They did *not* make the crops grow, or manage the affairs of wild beasts; on the contrary, both men and women sacrificed to them for good luck. The Treveran agreed that his women knew more about them than they would tell to men, but the cult was in no way secret. I explained to Acco that this proved that the

Three were not related to our single Goddess. He remained un-convinced, and very melancholy.

In the evening Crassus sought us out, and was pleased to find us looking after other men's horses. I had not planned to be discovered at this task, on purpose to curry favour with the commander; it was just that neither Acco nor I could endure to see good horses lose condition for lack of attention. Also, in any war-band it is very useful to store up a credit balance of favours done; if tomorrow I wanted to chase a pretty girl, or rob a fat farmyard, any of my comrades would look after Star-light while I slipped away from evening stables.

Crassus had walked over from the Roman lines with only an orderly and an interpreter, to see how his Gauls were getting on. When he found most of them still drunk he sensibly kept out of their way. Otherwise someone might have struck him, just to prove that we were free auxiliaries, not slaves of Rome. Then there would have to be a crucifixion, which always lowers the spirits of the troops. Romans never pass over flagrant in-subordination; but Crassus managed with very few punish-ments because he had the tact to know when to be absent.

He recognised the two of us by the ornaments on our swords (later he told me that to Romans all Gauls look alike; they can see nothing but our long hair and moustaches). He called us to him, and spoke pleasantly to his interpreter.

'These men brought me out of that disgraceful scuffle two days ago, when I was in half a mind to get myself killed. I was so ashamed of the wretched cavalry I have been training for the last three years that death seemed preferable to another sticky interview with Caesar. Make a graceful speech of thanks to my rescuers, using all the honorifics due to their nobility; and in-vite them to call at my tent tonight to receive a more tangible reward.'

'Thank you, my lord. You are very gracious,' I said in my best Latin before the interpreter could open his mouth. 'We Gauls feel nervous when we face German cavalry, but you will admit that today we did all that was asked of us.'

'Oh, you can understand Latin, and speak it more or less correctly? Then I can give you a bigger reward than a few gold coins. There are never enough interpreters. Does your companion also understand Latin?'

I said that though Acco spoke only Gallic he was as skilled in everything relating to horse-management as I was myself, and I was heir to the horse-master of the Elusates. I added a few words about Acco's very noble birth, for, though that carried no weight among Romans, Crassus was intelligent enough to see it would be an asset in dealing with Gauls.

Then we walked back with Crassus to the Roman camp, and the guard turned out to salute us. Crassus was not only commander of the auxiliary horse; he was also son to a Consul who happened to be the richest man in Rome, one of the three leaders of the state. If young Publius had been just one of the smart young knights who carried Caesar's despatches the sentry would still have turned out the guard for his father's son.

His tent was roomy and warm, for he had the money to buy the best equipment. At the back I saw bronze-mounted couches and inlaid tables; but Crassus knew that few Gauls are at ease if they must talk lying down, and we sat together on little stools by the entrance. The interpreter, an Aeduan named Gnaeus Pompeius (though he was not in fact a citizen), engaged Acco in polite conversation, asking him to relate the famous deeds of his ancestors; while Publius Licinius Crassus, Roman knight, son of the Consul, commander of all Caesar's horse, spoke to me as to an equal.

He drew me out about my past life, expressing great interest in my father's office of horse-master. He said that there was no equivalent in the Roman constitution, though it made provison for most eventualities; yet long ago there must have been something of the sort, in the days when Roman knights went to war on horses provided for them by the City. He asked whether I was ready to succeed my father if he were killed in battle tomorrow, and whether I had ever bought horses on my own responsibility. Perhaps I boasted a little in my replies, stretching the truth without actually telling a lie. Crassus listened carefully, and answered after a pause:

'You and your friend saved my life, and for that alone I ought to promote you. But since you speak Latin and understand horses I can give you important work which must be done, and which you are fitted to perform. That's better than inventing sinecures for deserving heroes. The army replaces horses killed in action or foundered by forced marching. I must buy more than a hundred horses to replace those killed in the recent rout. I have Roman experts on my staff, but they wouldn't be here, so far from civilisation, unless they were out to make a quick fortune; and anyway they don't know local conditions. The last lot of showy African gallopers proved useless in Gallic mud. You will be attached to my staff as local expert in charge of remounts. You will have to do most of my quaestor's work while he catches up with his drinking. Can you write? No? What a pity. We must find an honest clerk. Your friend can be your deputy, just to keep it all in the family. He will draw only half your extra pay, for you will be down on the pay-sheet as both interpreter and horse-buyer. Does that suit you?'

I accepted with enthusiasm. So did Acco, when the proposal had been explained to him. Then I plucked up courage to ask one further favour.

'Must we mess with our squadron? Or shall we be counted as members of your household?'

'You are members of my household. In camp you will inspect the horse-lines; on the march you make yourself useful as interpreter; and in battle you join the bodyguard which Caesar has detailed to ride beside me. He told me last night that he personally didn't care how I got myself killed; but he didn't want to lose an election in Rome because my father held him responsible for the death of his son.'

That was how Caesar talked of himself. But that was not how his soldiers talked of him. They knew he was the greatest general in the world; as a young man he had won the Civic Crown for saving the life of a comrade, and two years ago had fought on foot, in the front rank, to repel the Nervii. Even at that time his whole army adored him; later they followed him when he made war on his own City.

I thanked Crassus with genuine gratitude. For saving his life I deserved a reward, but this reward was greater than I had expected. Acco's enthusiasm got the better of his good manners. I was always telling him not to intrude Gallic customs into Roman social life, because the Romans are a discourteous race who cannot master the rules of ceremonious behaviour; now he fell on his knees and swore by the Raven, his ancestral sword, to be a true comrade to Publius Crassus until death. He looked rather foolish kneeling with his hands between the knees of his lord, until Crassus made a lucky guess and raised him graciously to his feet.

'What does all that mean, Camul?' asked Crassus with a smile. 'Has your friend adopted me to be his father?'

'Not quite, sir, though you are not far out. He has taken the oath which makes him your sworn comrade. By the custom of Gaul you now command his sword, and if you are killed in battle he must avenge you or die in the attempt. In return you must keep him in comfort all his days, and if need be share your last crust with him. You may reject his service, but if you accept it you should by rights give him an arm-ring.'

'Well, well. With the City in its present state a politician needs all the faithful swords he can find. I should like to accept the oath, but I don't wear arm-rings. Will this dagger do instead? A weapon as a gift seems in keeping with the spirit of the ceremony.'

Acco was delighted with his ivory-hilted dagger. I knew, and told Crassus, that he would be a trustworthy and wholehearted comrade, for he took the obligations of honour very seriously indeed. I myself nearly took the same oath, now I knew that Crassus was a gentleman who would keep his side of the bargain. But on second thoughts I considered it rash to bind myself more strongly than is customary among Roman soldiers. While Rome paid me I would serve her faithfully; from a life-long promise I shied away. That was as well. I kept the promise I made, and now it is ended.

Next day we began a new life. Grooms strapped our horses and servants polished our weapons. We rose in the morning with the officers, in time to inspect the parade, and went to bed when we had finished our work, which was often long after lights out. The Roman veterinary officer and buyer of remounts was as incompetent and corrupt as Crassus had supposed; I spent most of the day treating sick horses, while Acco chaffered with Gallic dealers.

Acco held himself bound to the service of Crassus, and therefore refused even the small commission the dealers offered unasked. I made up my mind not to take bribes unless I needed money urgently, and money could buy nothing while we lay encamped on the Rhine; though I made no rash vows about the future. In consequence not only Crassus, but all the Roman headquarters staff, found official funds went further when we had the spending of them. We quickly became popular and trusted.

We did not eat with the Romans officers. Language barriers would have made that awkward, and we disliked their custom of lying down to dine. But socially they treated us as equals, which was a pleasant change for men who had recently been troopers. We messed with the small group of Gallic interpreters and guides who were permanently attached to headquarters. We had no master except our sense of duty.

In the mess we had early information about the army's future movements. Everyone was preparing for Caesar's raid into the unknown island of Britain; for that maps were being drawn, and ships were being built, in the thorough Roman fashion. But first came an unexpected, improvised foray: the first recorded invasion of Germany from our side of the Rhine.

During this invasion there was no fighting, because the Germans fled before us; and western Germany looks disappointingly like eastern Gaul. But the expedition was far from useless. It terrified the Germans, and impressed the Romans themselves with a consciousness of great deeds accomplished. We of the Gallic horse had nothing to do except to look on; the building of that famous bridge over the Rhine was a feat worth watching.

Roman legionaries are fine warriors; but what makes them really formidable is that they are all skilled craftsmen. They began absolutely from scratch, by forging the iron 'dogs' which would hold the trusses in position, and felling timber for the piles. When their material was assembled they began building from the western bank, driving the piles with blows from a mighty engine of Caesar's invention. It was most impressive to see all those men working at their different tasks, while the bridge grew before our eyes.

I was sitting on the bank, absorbed in watching this marvellous work, when Crassus came up to me. He was proud of his auxiliaries, and enjoyed telling us what the army was doing.

'Well, Camul,' he said cheerfully, 'have you ever before seen a bridge like this?'

'Never, sir. Nor has there ever been one like it, over the Rhine.'

'But the forging of those iron "dogs"? Could you manage that?'

'I couldn't myself, because I am a warrior. I expect our smiths could.'

'And the timber-felling?'

'Oh, I could do that easily, if someone marked which tree I was to cut.'

'And putting the piles and struts in the right place?'

'There again, that's quite easy, after someone has shown you how.'

'Exactly, Camul. That's why we Romans are in Gaul. We want to show the Gauls how to do things. The Rhine has never been bridged. Yet there is nothing here that a Gaul cannot do. If you choose to serve us loyally you will have bridges, and stone temples, and paved roads, from end to end of your land. I don't say you will be our equals straight away; we are teaching you, and the teacher is master of his pupils. But your children, or perhaps your grandchildren, will be equal partners in the Roman dominion, the greatest state the world has ever seen. When you charge behind me remember that you are fighting for a civilised Gaul, not just for next month's pay.'

'I see, sir. But supposing we don't wish to serve you?'

'Then you will serve us just the same, but as slaves. Face facts, Camul, even unpleasant facts. This is the army that drove out Ariovistus, that conquered the Nervii. We could, if we tried, beat all the Gallic peoples together, though you know as

68

well as I do that hall te peoples will never fight together.'

'No man can be made a slave against his will,' I answered quickly. 'There is always a way out,' and I touched the hilt of my sword.

'That's true. In Spain the warriors fought to the death. But when they were dead their women and children submitted. Anyway, there are a great many able-bodied slaves in Italy. When it comes to the point life is sweet, even in defeat.'

(I must tell the truth. Later we both of us made the choice between death and slavery, and Crassus chose more nobly.)

'Very well, sir. I shall serve Rome. I like the Romans, not least because you worship decent manly gods.'

'I'm glad to hear it; though we have goddesses in Italy. However, I have explained my philosophy, and I hope I have made a disciple. I sought you out because I have a suggestion to make. I shall leave this army before it embarks for Britain. Next year my father leads a great expedition to the eastern border, a long way from here. My Gallic horse will join him when he leaves Rome. I myself leave for Italy in a few days, and I shall take a few staff officers to buy remounts, collect rations, and engage billets. I want you and your friend Acco to come with me. Even if you aren't killed you may never return, so I don't order you to come, I make a request. Will you come with me?'

'To see Rome, and the wonders of civilisation? I will come gladly, sir. Since Acco has taken the oath of a comrade he must go where you go. You need not ask him.'

'Then that's settled. You will come as members of my personal staff, and you yourself will have the rank of military tribune. Strictly speaking, a barbarian cannot hold that rank, and Caesar would not make you a citizen when I asked him. He has been making too many Gallic citizens lately, and there have been complaints. But my father will grant you the citizenship in due time. Anyway, no one checks these things, so long as you don't vote, or fight a lawsuit. You speak fair Latin, and you will be a citizen one day. Call yourself one when we reach Italy, to make your stay more pleasant. Do you mind passing under the name of Publius Licinius Camillus, that is Camillus for short? You take my forename and clan, because I am your sponsor. Camillus is near enough to Camui, but you can alter the third name if another takes your fancy. Right. Publius, citizen of Rome, go and tell my oath-bound comrade to begin packing his baggage.'

CHAPTER III

Rome

We rode at speed from the Rhine to the Tiber, to reach Rome in high summer. I shall not describe the splendours of Italy. Their impact was lessened since we were led gradually through half-civilised Cisalpine Gaul and ancient but impoverished Etruria to the magnificence of the City. We soon became accustomed to sleeping in stone-built bedchambers which were used for no other purpose, eating in dining-rooms which were occupied only at meal-times, and bathing in ealborate heated halls, larger than any chieftain's hall we had seen at home.

This complicated bathing wastes a great deal of time, and does not really make a Roman any cleaner than a scrub with warm water in a wooden Gallic tub. But otherwise we fitted easily into the Roman way of life. Roman manners are direct and businesslike, and Romans talk mostly about money or political power; since in Rome we sought neither, Acco and I could remain silent in the background.

At a posting-house outside the City we left our horses in clean and well-ventilated stables, for the steward of Marcus Licinius Crassus, the Consul, met us there with litters and porters to carry our baggage. Publius Crassus explained that it was reckoned bad manners to ride a horse in the City, and that traffic regulations prohibited baggage-waggons. I had never before been carried on men's necks as though I were a corpse or a pregnant woman. I expected to find it humiliating, but I found instead that it makes the human baggage feel very proud and pompous, as he looks out through the curtains at scurrying pedestrians.

Within the City Acco and I were carried to a tall lodging-house, where a large room and a tiny kitchen, with three slaves attached, had been hired for our use. We were told to present ourselves at the great Licinian mansion early every morning; the porter would admit us without question, and we were to wait in the hall until we received orders for the day.

By this time I was wearing Roman dress, including the toga which may only be worn by citizens. These clothes are comfortable enough for lounging in the sunshine, which is all Romans do while wearing them; in a toga you can neither ride nor fight, and to my mind there is not enough ornament on it to make it suitable wear for a gentleman. But it is a convenient uniform, which even the poorest citizen can afford.

Acco was encouraged to wear his most elaborate Gallic costume. I lent him my belt, torques and arm-rings, which were better than his own. Of course he was stared at by every idler, and young Crassus feared this might embarrass him. But as a noble of high birth Acco thought the lower orders ought to be impressed when he deigned to walk before them. He enjoyed being followed by street urchins, and could not understand the remarks they shouted after him.

On our first morning in the City we dressed by lamplight (Roman lamps burn brightly, and indoors no Roman is bothered by darkness), and hastened at dawn to wait on our patron. His mansion lurked behind a high blank wall, pierced only by a single door; but within it spread over many courts and arcades. In the great hall, so large that the roof was supported by columns, we found a crowd of other clients. Presently a servant came round distributing presents, and I was glad to see that some Romans had an idea of the generosity expected from a great man to his followers. But, as I have said, these gifts were distributed by a servant, not by the lord in person; and they were small sums of money, or baskets of food, not arm-rings and weapons. Even when the Romans have guessed at the proper rules of courtesy they thriftily spoil the effect by making a present look like wages.

Soon after sunrise Publius Crassus bustled in, to walk quickly round the room greeting each guest with a perfunctory nod. Then he made for the front door, and a servant indicated that we should join the group who followed at his heels. Most of the clients waited behind, for they had come to greet his father the Consul. As we went out I gave the porter the cold roast fowl wrapped in a linen napkin which the steward had pressed into my hands. I had thought it unmannerly to refuse my patron's gift, even such an unfitting gift; but obviously a gentleman cannot appear in public carrying his own dinner, and it is never discourteous to tip the servant of your lord. Acco had been given a small purse of silver coins, which we kept. Silver can be considered an ornament, and a gentleman is entitled to accept jewellery.

In the street we all set off at a great pace, on foot. Publius led us across the town to the even bigger mansion of his father's colleague in the Consulship, Pompeius. There we found a great press of clients, whom Publius joined with his own following. We were just in time to greet the Consul, who walked round the hall smiling graciously before making for the street at the head of what was now a small army. We trooped after him to a temple on the Capitol, where men were waiting with an ox decked for sacrifice. The other Consul, Marcus Crassus, met us there at the head of another army of clients, and after the ox had been killed by the blow of an axe they both glanced at the liver and pronounced all well. The ceremony was over in a few minutes, and it seemed to me that no one took it seriously or bothered about the meaning of the omen.

Then the Consuls went home again, and Publius led his clients to the Forum, where we marched solemnly round the crowded square greeting some citizens – and not greeting others. Acco and I soon got the hang of it; we bowed and smiled with affable politeness, or scowled fiercely, as our patron indicated. By now it was three hours after sunrise, and I had not spoken sensibly to anyone. It was more like one of those parades in Caesar's army, where we stood about endlessly while the officers learned how to drill us, than like anything I had imagined as the home-life of the Romans. During the morning Publius made a point of speaking personally to each of his clients, and when my turn came I asked him how soon we would get on to our proper business of buying remounts for the army. But he only answered that there would be time for that in the autumn, and smiled at the next client who stood waiting for a greeting.

At last, when it was getting on for midday and we were all hungry and tired, Publius turned to address us in a body. 'Good day, gentlemen,' he said with a mechanical smile, 'I look forward to meeting you tomorrow. Same time. Same place.' Then he was whisked away in a litter, and it seemed we had done our duty for the day.

For the next ten days that was our routine. We got up very early, paraded through Rome behind our patron and at midday were dismissed. We never had a chance to talk to him quietly, and we never met a horse-dealer. We found it very difficult to get through the afternoon and evening, for it is not the Roman custom to keep open house; after the clients' reception invited guests only were welcome in our patron's mansion. We had to buy our supper, with silver coins; for though in Rome bread is cheap, beef is remarkably expensive. On the third day we took a servant to the morning reception; he waited by the outer door to take away whatever present we had been given and spare us the indignity of carrying it; for even a basket of apples was now too precious to be wasted. I was very bored, but prepared to stick it out; for it seemed no worse than drilling with Caesar's army. Acco was more than bored; he suspected that someone was insulting him. He proposed that we should leave the City and join the first band of brigands we met.

I persuaded him to be patient, reminding him that he had taken an oath to follow Publius Crassus. His lord neglected his obligations, but that made it all the more necessary that a well-born Gaul should set an example among Romans. He saw the forces of this and came quietly, though with a bad grace, to more of those dull and meaningless receptions.

'But why did Crassus bring us here?' he burst out, on the tenth evening of our stay. 'We are warriors and horsemen. In

Romen even Publius walks or is carried in a litter like an old woman, and as far as I can see he has no enemies for us to fight. Even his mean little daily gifts must cost him something. Perhaps he would be pleased if we offered of our own accord to go back to Caesar?'

'No, he wouldn't like that,' I answered at once. 'I think we are here for a definite purpose. We are here to remind the Romans that Caesar did not conquer Gaul single-handed. The Romans are very proud of that conquest. They used to fear us Gauls, for their legends tell them that once, long ago, a Gallic army sacked the City.'

'When was that?' asked Acco, interested at last. 'I have never heard of it, so they can't have been my own ancestors. Who was their leader?'

'I can't say more than that it was a long time ago, and the Romans never learned the name of their leader. They call him Brennus, as though Brenn were a name, not a title. I suppose some nation from this side of the Alps rode south on a raid, and thought so little of their victory that no one made a song about it. But the Romans have never forgotten.'

'Well then, Gauls once conquered Rome, as Romans now conquer Gaul. It is what you would expect. Every people have their turn, if they last long enough. That does not explain why Publius dragged us here under false pretences.'

'It does, if you stop and think. At present three men rule Rome: the two Consuls we see at the daily sacrifice, and Caesar with his great army. They share supreme power because they work together against all rivals. But that does not mean they are truly friends and allies. Pompeius, the stiff-looking Consul, has won wars in the past; at present he is raising an army to fight in Spain, and he is bitterly jealous of Caesar. The affable Consul, our patron's father Marcus Crassus, has never had a chance to prove his valour; though when he was a young man he wiped out a band of rebel slaves. He is now gathering an army to enlarge the eastern frontier, the army we are to join. Each of the three is convinced that he is the greatest soldier in the state, but not yet great enough to take on the other two combined. Caesar is the famous conqueror of Gaul. Publius

wants to remind the Romans that Caesar had help. There must
be Gauls in the Licinian train. I am supposed to be a citizen of
Gallic birth, to match the Gallic noblemen enfranchised by
Caesar. You are an eminent foreign ally of the Roman people,
to match the queer envoys from distant lands whoc all Caesar
patron. That is why the steward encourages you to wear Gallic
dress and look as foreign as possible. When we walk behind
Crassus the Romans remember that Publius commanded
Caesar's horse, and that Marcus his father is also a great
soldier.'

'So we are really trophies of victory? I am not sure I like
that.'

'Perhaps, but trophies who can walk about freely. That is
better than being dead heroes or conquered slaves.'

That set us off once again discussing the Romans, and the
attitude we ought to adopt towards them. Acco could not make
up his mind. The Romans made marvellous things; and they
owned many beautiful things which others had made. On the
other hand, they were ugly people with crude manners; and
they never regarded a Gaul as an equal, even when they were
outwardly civil to us.

One day I would go home, while Acco was in exile for life;
so I did not care very much about the Romans and what they
thought of me. If they despised me as a barbarian, I despised
them for boors. When I could stand their discourtesy no
longer I would leave; but in the meantime they paid good
wages, and I would serve them faithfully.

Neither of us gave a thought to the Goddess, far away in her
valley.

Then one day at the morning reception the steward came up
with a written paper, which he said was a message for me. He
looked at me curiously when I explained that I could not read,
for that is a thing nearly every Roman citizen can do. He read
the message to us quietly in a corner, and then advised us how
to answer it.

This steward was a decent unwarlike man called Pyrrhus,
who had been born of slave parents on the Licinian estates.
After long and faithful service he had been freed, and Acco

76

decided that we might treat him as an honourable freeman. Since he had been born a slave he had never enjoyed the choice between death or slavery, and should not be blamed for his misfortune. It was a point that would not have occurred to me but Acco liked to think these questions out for himself.

The letter which Pyrrhus read to us was an invitation to dinner, sent by an eminent Roman nobleman named Publius Clodius. Naturally we were eager to accept. At last our noble birth was being recognised as it should be. But the steward would not write our answer until he had consulted Publius Crassus; after a long private conversation he came back to tell us of our patron's decision.

'My master says you may go if you wish, and indeed he advises it. For you will find the party amusing. But you should understand the reason for your invitation. Clodius is the most scandalous rake in Rome, but he is also Caesar's agent. Perhaps he wants to pump you about the Army of Syria; though that seems unlikely, for he can find out that sort of thing without asking questions of foreigners. More likely he will try to persuade you to join his faction. My master takes it for granted that Gallic noblemen who follow him of their own free will cannot betray him. He asks you to keep sober as long as you can to listen to any proposal without showing anger, and to report afterwards on the general attitude of Clodius, and on anything else that may be of interest.'

'Now we are to be spies,' said Acco.

'Not unless Clodius insults you by seeking to buy you,' Pyrrhus answered quickly. 'If he tries to persuade you to treachery you are justified in betraying his confidence.'

The freedman had no honour of his own; how could a man in his position afford such a luxury? But he was clever at seeing into the minds of others, and he understood Acco.

So on the afternoon of the next day we set out, in two smart litters lent by Publius. Before starting we each swallowed a small measure of olive-oil, since that is a well-known remedy against drunkenness. But we thought we could drink any Roman into unconsciousness without artificial aid, for Romans dilute their wine with great quantities of water. At home we seldom taste Roman wine, but when we do we put it down neat.

This was our first Roman dinner-party, and we had heard great things of them. I was disappointed to be shown into quite a small dining-room, smaller than the hall of the Licinian mansion. We were only eight guests, making nine in all with our host; whereas in Gaul we don't call it a party unless there are at least fifty drinkers present.

Clodius himself was a very charming and handsome young man, so handsome that he was nicknamed 'the Beautiful'. I knew he had been a gallant soldier; though that is true of every Roman politician, since Roman politics is no business for cowards. The six other guests were young men of affable manners, with an air of aristocratic recklessness which reminded me of Gallic nobles.

Acco and I were placed at the third table, since we had no Roman precedence. Our companion was a handsome young man named Scribonius Curio, who laid himself out to put us at our ease. That was not such a difficult matter as the Romans imagined; we were not worried lest we broke the rules of their etiquette, for we knew that our own Gallic manners are really more courteous than theirs.

A Roman dinner may last anything up to eight hours, and it is assumed that all Romans have enough to eat at home. So the host does not allay his guests' appetites with huge joints of meat and buckets of wine. The food is brought in little by little, and valued more for its savour than its bulk; and the wine is heavily watered, that the guests may continue an intelligent conversation after drinking for several hours. The pleasure of the party is supposed to lie in conversation, or in the antics of the dancers and singers who perform in the middle of the room.

This party began quietly, with Curio asking intelligent questions about the war in Gaul while boys danced before us; one of them was supposed to be an eagle who fell in love with a youth and eventually carried him off to the sky, and a chorus sang the story while they danced it. This is a well-known legend of the Roman religion, and therefore perfectly respectable; obviously it offers great scope as a spectacle. In Rome it

78

is the fashion to make more fuss over pretty boys than over pretty girls; if it amuses them they may do as they like, but it does not amuse Gallic noblemen.

As the evening proceeded the entertainment grew more riotous; but in less than two hours it ended, with a boxing match between teams of German women. The owners of these performers charge enormous sums for their hire, and even the spendthrift Clodius could not afford more than two turns.

By this time everyone felt mellow, and the talk was very free. It should have been enjoyable, for I was among witty young men who were having a very good time; but I was continually worried over Acco. At any moment he might declare war on some fellow-guest. He disapproved of the goings-on round him, and if a Roman made amatory advances to him there would be the honour of a Gallic nobleman to avenge. I was relieved when our host engaged us in conversation, calling across from the centre table.

'I hear you foreign tourists have been wasting your time, when you might have sampled the amusements of the gayest city in the world,' he shouted cheerfully. 'Is it really true that you study our politics by trailing round among the clients of young Publius Crassus? I know he's your patron, and I'm not suggesting you should leave him. But if you want to learn how the City really manages her affairs you ought to come out one afternoon with my friends for a tour of the Forum. Why not join us tomorrow?'

'We have to be careful in the Forum,' answered Acco. 'I am not a citizen, and Camillus thinks it wrong to vote until he understands the issues at stake. But we would both be delighted if you would show us the public buildings. We have seen nothing except the temple where the Consuls offer sacrifice. I don't like wandering about without a real Roman to vouch for me, in case I go somewhere forbidden to strangers.' By now Acco spoke some Latin, very slowly and grammatically; for he feared to look foolish if he made a mistake. I never minded blunders so long as my meaning was clear; though some of the adjectives I had picked up in the army caused surprise when used in general conversation.

All the same, I answered now; for to this company Acco's reason for refusing would seem absurd. 'We are in Rome as Licinians,' I said. 'If Publius leads us to battle in the Forum we shall follow gladly. We ought not to join another band without his permission.'

This was very plain speaking. Curio looked anxiously to see how our host would take it. Luckily Clodius chose to be amused.

'Pompeius marched his veterans in rank to the Forum to persuade his fellow citizens to vote him the Consulate. I didn't know Crassus was also calling out his soldiers. If I am to keep my place in politics I must find some troops of my own.'

'What the devil are you talking about?' asked Curio quietly, as our host turned once more to his neighbours. 'Did someone tell you that Clodius leads an armed gang in the Forum? It happens to be true, but we don't discuss it.'

'I didn't know,' I answered truthfully. 'It's just that I picked up my Latin in the army, and I talk in the army way. So far I have never inquired why clients follow their patron through the Forum, but if we are not there to fight at his command why does he bring us?'

'Oh, to vote as he tells you, and to make him look powerful. Never to fight, for that would be unlawful. We Romans revere our laws.'

'All the same, I wish someone would show us over the temples,' Acco put in. 'We have nothing of the kind in Gaul; whereas our nations often choose their rulers, and we know all about contested elections.'

'Then you have come to the right address,' said Curio sardonically. 'Our host is an expert on all religious affairs. For example, he knows more about the rites of the Good Goddess than any other man.'

'Don't take away my character before these distinguished foreigners,' called Clodius, grinning broadly. 'I often go out at night, and on some mornings even I myself cannot remember where I have been. But on the night of that festival I was never under Pompeia's roof. So a jury of my fellow citizens decided, and you must accept the finding of a jury.'

Acco was at once on the alert. 'Who is this Good Goddess?' he asked.

They all began telling him at once, though in fact they knew nothing definite, for this Roman Goddess is worshipped only by women. The point of the joke was that a few years ago Clodius had attended her secret mysteries disguised as a girl. He had been recognised, and later charged with sacrilege. But the jury had pretended to believe his denial of the charge.

The trouble was that we had now become the centre of attention, just when Acco was too excited to remember his manners. Clodius was beginning to feel his wine, and with drunken persistence pressed us to join his following. I was determined to keep clear of Roman politics, for if enemies made inquiries they would soon discover that I was no citizen.

Luckily our fellow guests were soon distracted by another interest. The manager of the entertainers sent in word to ask if there was anything more they could do for us. Curio had a bright idea; he persuaded Clodius to order the women boxers to dance Ganymede and the Eagle, and the boy dancers to fight with metal boxing-gloves. Soon everyone was shouting, and throwing apples at the battered performers. In the confusion Acco and I slipped out without saying goodbye to our host.

We passed the next morning, as usual, in attendance on our patron. We were growing very tired of this servile foolishness. But we knew that our undignified way of life would not continue long, for the Army of Syria must march before spring; and Acco would not desert the lord to whom he had sworn fidelity.

I made discreet inquiries among the other clients and gathered that we, the followers of Publius Crassus, were unlikely to fight in the Forum. Marcus Crassus the Consul was the richest man in Rome, and he preferred to win elections by the simpler method of bribery.

On the evening after the dinner-party Acco returned to his hobby-horse. Whenever he heard talk of a Goddess he could not rest until he had decided whether she was the nymph Pyrene under another name. At dusk he went out alone, and presently returned with a seedy Gallic vagabond, a professional

6

soothsayer and fortune-teller.

When this rogue had been given an enamel brooch and a jug of wine, as though he were a genuine bard, he proceeded to make our hair stand on end, speaking fluently in the low and ungraceful Gallic of the Roman Province.

'You have heard of the Isles of the Dead, far out in the Ocean, my young gentlemen. I know them also, for I know all the lore of the Druids; as well as the magic of Egypt and the horrid necromancy which brought down the wrath of Heaven on Carthage. But I tell you that Rome here, pleasant Rome where young gentleman have such a good time, is more uncanny than even the Isles of the Dead. Do you know that under the Capitol lies a bleeding human head? Yes, they have been building on the Capitol for centuries, yet whenever they dig a new foundtion they find the head, freshly severed and still bleeding. The magician who buried that foundation-sacrifice was a Druid of power! Under the Forum, where you walk every day, lie men and women who were sacrificed to the Infernal Gods: Marcus Curtius the gallant horseman, and nameless Gauls They were alive when they went below. Who knows whether they are still alive today? And the Palatine, the holy hill where stands the house of the Pontifex Maximus (your old commander, Caesar) – the Palatine is the Gateway of the Underworld. They show you a pit there, the Mundus. Of course they keep it sealed with a heavy stone. But thrice in the year that stone is removed, and only the Pontifex knows what beings come and go. You have seen the Cloaca Maxima, the great drain they are so proud of. Did you see nearby a notice warning you not to spit? You mustn't spit there, because there is something buried underground which wouldn't like it. Ah, Rome is a terrible place, most dangerous to young foreigners; unless they get a wise old Gaul to show them how to deal with the spirits in it.'

'We are not interested in spirits,' Acco interrupted sharply. 'I myself am a trained Ovate. I can bind small ghosts by the power of certain names which have been taught to me; and to appease the great ones I know how to pour the blood.'

'An Ovate, noble sir? But I am a full Druid, though it so

82

happens that because of my long exile I have forgotten some of the signs. I am a full Druid, I say; yet even I dread the underworld guardians of Rome.'

'That's as may be,' murmured Acco, making queer motions with his fingers. The old fraud either missed the signals or did not know the correct answers. Acco continued in a brisk and resolute voice: 'Well, Agedincus, you may be a Druid long in exile, or you may not. Let us dismiss the matter, and the spirits of the underworld. My friend and I wish to know whether the Goddess bears sway in Rome. I ask you to help us with your information, merely because you take an interest in religion and have lived here many years.'

'There are many goddesses in Rome,' answered the soothsayer, falling once more into the tone of a guide telling a familiar story. 'On the Capitol they worship Juno and Minerva. The people also serve Diana, a maiden who hunts in the countryside, though the magistrates neglect her. What usually interests strangers is the worship of Venus. If you care to come with me tonight I can show you some curious rites held in her honour; very curious indeed, and most interesting to travellers who have left their wives at home.'

'We know every mode in which Venus is worshipped,' I said angrily. 'We are guests and clients of Publius Licinius Crassus, son of the Consul; not guileless strangers in need of a pimp. You are supposed to be a prophet. Can you tell us whether here in Rome there is one great Goddess, who rules the women and keeps her doings secret from men? In our own land such a Goddess rules, as we know to our cost; though we were warriors grown before we knew her importance.'

Agedincus looked up sharply. The fawning smile vanished from his lips, and for a moment a serious seeker after truth looked out from his bleary eyes.

'I beg your pardon, noble gentlemen,' he said more proudly, with some attempt at the dignified speech Gallic nobles use in talking to one another. 'I have been many years in exile, earning my bread by telling travellers whatever they wish to hear. How could I guess that you were fugitives from the wrath of the Goddess? Most warriors end in the hero's barrow without ever hearing of her. Of course the Goddess rules in Rome. She rules everywhere, if you choose to look below the surface. I will gladly tell you what I know of her.'

'Come, that's more like it,' said I, giving him a piece of silver money.

'But don't run away with the idea that we are afraid of her,' added Acco. 'I have already killed her bear, with a javelin, in her own valley; and if she pesters me in this city I shall try what my Raven can do.' He nodded at the heavy old-fashioned sword hanging from a peg on the wall.

'Of course, gentlemen of your birth will face any foe rather than admit to fear. I am truly a Gaul, and I remember that from my youth,' said the charlatan wistfully. 'When I was young I also outfaced every danger. Perhaps the heroes of the songs died heroes because they were killed in the bloom of their youth. Now I am old – and careful. The Goddess is most dangerous and you must walk warily.... Or perhaps since there is no escape from her wrath it is more manly to brazen it out. ... I don't know.'

He sighed, and drained the jug of wine.

'You have seen the Consuls at sacrifice,' he went on. 'That is the only religion practised openly by Roman citizens. They honour Skyfather by the name of Jupiter, and give the Wargod his share of all the plunder they win from their enemies. But the Goddess is perpetually worshipped by their womenfolk, until even stupid practical Romans take notice of what goes on under their nose. On one day in the year the house of the Pontifex Maximus is given over to the rites of the Good Goddess. You can imagine how terrible she is, if her votaries flatter her by that name. Men keep away from those rites. Your friend Clodius intruded on them, as we know. He got away alive, but avengers still pursue him. He will be cheated of the promised Consulate which would have made his name immortal; and when he dies, within less than three years, the holiest temple in the City will burn as his pyre. Don't dine with him again, I beg you.'

'We don't need your advice. We want information about the Goddess,' I said, seeing that the old man was falling again into the ominous cant which earned him a living at street corners.

'Ah yes, the Goddess, where was I?' he went on more quietly. 'Once a year she is Bona Dea, as I was telling you. The temples of Isis are open every day, though I am not sure she is Isis as well. I have never been initiated into those mysteries. Why don't you try them, if you are still curious?' he shot at Acco, probably to frighten him.

'If they let me bring Raven with me, I might visit those mysteries,' said my friend proudly.

'But that's only the open worship, mark you, the things men are aware of, though they don't know what goes on. Besides that there are the Vestals. They tend a sacred fire, and keep a registry of public documents; what other rites do they perform in their round thatched hut where no man may enter? What did they bury in the Doliola, the sacred spot where you may not spit? It was buried long ago to save it from your ancestors and mine, when a Gallic Brenn sacked the City. Perhaps if we Gauls had it we would rule in Rome. So the Goddess is Bona Dea, and Vesta, and of course Hecate of the three shapes and perhaps Diana as well. I don't know about Isis, but Juno and Minerva are just satellites of Skyfather. Have I told enough?'

'She is worshipped here,' answered Acco, 'but is she strong in herself? Are the things done which please her? I won't put it into words, but you will know what I mean.'

'This is no good place for the Bride, or for the Mother. But the Mistress of Beasts must be very much at home. Rome stinks of blood, and cruelty and untimely death. In the autumn you will see the opening of the new Theatre. They may not know it, but that will be a most pleasing sacrifice to the Terrible Lady.'

'You have said enough, Master Agedincus,' said Acco, more politely than he had spoken hitherto. 'Your information is most valuable, and I hope you will consider this golden arm-ring a proper recompense. While there is an Ovate in the City you should not try to pass as a Druid, but I acknowledge that you are skilled in the affairs of the underworld. Before you go please taste this jug of wine. I should value your opinion of it.'

He went through all the ceremonial of an honourable leave-taking, and the charlatan answered as well as his sketchy knowledge of Gallic etiquette would permit.

When at last we were alone Acco took down Raven, and went over both edges carefully with a good whetstone. 'It's a pity, Camul, that in your ridiculous costume you can't carry a sword,' he said when I pointed out that it was after bedtime. 'Since Raven must work for two I shall keep her sharp and keen. At first the old man was trying to frighten us. Later, when he realised that I knew what I was talking about, he told the truth. I shall be glad to leave Rome, even if this war in the east proves as dangerous as they say it will be.'

'Wouldn't a good amulet be more use than a sword?' I suggested. 'You surely don't propose to fight hand-to-hand against the Goddess, or her messenger?'

'Why not? I fought her bear, and killed it. Besides, where do they sell amulets that can turn away the wrath of the Goddess? There may be no defence. But if I die sword in hand at least I die like a gentleman.'

A few days later our patron, Publius Crassus, asked us to come home with him after the usual morning walk through the Forum. I remember that walk particularly because of a ridiculous incident. The time was drawing near for the annual elections, and the Forum was dotted with the stately figures of citizens seeking office. These office-seekers were forbidden by law to ask for votes, or to offer their bribes in plain figures; all they could do was to stand about, in togas specially whitened, smiling at the crowd and demonstrating what a lot of citizens they knew by name. As great men came by at the head of their clients they would greet the candidates they supported, and ignore representatives of the opposition. On this morning Publius encountered a young friend who was standing for the quaestorship, the lowest elective post and the normal entry to a political career. He wanted to do something extra, to demonstrate that this candidate was not only a political ally but also a personal friend; so he greeted him with a hearty clap on the shoulder.

The young man had overdone the pipeclay on his toga; we

all sneezed in a sudden cloud of white dust. For the rest of his walk Publius Crassus had a large white smear on his grey toga; someone asked him in jest whether he was himself standing for some minor office, since he seemed to be half a candidate.

That little incident brought it home to me that all the high-sounding Roman talk about a free community governed by the freely-elected magistrates of a free people was so much wind. That young man, who couldn't even train his valet, would next year be quaestor in charge of the treasury in some helpless Province. He would be elected because Crassus backed him. Presumably he had fought a few campaigns without disgrace, because no one might stand for election without a good record of military service. Otherwise he was the son of his father, and a friend of the Consul's son. The Roman People would submit to his rule without complaint, and I dare say he would govern reasonably; but no one had ever weighed his personal fitness for the post.

When we reached the Licinian mansion and Publius ushered us into his private study, my mind was already running on Roman politics. Acco was as usual pondering on the influence and powers of the Goddess, and found it hard to bring his mind back to the Forum; that happened often, and made Romans think I was more intelligent than he, though in fact he thought more deeply.

Publius began at once, 'I have work for you at last. The African horse-dealers are bringing their herds from Tarentum, and in a few days you may begin choosing remounts for my Gallic cavalry. Everything is arranged. My father can begin to levy his army, and in the autumn we march. We shall move by easy stages all through the winter, and bring our horses fit and plump to Syria in time for a spring campaign. Until yesterday's vote the whole expedition was in doubt. Our rivals didn't want my father to command a great army, and they raised the ridiculous excuse that the Parthians have done us no harm and that there is no reason to fight them. If our ancestors had argued on those lines our frontier would still stop short of Veii! Now you will ride with me to the conquest of a great kingdom!'

'That is very good news, my lord. I suppose we can draw

87

money from your steward?' I answered, standing straight like a soldier since we were again under orders.

'Yes, and there's no need to pinch. This army will be splendidly equipped. My father is tired of sending silver to Caesar, silver which Caesar uses only to increase his own fame. From now on the family fortune will be spent in the cause of Crassus.'

'But we remain Caesar's friends?' I asked hesitantly. 'We don't want to draw down his vengeance on the Elusates.'

'Officially the three leading men in the state are in close alliance to carry out an agreed policy. In serving my father you serve Caesar. I need not tell you that in fact each of the three is striving to overcome the other two, for you will have already seen that for yourselves. It doesn't matter. With the wealth of Parthia behind him my father must become the greatest man in Rome. Those Parthians are savages, but they rule a prosperous land. After we have carried the Eagles beyond the furthest bounds of Alexander's empire Caesar will be forgotten. When my father retires I shall succeed to his position. You, my faithful followers, will then be the trusted companions of the ruler of the world!'

'Do you wish us in the meantime to pass our mornings in your train?' asked Acco, suddenly waking up but showing no elation at this splendid prospect. 'It takes up a great deal of time, my lord, and I should like to see more of Rome before I leave it.'

'Go out and enjoy yourselves – when you are not judging horses,' Publius answered affably. 'You will come in my train to the opening of the Theatre of Pompeius, because otherwise a foreigner might not get in. You have both been dutiful and assiduous clients, and I congratulate you on your fidelity when Clodius tempted you. But your presence has now produced its full effect; the Roman people have been reminded that Caesar was not the only soldier to have a hand in the conquest of Gaul. They tell me you are interested in temples. Go where you like, and if anyone bars your way say that Crassus the Consul vouches for you as loyal friends of the Roman People.'

Then we began to talk of money, in which Crassus was an expert, and horses, on which Acco had plenty to say. I had bought horses before, as agent for the Elusates; but I had never dealt on this scale, buying them by the hundred, with great sacks of silver behind me. The prospect was most exhilarating.

That evening I suggested that we should celebrate the good news in some appropriate tavern; but, as often happened, when I was elated Acco was depressed. 'I have no home to return to, and my oath binds me to Crassus,' he said gloomily, 'but you Camul, should go back to Gaul. This war will end badly. Marcus Crassus is drunk on dreams of glory, and his son has caught the infection.'

'Why do you think that? No one begins a war unless he expects to win it, and Publius seems level-headed. Certainly he still keeps an eye on the spending of his money.'

'Never mind why I think it, I am an Ovate. What I said came into my mind. Perhaps some god speaks through me in warning.'

'Was it perhaps the god of the Parthians? A few days ago you sharpened your sword against a goddess. Whatever the gods may decide, courage is what wins wars – and we know Publius Crassus for a brave leader.'

But nothing I could say made Acco cheerful.

As the summer waned Rome became more lively. For every Roman war is the chief business of life, and now three great armies were being recruited from the citizens. Caesar was levying fresh legions to conquer Gaul, Pompeius was enlisting a new army to bring order to Spain, and the great Army of Syria would be larger than any force the Romans had hitherto sent to the east. Everywhere the talk was of battles and plunder.

The citizens in the Forum did not intend to enlist in the legions. Many were middle-aged veterans, discharged after twenty years' service. Veterans are granted a farm on discharge, but most of them sell it to live in Rome on the purchase-money, which they supplement by selling their votes. The more youthful looked down on the life of a soldier; though they were willing to try the supply-train, where quick money can be made. As usual, recruits for the regular foot must be found in the country districts. The Romans do not even try to raise regular horse, for their citizens are shockingly bad riders.

When we visited the horse-fair outside the walls we encountered rural recruits coming in to enlist. Naturally they were interested to see Gauls, and it was easy to chat with them. Very few of them planned to join the Army of Syria. For the last three years Caesar's Army of Gaul had been the talk of Rome; young men seeking glory wished to serve under the most famous commander of the day. The sons of veterans, and the few old soldiers willing to re-enlist, mostly sought places in the Army of Spain. Pompeius was famous for the lavish way he looked after his men, and as the most powerful politician in Rome he could guarantee promotion and a good farm on discharge; besides, Spain was known as a good station, not too far from Italy and well provided with taverns and pretty girls. When Gaul promised glory, and Spain offered comfort, Syria must come third.

I mentioned to Publius my fear that his father might not fill the ranks of his army; but my patron made light of it. 'Farming is a hard life,' he said, 'and there are a great many Roman citizens. Of course, ardent boys seek the glamour of Caesar; you felt that glamour, and so did I. Yet the east is fabulously wealthy. We may set out with weak legions, but after we have sacked a few cities recruits will bribe our quartermasters to accept them. When we have crossed the Tigris, into an unknown world, Caesar's petty raids across the Rhine will be utterly eclipsed.'

That sounded reasonable, in the Roman Forum, surrounded by trophies of Roman victories in three continents.

Meanwhile we were inspecting the wonders of the City; for you cannot buy horses at the right price unless you go about it slowly, and we had plenty of time on our hands. I don't like Romans as people; they are greedy, cruel, and too forthright in their wickedness to be interesting to a student of human nature. But they live splendidly, in their splendid City; a wise man could fill a life-time just by looking at the buildings of Rome. Even Acco, who disliked them more than I did, admitted the magnificence which set off their sordid lives.

As we came away from the Capitol, where stand the most holy

90

temples, he thought deeply and then gave judgement; for he was better trained in spiritual matters than any of these Romans who spend their days reading and writing.

'The buildings themselves are fit for gods to dwell in; but I can't make up my mind about the statues. Surely Skyfather is more than a kindly old gentleman, and the Wargod more than a handsome recruit? If gods are just big men, handsome and a head taller than us, why should we bother to worship them? As for the images of goddesses, most of them would improve a brothel and the rest would look well in a nursery. The Goddess who hunts us is neither a big-bosomed foster-mother nor a pretty little bitch. We know, from Agedincus, that the Roman women serve our Goddess; but it seems that their husbands, who pay for these statues, have never heard of her. I don't think these grand Roman temples help men to see the gods, as do our unroofed shrines in Gaul. I like the Forum better, here below the sacred hill.'

'Why is that?' I asked, because he waited for me to speak. Acco, launched on some theme that had captured his imagination, might talk for half an hour without really stopping; but in every half-minute he would pause for an answer, because he feared to be discourteous if he did all the talking.

'I like the bronze men in the Forum because they are men, and of bronze. There is something splendid about setting up the image of a dead hero, deliberately making it the same size as the statues of the gods. When he was alive the hero must have challenged the gods, because that is what makes a man a hero. Now his people render the challenge eternal, putting him where he outfaces the gods for as long as bronze shall endure. It seems to be better immortality than the songs of our bards. I am not babbling Druid secrets, this is something I found out for myself. But surely you see as clearly as I do that the gods are the enemies of all that makes man heroic? Oh, Skyfather sends the right weather to honest farmers with their eyes on the mud, and the Wargod helps us to murder one another. But anyone who makes something fine, whether with words or with cunning ornament, *knows* that the gods are his foes. We do right to placate them with oxen; oxen are just what they like.

91

They wish *us* to be oxen – dumb, busy at the plough, and castrated.'

'And the Goddess, is she just another foe?' said I.

'Not in the same way. The Goddess may get me in the end, but I don't dislike her. I feel all the more a man because I have incurred her enmity.'

'Then you should admire the Romans, for they neglect their gods. They spend money on tall temples and costly sacrifices, from pride. But not one of them would do anything unpleasant, or forgo a pleasure, just to please the gods.'

'So far they are right. All the same I don't like them, because they are ugly and cruel.'

'I think I like them in the mass, though of course I am repelled by their bad manners when I talk with them. What fascinates me is to watch them working together. That Theatre of Pompeius, now, that we are to see inaugurated. Just think how some men hewed marble in Numidia over the sea, and others built boats to carry it here. Then craftsmen carve it and smooth it, while others square great blocks of stone. In the end crowds of ignorant slaves hoist the pieces into their true position, so that the wall stands straight and sheer with never a bulge, just because one man in charge can read the plan in his hand. A really good ambush, with every detachment turning up on time so that the enemy is completely surrounded, is a very pretty thing. The building of that Theatre seems to me just as pretty and amusing.'

'Oh yes, pretty and amusing. But not beautiful. As performing animals the Romans have no equals. It's more fun to watch them build than to watch ants moving their eggs. But I can't think of them as genuine men. When they have built that Theatre of theirs they will use it as a place where men are killed for fun. Men must be sacrificed, since the gods are stronger than we are. But when the Archdruid burns his victims in their wicker cages the ceremony is awe-inspiring and terrible, because we all know that the Great Sacrifice is a terrible thing. Only Romans would think it funny, and lay bets on the result.'

'Come, Acco, we don't know that. Everyone talks of their wonderful Games, but we haven't seen them. If they are the chief interest of the men who built those roads and bridges and harbours we saw on the way here, they may be the most marvellous and inspiring spectacle in the world.'

When we saw the inauguration of the great stone Theatre of Pompeius we were both proved right. It was marvellous, it was disgusting, there were moments of terrible beauty and long stretches of the most prosaic squalor.

We attended the inauguration in the train of our patron, for this was an important political event. Of the three chief rulers of the City Caesar had begun to draw ahead of his colleagues. His conquest of Gaul was unlike anything that had been done before; he was winning lands no Roman had visited. Soon Crassus would do something equally remarkable, in the ancient and wealthy east. Pompeius, who commanded only in peaceful Spain, had to invent a striking gesture that had nothing to do with fighting. Since he could not parade captured prisoners he must parade bought slaves and beasts taken in nets.

On the day thus consecrated to the glory of Pompeius, Marcus Crassus must demonstrate that he was the equal of any man in Rome. Publius brought every client he could muster, most of us in new togas. Besides Acco in his Gallic dress, foreign merchants from the east attended in their most outlandish clothing; if they were in the habit of dressing like ordinary Romans, Marcus invented a national costume for them, and paid for it out of his own purse. As we marched across the Forum all could see that Marcus Licinius Crassus was a man to be reckoned with.

Approaching the Theatre we saw first a big masonry wall, curving away so that one could not estimate its extent; though it was higher and steeper even than the mighty civil walls we had seen on our journey. But once through the narrow passage which led to the unroofed interior I caught Acco's arm in astonishment and wonder.

The sloping oval was bigger than anything I had imagined. Every surface was of sheer carved stone, until I turned dizzy trying to reckon the number of chisels that had faced it. Below stretched a smooth pool whose surface was sand, not water. All round us were the crowded ranks of spectators, packed in close order; save where Pompeius the Great, the diviners, and the Vestal Virgins sat in majesty, robed liked gods.

'The men who built this are more than men,' I whispered. But Acco answered: 'Wait. Let us see what they built it for.'

Then a procession of priests marched round the arena. They wore dignified gowns, reaching to the ankle, and garlands which might have been royal crowns. They were got up to impress the crowd, and they did. But Acco and I had seen Druids on their way to the midsummer divination, men in the garb of the Great Gods; these were only minor politicians, appointed to priesthoods as a move in the game of politics. The solemnities of Roman religion are wasted on experienced Gauls.

A few grains of incense burned on a little altar, while the priests intoned and the audience stood in reverence. A neighbour whispered to me that they were dedicating what would come to the spirits of dead men whom the great Pompeius wished to honour. Acco whispered in my other ear: 'We in Gaul offer the Great Sacrifice because we must, and we are sorry for it. To these Romans it is a pastime.'

He was right. Though the crowd stood decorously they did not keep silence. Some called to friends among the priests, others shouted bets from one bench to another; at the back a vulgar voice entreated the priests to finish their prayers and get on with the killing.

Then the priests withdrew, and warriors in splendid armour fought to the death for our amusement.

Though the Greeks, and the rest of the civilised world, profess themselves horrified at this Roman entertainment, it is most enthralling. The fighters were either criminals or cheap slaves, and no one cared whether they lived or died. Their showy armour was designed to protect the limbs while leaving the vitals exposed, so there were no crippling wounds; a swordsman either ran in glorious activity or lay dramatically dead. We were too far off to see the expressions on their faces, shadowed by fantastic helmets. It seemed the most natural thing in the world that these figures capering on the golden sand should leap and clash and then lie still; that was why they were there.

Presently most of the swordsmen were dead, and the few survivors left the arena. Then from a gate at one end issued black men, quite naked; they bore shields of wicker and stout spears. From the other end bounded a troop of lions.

I expected the beasts to gobble up the naked blacks at once; but it turned out to be quite a fair fight. The men approached in line, and when a lion sprang his victim tried to lie flat under the shield while others stabbed the beast in the back. But the lions were very quick, and sometimes caught an antagonist standing. Of course, the shields were not quite big enough, and if the black protected his head he exposed his feet.

More and more lions bounded through the gate, as their travelling-cages reached the mouth of the tunnel that led to it. More and more spearmen came in at the other end, though Pompeius had not been able to collect a whole regiment of blacks; some of the rearmost were ordinary white Spaniards. This made the crowd whistle in protest. On these occasions the mob is always on the look-out for evidence that the giver of the Games has been stingy. Soon the whole arena was crowded with fierce beasts and fiercer men.

'Five hundred lions!' Marcus Crassus cried in a tone of vexation, 'I kept tally as they came out. There has never been a display to match this! Tonight every rascal in Rome will cheer for the great Pompeius.'

'Never mind, father,' Publius answered him. 'Think of the money it has cost. He could have armed a legion for less. When we meet him in the field, as must happen one day, a legion will be more valuable than all the cheering voters in the Forum.'

Marcus smiled agreement. Father and son were of one mind: that what gave power to a politician was money.

At first the mob was entranced, delighted that a great man had thought proper to provide such a mass of expensive living flesh for their amusement. But what was happening in the arena was also rather disgusting. Instead of a gallant swordsman falling dead with a blade in his breast there were naked, shrieking figures crawling at random over the sand, bleeding to death from gnawed ankles or clasping trailing intestines. The lions did not fight willingly; they preferred to crouch, eating, over

95

the first man they had killed. The stink of blood and guts over-came the scent of incense. By the time this act of the spectacle was finished, with the downfall of the last lion, the crowd was feeling restless and perhaps a little ashamed.

The arena was so crammed with carrion that before the next performance it must be cleared. Servants dressed as demons of the underworld came out with ox-carts and piled the corpses tidily, stacking them like faggots. The sand was raked, and more incense burned against the stench. The people near us were silent and uncomfortable, worrying whether they had appeared undignified when they yelled for more blood. Acco spoke to me in an undertone: 'Our wicker cages are better. The smell is just as bad, but you don't see everything.' I nodded agreement.

This third act would be the last part of the spectacle, and presumably the best. We could hear a great disturbance of shouted orders and shifting planks from the other side of the gate, as though something extraordinary was being moved into position. Then the tall entry was flung open, and with a blast of massed trumpets a line of great beasts appeared.

There were seventeen elephants marching in single-file, and at sight of the huge grey moving mountains the crowd went mad with excitement. Although the Romans are familiar with ivory, which is used as a badge of office on the thrones of their magistrates, living elephants are rarely transported over the wide sea. Few members of the audience had seen an elephant before; no one had seen seventeen at once.

The creatures are so tall and strong that they carried on their backs boxes like forts, each manned by half a dozen archers. I believe, from the designs I have seen on certain coins, that they ought to have been guided by a man sitting on the neck; but it had been thought more amusing to drive them uncontrolled into the arena. Nevertheless they plodded sedately, for they are placid animals; until from the other end a body of foot advanced against them, armed with javelins and long battle axes.

The trouble was that the elephants did not know they were supposed to fight. Unguided, they strolled placidly about, flapping their ears in mild curiosity. The hunters, naturally afraid, were reluctant to begin the battle. They also loitered in a timid group, from which presently flew a tentative javelin. It pricked an elephant in the trunk, and as he screamed with pain great tears rolled down his cheeks.

Thereupon the unpredictable Roman mob decided that it could not tolerate such disgusting cruelty to harmless animals. The lower orders, from their seats high in the raking slopes, shouted to Pompeius to stop the show and let the beasts go free; the cry was echoed from the lower benches, where every envious rival and political opponent was glad to lend a hand in spoiling the famous Games on which the Consul had spent a fortune. Right across the theatre I could see the great man rise from his seat and give the order for clemency.

But there was no interpreter to explain this to the elephants. They were excited by the uproar, and presently decided they were among foes. Just as the hunters were about to retire, gratefully, through the door by which they had entered, three elephants charged them, trumpeting. The armed men defended themselves, the crews of the elephant-castles joined in, and the fight was on. Someone with a battle-axe, who had thought out his tactics beforehand, dodged round to hough one animal with a cut to the hindleg. The victim's scream roused all his comrades to action.

I was watching the interesting spectacle with close attention when I became aware of a tumult behind me. The mob had issued its command, and the Consul had failed to comply with it. The dregs of the amphitheatre, who consider themselves the sovereign People of Rome, felt insulted at this disobedience. Sturdy gangsters and tough ex-soldiers were climbing over the stone benches, intent on bringing the great Pompeius to a properly submissive frame of mind. When a shoe whizzed past his ear, and a man with a broken jaw tumbled into his seat, Marcus Crassus called to his followers and led us swiftly from the building.

Closed up for safety, we crossed the City to the Licinian mansion. Behind us the clamour from the riotous theatre filled the sky, and as we passed merchants closed their shops. Then we smelt smoke, and Publius Crassus halted us to hear his orders.

'Tonight you will all be armed, and divided into watches. We must guard the mansion as though it were a fortress. To-morrow or the next day Pompeius will restore order. Recruits for his Army of Spain are training near the City, and they will obey his orders. But until trained soldiers arrive the mob is in control, and they will crown this day of festival by plundering the houses of the rich. They may also plunder the homes of the poor. But Crassus guarantees full compensation for losses incurred in his service; while if Crassus is plundered you also are ruined.'

The renewed harping on the wealth of his father struck me as vulgar in a young man of noble birth; but the other clients saw nothing wrong in it, and we did as we were told.

By afternoon of the next day things were back to normal, which in Rome is not saying much; the City is most disorderly. We heard from eyewitnesses that the riot in the Theatre had proved a splendid finish to a brilliant and costly festival. In the course of the fighting all the elephants were killed, as well as the huntsmen and a large number of the audience. The Theatre itself, built throughout of dressed stone, would not burn; but several large houses and well-stocked shops had been sacked and destroyed. Some wiseacres held that the whole thing was a cunning Caesarian plot to weaken the effect of Pompeius's lavish generosity; but I was there, and I am sure the riot was spontaneous. Romans enjoy a riot; they like killing, and don't mind very much if they get killed themselves.

There was no business for us to do on the day order was restored, for of course the horse-dealers had left the City in fear of being plundered. Acco and I planned to spend our free afternoon in a tour of the wine-shops, since now we had plenty of money; but we found them all closed by the legions of Pompeius.

As we turned away from the fourth tavern the sentry on the door took pity on our disappointment. Without thinking I had received his orders standing at attention, and he spotted us as ex-soldiers.

'If you want only a skinful of wine, with no funny business after, why don't you try our canteen? You might meet a few old

98

comrades. Which was your legion, citizen?' he added, to me.

'No legion, soldier,' I answered, knowing that among veterans I could not pass as a Roman. 'My friend and I both served in Caesar's auxiliary horse, and I was lucky enough to be granted my citizenship on discharge.'

'Fancy soldiering, eh? Peacocking about on horseback when honest Romans are too sore to sit down anywhere, what with the centurion's cudgel and one thing and another? No, don't take offence, my good barbarian,' as Acco frowned. 'In Caesar's army everyone fights, even the cavalry. I know, my brother's in the Thirtieth. Well, any soldiers of Caesar who find themselves in Rome deserve a party, even if we *have* closed the taverns. That house on the corner is now our guardroom. Say I sent you, and save a cup for me when I come off guard.'

In the house on the corner a dozen legionaries dozed in their blankets. In the court at the back the regimental sutler had set up his casks, and an oddcrowd of semi-military hangers-on were drinking seriously. It was not what we had come outfor since it was not typical of Rome; but I was quite pleased tobe back in the atmosphere of the army.

A burly man in a plain tunic insisted on paying for our drinks. He was standing treat to all comers, and explained that he had just enrolled a big batch of recruits and been paid the usual bounty. A retired centurion, he was now employed in the baggage-train; and he spent his spare time 'reinforcing the army', as he called it.

He was interested to hear that we were bound for the Army of Syria. 'Though why on earth you want to leave Caesar beats me. Why, if you stuck to him you might visit the Hyperboreans, in their warm home at the back of the North Wind. And next year, for sure, his men will fill their helmets with British amber and pearls.'

'You forget, sir, that we are Gauls,' I answered politely. 'We come from a land very like Britain. I have met British traders, and they seemed no richer than anyone else. Caesar also led us into Germany, and after one look I want to see no more of that beastly country. But Crassus marches to the wealthy east. How many cartloads of treasure did Alexander find in Persepolis?

99

It's time that country was plundered again.'

'Oh yes, the east's worth plundering. I hope you and your comrades can plunder it. But you will find those comrades a queer set of men. Caesar offers glory and Pompeius offers ease. No one volunteers for the east unless the other armies won't have him. After all, though Crassus is Consul, what has he ever done? Crucified a lot of slaves, while his rivals were conquering provinces.'

'We follow his son, a gallant captain of horse. I know that, for he led us in Gaul,' I answered, still with politeness.

Luckily Acco was not listening, or his honour might have flared up. 'Besides, sir, we must all begin somewhere. If our great leader has not yet won famous victories, it may be because he has never served in great wars.'

'You may be right, and I am glad to see you loyal. Let's hope you carry all before you in the east. But in the old days I served under Lucullus, and I tell you these new legions for the Army of Syria are not the right stamp. Besides, in those days we were defending our own from the ravages of King Mithradates, and the gods favoured us. You will attack peaceful neighbours without provocation, or so they say in the Forum.'

'That's as may be. We are men under orders, fighting where our leader bids. My friend is a foreigner, and it happens that I have never voted. So we are not to blame for the foreign policy of the Senate and People of Rome. Now it's my turn. what will you drink, sir?'

He took the hint, and turned the conversation. We passed the rest of the evening drinking quietly, and listening to stories about the difficulty of keeping order in the tumultuous City.

All the same, next morning I remembered this conversation. We were busy now, since at last the expedition was getting under way; but I found time to stroll through the Forum in the afternoon, when official business was over and private speakers harangued the citizens. The veteran had told the truth; on every side I heard denunciations of the wickedness of this unprovoked attack on the blameless Parthians, who wished only to live in peace with Rome.

I was not convinced. We Gauls also had no quarrel with

Rome, but no orator maintained that Caesar should stay in his Province until Roman territory was attacked. For two hundred years the Romans have invaded their neighbours without waiting for an excuse, merely because the neighbours are weaker. If now some of them held such conduct wicked it was because they opposed Crassus, not because they thought barbarians have a right to freedom.

I mentioned the matter to Pyrrhus the steward, when he called on us with money for the horse-dealers. Nowadays we were too busy to attend the morning assembly of clients, and I did not wish to bother our patron with what might prove an unnecessary alarm. Pyrrhus told us not to worry. He explained that a clique of elderly Senators had for years carried on a feud with Marcus Crassus, whom they hated because he had made money for himself instead of inheriting it from his ancestors. They had delayed the Parthian expedition as long as possible, and now that all their efforts had failed, and the army was at last mustering, they were putting up hired speakers to give the whole enterprise a bad name.

Though they knew it was nothing but a political move, many citizens were persuaded. Our horse-dealers complained of a hostile public opinion, which was spoiling the pleasure of their visit to the City. But Acco and I could go anywhere in comfort; we were always taken to be followers of Caesar, who was immensely popular with the lower classes.

The veteran in the canteen had been right about the new legions, as I realised when I delivered the first draft of re-mounts to the camp in Etruria. The centurions and rear-rank men were ordinary Roman soldiers, who would do their duty in a tight place and shirk fatigues if there was no enemy about. The new recruits I saw drilling were not so impressive. Some had the shifty deference that is the indelible mark of the slave-born; others were clumsy farmhands, too slow and loutish to be to be made into good swordsmen; many were obviously petty thieves. They were proud to be soldiers, which sounds a good quality. But their pride had in it a trace of surprise that anyone should have trusted them with weapons.

I had visited the camp alone, but Acco was beside me a day

101

or two later when we watched a cohort march in for the ceremonial parade which would officially open the campaign. Though I had not prompted him he thought as I had. 'This is a new kind of soldier,' he said in a whisper. 'They are not like the men who beat the Nervii.'

'They are Romans, all the same,' I answered. 'Perhaps the Parthians are worse. Among the Gallic horse we shall be in good company, and Publius will lead us bravely.'

As the autumn deepened into winter that was our consolation. We were both tired of Rome, tired of these proud, cruel, thieving strangers who would never accept us as equals, tired of the noise and the smells and the echoes bouncing back from steep hot walls, tired of the jostling and the lack of dignity. Soon we would be riding among Gallic cavaliers, men of honour with ceremonious manners. We were loyal to Publius Crassus, but we did not like his friends and fellow citizens.

At last the day came when the army was to march out. This formal marching-out was an important ceremony, for it marked the end of the Consulate of Marcus Crassus. Detachments of the best men from every legion (not very good men, all the same) had been specially sent into the City as escort for the new Proconsul of Syria.

Even now the memory of that procession can give me nightmares. I have seen more terrible sights, but none more ominous; and though we knew that political trickery was at the back of the evil omens, still they were evil omens. There could be no arguing about that.

Acco and I, foreign auxiliaries, had no place in a parade of Roman legions. We waited by the city gate among a crowd of sightseers, ready to join our drove of horses as soon as the troops began to march at ease. We had a fine view of everything.

We had early learned to recognise the insignia that mark the Tribunes, a thing foreigners in Rome must know if they are not to break the law. For these sacred officials may never be touched, or hindered in anything they set out to do (But they hold office for one year only, and may be prosecuted after, which keeps them within bounds.) We saw an elderly Tribune come down the road, and we were among those who got out of his way when he announced that he wanted a clear view of the parade. Someone told me his name was Ateius Capito, an opponent of both Crassus and Caesar. He looked a decent, respectable man, though not perhaps noble, as we reckon nobility in Gaul.

Then we heard the bellowing of brazen trumpets, and knew the troops were on the march. Everyone looked up the street, forgetting the old Tribune. The first standard came in sight and the crowd fell silent; for these eagle standards rank as the most holy gods of the Romans.

When the marching column had nearly reached us old Capito darted out into the middle of the road, followed by a slave bearing something on his head. The something turned out to be a small bronze tripod. As soon as it was set down the Tribune busied himself with lighting a pinch of incense with flint and steel (he was clumsy, but energetic, and he soon got it smoking). He crouched by the tripod, cowering down to the earth; and he drew his toga over his head.

At last I understood what he was at. He was praying, presumably for the success of the expedition. Romans always cover their heads to pray, and since they hardly ever cover them for any other reason you can be sure that a man with his toga over his head is calling on the gods. No one else was doing anything except cheer, and the army had just come from the solemn state sacrifice; but many Tribunes grow eccentric, since no one dares to check their actions. Presumbaly Capito thought another prayer would do no harm.

The troops began to march by, and the Tribune continued to pray. The crowd was peering at the soldiers, trying to recognise friends or criticising the marching. There was a lot of noise, and no one could hear what the devout Capito was saying.

Cheers rose to a roar as the commander came in sight. Marcus Crassus stood upright in a two-horse chariot. He wore the dress of his military rank; a cuirass of gilded linen from neck to hips, swaying strips of thick leather over his thighs, and tall bronze greaves from ankle to knee. On his head was a splendid bronze helmet embellished with a tall horsehair crest, and his long scarlet cloak fell behind him in one sweep from the shoulder. A trusted guardsman standing beside him in the chariot held an antique shield worked with many little figures in combat. The full dress of a Roman commander is a most impressive costume.

But it did not suit Marcus Crassus. I had seen him often during the past summer; but always wearing the ample toga of a Consul, in which he looked a statuesque figure of benign state-craft. Now he seemed a crapulous and bloated old man. The cuirass was moulded to suggest the muscles of a Hercules; but it could not suppress his prominent belly. Behind the bronze greaves his spindly legs seemed too fragile to support such corpulence. His bare arms were skinny with age, and he peered from under his helmet as though he were extremely short-sighted. He was in his sixties, which for a statesman is the prime of vigour; dressed as only a young warrior should dress, he looked a silly old dotard.

The crowd gave him a cheer because he was the leader of their army; but among the hurrahs were sniggers and catcalls. The officers of his staff, including his son Publius, marched on foot immediately behind his chariot, they looked worried, and I guessed that throughout the procession there had been a constant risk that encouragement might turn to mockery. All crowds are cruel, but a Roman crowd is utterly ruthless. I nudged Acco, and cheered at the top of my lungs to set an example.

Suddenly I heard my own voice against a background of silence. The old Tribune by his smoking tripod had commanded quiet, and in Rome a Tribune is obeyed without question. Squatting in a complicated position, as though every movement was ordained by ritual, he inclined his face to the ground and began to speak.

Even I, a stranger, knew at once that he was addressing the Gods Below; for the underworld lies below every land, and all men are aware of it in much the same way. Even I could guess that it was contrary to ritual to shout as he was shouting; I knew that he was addressing the People of Rome as well as the gods of death. 'This is politics, not enchantment,' I whispered to Acco.

But the people were impressed, for old Capito performed his ritual with conviction. He began by calling over a long list of what were to me meaningless words; they were the old names of the old gods, seldom heard by modern Romans. Then he pronounced what was very nearly the ritual dedication of the sacrifice I had heard when the Consuls slew their daily ox for the good of the City. It was not quite the same, for that was a thank-offering, and this was not given in gratitude but in aversion. Last of all he named the thing he was sacrificing.

'Take, ye powers,' he chanted, 'take Marcus Licinius Crassus and all his host. We devote them to early death, to turn away the vengeance. Innocent blood will be shed without cause. Impute it not to the People of Rome; impute it only to that Crassus and his infatuated following. Even now they leave the City, bearing their pollution with them. Suffer them not to return!'

The troops had halted to hear the Tribune, as is the duty of all Romans. Now the Tribune had finished. Overturning his tripod, he stamped out the smouldering incense with a gesture of complete finality. In dead silence he returned to the crowd beside the gate. Crassus, in a clear expressionless voice, gave the order to march on.

In silence we watched until the last mailed legionary had marched forth under the carven arch. Then Acco turned to me with a thin smile.

'The old man might have spared his breath. I am an Ovate, and I knew it before he spoke.' He bent down to pat the earth. 'So, my masters, you expect us. But we all come to you in the end, by one road or another. My road runs through the ancient cities of the east, where man first learned wisdom. I shall see the greatest beauty man has ever made. Then you will take me. That is my fate, and I would not have it otherwise. Come on, Camul. We must get the remounts moving before those grooms lose them and find wineskins in exchange. The army has marched and we are on campaign.'

He was quite self-possessed, and I think quite happy. But he had already journeyed a little way out of the sublunary world of ordinary men.

CHAPTER IV

Greece

It was pleasant to be back in the army. I was now quite
accustomed to Romans, and no longer felt shy in their presence. I had lived among them long enough to share some of
their background, and, though neither Acco nor I ever thought
or felt as Romans, we knew enough about them to understand
how they would think and feel.

In particular we had learned all we could about their newly-
conquered dominions in the east, the lands whither our patron
intended to lead his troops. Veterans who had followed Lucullus and Pompeius had boasted before us of their deeds in the
long wars that had devasted Asia and Armenia. Traders from
those parts called frequently at the Licinian mansion, with
hair-raising descriptions of the great deserts of Mesopotamia,
and bitter complaints against the thieving nomad Arabs who
lived there by robbery. These Arabs, and the great beasts
called camels which are their wealth, seemed to me most interesting; a people who preferred freedom to prosperity were
obviously a rarity in the Roman world. All our informants
agreed that the Arabs, who should have been noble savages,
were in fact untrustworthy and dishonourable cowards. But
then Romans are apt to accuse all orientals of cowardice; they
despised the Parthians, and yet they had assembled a mighty
army to plunder their kingdom.

Probably we knew as much about the east as any Roman in
the army who had never been there. With one part of my mind
I was almost a Roman, but I never tried to hide the fact that I

was a Gaul; for after seeing the City and the methods by which it was governed I had lost my awe of civilisation. In my Gallic trousers I felt myself the equal of these other soldiers in their different campaigning dress.

We no longer suffered from the irksome parades and inspections which had harassed us when we were Caesar's recruits. Now Acco and I were attached to the staff of the cavalry commander, who was also the son of the commander-in-chief. The position we held could not be found in any Roman drill-book or muster roll; but then the Roman army makes no provision for cavalry, who are always irregulars, mercenary or allied. I think our pay came from our leader's private purse, and we were rather members of his household than soldiers under his command. Marcus Crassus was spending large sums of his own money on his army, which is a common Roman custom; he would get it back from the plunder of our enemies. I never gathered exactly what was supposed to be our rate of pay. We had a clerk, a slave from the Licinian counting-house, to handle our affairs; he carried a bag full of sealed documents on which local merchants would advance money and he gave us whole sacks of silver at a time. When we bought forage or engaged billets we also took enough for our private expenses, and no one asked to see our accounts.

We always told Publius, or his steward, what we planned to do; and if it was suggested that we should do something else we complied at once. So we seldom received a direct order. We slept at headquarters, and made a point of getting back there by lights-out. We seemed free to live as we pleased, because we took care never to overstep the mark.

Of course, at the beginning I had been tempted to pick up as much silver as I could carry, and disappear into the mountains where the Romans would never find me. Acco pointed out that a few bags of silver would not be enough to support the life of an outlaw, who must buy shelter and food by bribery; if I ran away I would live a poor man as well as a hunted one. He himself must remain loyal to Publius, he added; for Publius was his lord, to whom he had given his oath. Acco also devised a sensible way of dealing with the bribes which army contractors

107

pressed on us. We took them, which pleased the contractors; and then handed them in to the military chest, so that Publius and his father were pleased with us also. We needed no more money than came our way honestly. We already possessed sound weapons and handsome ornaments, better than we could buy in the Roman world; our dignity would suffer if we made a habit of drinking more than we could carry; there was no point in loading ourselves with savings which would be stolen by some camp-follower while we were busy fighting.

For, of course, though at present we were buyers of remounts and forage, when the time came for fighting we would join the Gallic horse. Publius had promised as much. But when the army marched the Gallic horse were still north of the river Po. They were to catch up with us later.

I cannot remember the names of the little Italian towns through which we marched, though I can recall the main outlines of our journey. From Rome the legions marched to a seaport named Brundisium, and embarked on a short voyage to the opposite port of Dyrrhaccium. There we halted for some days, to sort the baggage after the disturbance always caused by any dealings with ships and sailors. We had a long spell of marching before us until we reached our next base of supplies, the wealthy city of Thessalonica. There we were to halt again, to await the Gallic cavalry and the other auxiliary troops.

At headquarters the officers were always sketching maps in the dust as they planned future marches, and the Proconsul had in his baggage a copper plate on which were engraved all the seas and mountains of the known world. As far as I could understand these plans, we seemed to be marching round three sides of a square, with the sea in the middle. The normal route from Italy to Syria is by sea; but such a great army would have needed a huge fleet of transports, which a storm might have scattered through all the ports of the east. In any case the Romans, very sensibly in my opinion, would rather march a hundred miles by road than sail ten miles in a ship.

From Dyrrhaccium a magnificent road leads through the mountains to Thessalonica. This road was made by the Romans for their armies to march upon, and thousands of troops use it every year; at every halt there are barracks and post-houses, and local merchants supply plentiful rations and forage. Over this stretch of our journey there would be no difficulty about subsistence. We, and the quartermasters, might ride quietly with headquarters.

Not far to the south lay all the famous cities of Greece, cities that were famous even in distant Gaul. Acco boldly asked permission to leave the army, so that we might visit the sights of Athens.

He hated asking permission to do anything, and came out with the request as though daring his leader to refuse. But Publius understood his simple, prickly character, and liked him. He answered that at the outset of a long campaign it was difficult for him to grant leave to members of his personal staff, since if our colleagues saw us go off on a pleasure trip they would ask for leave to revisit their families in Italy; but that we might hurry south on business to Piraeus, the port of Athens, if we took our clerk to negotiate contracts with the great international merchants whose offices lay there.

'Go to Athens on duty,' he said with a smile, 'and before you leave us complain about the fatigue of the journey. Then the others will not be jealous. I suppose you really want to see temples and shrines, and there's no harm in it. But if you discuss religion with the priests and oracle-mongers of Greece don't make too much of that political demonstration as we left the City. We don't want those rumours revived just as the troops are getting over their upset.'

That was the official explanation of the Tribune's curse; Capito had been furthering the plans of a gang of corrupt Senators with reasons of their own for wishing the campaign to fail. The old boy did not really believe in his curses, which he had been bribed to pronounce against his better judgement. His unpatriotic action deserved punishment, but inviolable Tribunes must be allowed to make their mistakes unrebuked. When the King of the Parthians, in chains, walked behind the triumphal chariot of Crassus, old Ateius Capito would look very foolish. Until that came to pass the incident was not worth serious discussion.

Of course, a political motive had lain behind the affair; though it seems to me that if you think your political opponents are doing something wicked you are entitled to curse them. However, the result of emphasising the political background had been to weaken the effect of the curse on the few soldiers who had heard it. These legionaries were all adherents of Crassus the Proconsul, who fed them generously and looked after their comfort. They had argued themselves into believing that a few old-fashioned Senators, who wished to keep the lower orders poor and humble, were working against their generous leader; and they were all the more determined to fight bravely, to show these well-born oligarchs that they had backed the losing side. Romans are stubborn, and unfavourable omens seldom deter them from their purpose; certainly not from such a congenial purpose as the pillaging of a wealthy Empire.

The Accursed March, as we called it, was never out of our memories; but we kept it in the back of our minds, and concentrated on doing the tasks that must be done today. That does not sound very sensible, but then soldiers are not sensible men; if they were they would have chosen some calling that is safer and better paid.

As we rode south to inspect the beauties of Athens, Acco sang cheerfully. He believed absolutely in the omen; but we had half the world to cross before we began fighting, and there was time for many things to happen.

So strong is the Roman peace that we rode through wild and thinly-peopled Epirus without an escort, just Acco and myself and the clerk with his bag of sealed bills of exchange.

Italy is much the same sort of country as Gaul, looking different because it is inhabited by a very different set of men; one could imagine any stretch of countryside in Etruria or Campania dotted with Gallic huts and barley-fields. But Greece is in itself, in the very bones of the landscape, unlike any other country on earth. The limestone mountains, the fertile valleys, the clear horizon never veiled by mist, combine into a background of beauty that uplifts the spirit. I liked the people as well, though they did not like us. Roman soldiers are

110

unpopular as conquerors, and barbarian soldiers of the Roman army are considered even worse. Travellers scowled, the innkeepers were surly, and shepherds looked for an excuse to set their dogs on us.

Fierce sheepdogs did not bother us, though they frightened our clerk; we have sheepdogs in Gaul, and no dog, however dutiful, will run on a drawn sword held in a steady hand. We did not feel insulted to be called barbarians, for in Greece that word does not mean 'savage' as it does in Rome. To Greeks anyone who cannot speak their language is a barbarian, and they use the term for Asiatics and indeed for Romans, no matter how highly civilised these foreigners may be.

We liked the Greeks because they are cheerful and cheeky, independent men who are very pleased with themselves. Their conceit is not contemptuous of others, like Roman pride. At the inns our fellow travellers treated us as equals; perhaps not the kind of men they liked, but free men who might be foreign, and behave like foreigners, if that was what we preferred. They recognised our right to be ourselves.

The little towns of Thessaly are all that little towns ought to be. They are strongly walled, because defence is the object of a town; their temples are imposing, because temples make a community; their private houses are small and flimsy, because in a city private life is not important. We were delighted with these little places. Even though we saw them through the fog of an incomprehensible language and the further barrier of our own unpopularity, they seemed to be just the right sort of home for poor but intelligent men.

When we reached Athens we revised our ideas. The little towns were all very well in their way, but this is the only place where any gentleman in the world will feel at home, no matter where he happened to be born. I cannot describe Athens. Every building, and indeed every prospect from the walls, is exactly right, and the heart of any stranger leaps with joy as he breathes its air. Of course, it is full of strangers, from the east as well as from the Roman dominions; amid Persian tiaras and Scythian necklaces our Gallic trousers passed almost unnoticed.

The Acropolis was damaged about forty years ago, when Sulla, the Roman Dictator, took it by storm from the adherents of King Mithradates. The Athenians were repairing the great fortified entry, and it was most interesting to watch the craftsmen working their pure white marble on the spot. But the chief temples within the enclosure stood unharmed in all their flawless serenity. I cannot describe that citadel; but it filled me with visions of the immortal gods, looking down on earth from a peaceful heaven.

Piraeus, the neighbouring port, is quite a different place. It was full of businessmen who spoke to us in Latin and bore Roman names; but they were not like the Romans we had met in Italy. The citizenship can be bought, if you know how to go about it. Most of these traders stank of crooked dealing, though our clerk advised us to deal with them all the same. He explained that, though they were grasping, they understood their business and would perform what they had promised. Of course they would overcharge the Roman People, but since they would be paid from Parthian spoil that did not really matter.

There were honest traders, of course, for no market can survive without a few of them. They were mostly in a small way of business, incapable of contracting for delivery in Syria in a year's time.

I found this trading a most fascinating occupation. It seemed a pity that a man of my birth cannot buy and sell for his own profit, for I am sure I would have been good at it. It was all the more enjoyable because I knew that if I made a mistake the Roman People would stump up. The Roman People can look after themselves; they will not starve if they are committed to a few expensive contracts.

I wished to have supplies and remounts waiting for a thousand cavalry who would find themselves in Syria at the beginning of the next hot weather, with many horses lame and out of condition after a long journey. Until spring, I was told, there was no worthwhile grazing in the pastures, and the horses would have to eat hay and thrahsed barley. Forage is never expensive beside the field where it was harvested, but it is bulky stuff to move. I was trying to arrange a line of depots which would be ready stocked when we arrived

Acco was quick at reckoning prices and spotting the little tricks of the merchants; when we talked over our plans in private I nearly always took his advice. But during the actual negotiations I had to keep him in the background or leave him behind in our lodging; for he would grow very angry, or even consider himself insulted, unless the merchants at once agreed with all his calculations. Between us we made a strong team; our clerk said politely that born Romans could not have done better. Perhaps he was telling the truth as well as flattering his superiors. After all, Gallic nobles are just as intelligent as Roman merchants, though at home we do not risk our silver in these complicated counting-games.

The merchants we dealt with were elderly men, fat and smelling of greasy perfume. They invited us to dinner, where we lay by the hour on stuffed couches, sipping watered wine and watching the capers of hired entertainers. Here in Greece even Romans hire only dancers and singers for their amusement; boxing and wrestling are considered pastimes that free men should undertake themselves, not shows to be watched during dinner; and bloody fighting is held too disgusting to amuse anyone. These performers usually sang or recited poetry in a tongue we could not understand, and altogether we found our complimentary dinners very boring indeed.

But we met one young merchant whom we liked. He lived in Piraeus as agent for his father, a rich tanner and leather-dealer of Antioch in Syria. We called on him to bespeak a supply of bridles and watering-buckets of sound supple hide, to be ready when we reached Syria. I took a fancy to him because he was young and slim, and smelled of the clean olive-oil used by athletes, instead of reeking with garlic and perfume. At our first meeting Acco was completely captivated; for when I began arguing over prices the young man answered with a smile: 'I have explained how much this leather will cost my father, if all goes well; and what it might cost him, if there are various misfortunes during the winter. As you know, we live by selling leather, and must make a profit. Let your friend decide the price, remembering these things. He is a nobleman and a man of honour, and I shall abide by his decision.'

Such straightforward dealing was refreshing; it was also good business; for of course Acco, flattered by the stranger's trust, fixed a generous price. Soon we were chatting pleasantly together, our business concluded and a free afternoon before us.

The young man told us he was named Marcus Licinius Nicanor; for more than twenty years before his father, Aristobulus, a citizen of Antioch, had been granted the citizenship by Lucius Licinius Lucullus, a famous Roman general. The family business was centred on the pastoral Arabs of the desert and the branch at Piraeus was unimportant; but he had persuaded his father to send him here so that he might also attend the lectures of the philosophers.

This was the first we had heard of modern philosophers. To us Athens was famous for its buildings and its history; we had not realised that it is still a centre of learning. At once Acco begged Nicanor to take us to the Porch where wise men instructed their pupils; and nearly cried with vexation when reminded that the wise men lectured only in Greek, so that he could not understand a word of their discourse. Since the Porch was no use to us we carried off Nicanor instead to the best tavern in Piraeus, and passed the evening talking with him of the wisdom he learned in the Athenian schools.

We talked in Latin, which to all three of us was a foreign language; and Nicanor kept on quoting long Greek words which it seemed just would not go into any other language, though it was impossible to discuss the quest for wisdom without using them. It was hard to make out what the learned philosophers were driving at. But before we separated for the night Acco had discovered enough to convince him that Athenian philosophy was not a necessary part of the education of a Gallic nobleman.

'Your teachers pursue two different inquiries,' he summed up, smiling to show that no personal criticism was intended. 'In the first place they want to know how the world is made, and why it is this particular world and not something different. That is a noble study. But our Druids know the answer. Even I,

114

an Ovate, have some hints of it; though I may not babble Druid secrets in a tavern. If your wise men are genuinely in earnest they should voyage to Gaul, or beyond Gaul to Britain, where the Druids are more learned. But your wise men will not travel, because they are certain that all wisdom resides in Athens. That's how it is. They cannot teach me anything about the world.'

'Their second inquiry is more interesting,' he continued, 'if I have got it right. They want to know how the just man should act, in cases where there are no rules of religion or laws of men to guide him. That again is worth learning, but again I know the answer. When there are no other guides, Honour must be the guide. I ask myself what my ancestors would have done, and Honour always gives a clear answer.'

'Were your ancestors wiser than you? Did they also call on their ancestors? Who was your first ancestor?' asked Nicanor, as though genuinely seeking information.

'That's one of your Greek traps, but it won't catch me. The founder of my house was the Wargod, who once carried off a mortal maiden. By calling on my ancestors I call on the Wargod,' said Acco proudly.

'Ah yes. Now who is your Wargod? Is he Ares, whom the Romans call Mars?'

I interrupted, to close the exchange before tempers were lost.

'Our Wargod has a name, thought I don't know it. Probably Acco has been told, since he once trained to be a Druid. But he cannot repeat the name to a Greek.'

'I understand. It is a mystery. Where there is a mystery reason and argument are useless. For that matter I myself learned at Eleusis certain names which I may not repeat to strangers.'

'There you are,' said Acco, with a triumphant smile. 'I thought you Greeks reverenced only reason, and worshipped the gods solely to make the crops grow. I see you have secrets also. I have a special reason for inquiring into these matters, since I have been driven into exile by the angry divinity of my native land. But the close of a supper party is no time to discuss such deep matters. Can we meet again, to have another talk and see the great temples on the Acropolis?'

We had concluded our business, and in four days must leave Athens for Thessalonica. We arranged to spend the next day but one with Nicanor.

On the intervening day Acco went off alone to inquire into the public facts about Athenian worship, which anyone will gladly tell to a stranger. When I came home in the evening after some final calls in Piraeus, I found him restless and excited.

'I have again met traces of the Goddess,' he told me. 'That armed maiden on the hill is an attendant on Skyfather, as we thought at first. But at Eleusis they worship a goddess by secret rites. They tell strangers of the annual pilgrimage to the shrine, and of the purification beforehand. There is nothing secret about it, except what they actually do in the temple when they get there.'

'Can anyone go?' I asked. 'We might try it ourselves.'

'It only comes once a year, so we can't wait for it. I think any Greek can go, and they dare not forbid Romans though they do not welcome them. Other foreigners are definitely forbidden to attend.'

'Then don't think about it any longer. I suppose Nicanor knows all about it, but he won't tell us. A man who would reveal the secrets of his mystery is not to be believed anyway, so we shall never find out.'

'Nicanor would not break an oath of secrecy, but when I have told him why the Goddess is my foe he may let us know whether the Goddess is the divinity worshipped at Eleusis. There can be no harm in that.'

Acco's perpetual search for the Goddess was beginning to bore me; but strangers meeting him for the first time were often captivated by his eager curiosity. It was likely he would get something out of Nicanor.

We started next morning at sunrise, for Greeks keep earlier hours than Romans. All the same, when we reached the Acropolis it was already crowded. Nicanor read us the inscriptions on votive offerings and told us the history of each building. But there is nothing secret about the Acropolis. The maiden-goddess is obviously one of the warrior-maids who serve Skyfather, and the other principal god, though his legs are carved as serpents, is merely the human founder of the city, deified in reward for his achievement. Everything is clear and straightforward and on the whole kindly. They will tell you all about the ritual, and they never mention the Great Sacrifice.

From the battlements of the many-coloured marble fortress we could see Eleusis in the plain below. Acco told of the death of Grane and the killing of the bear, and then asked Nicanor to give us what information he could, without revealing holy secrets.

'Gaul must be a very fearful place, and I'm not surprised you left it. But about Eleusis I can set your mind at rest. There we worship the mother of the fruitful earth, and her daughter who teaches the barley to grow. They are kindly ladies, and when we have fulfilled our ritual they grant us another gift as well which I may not speak of. They hunt neither men nor beasts, and blood is not offered to them.'

'Then they are not Pyrene,' said Acco with relief. 'Though she is sometimes both Bride and Mother, she is always then the Terrible One as well. If she is not single she must be triple.'

I saw that Nicanor was suddenly reminded of something unpleasant. A shadow passed over his face. But at the time he said nothing.

From the Acropolis we went on to the Theatre, where Nicanor spoke of Dionysius and the Bacchic rites. In this there seemed to be a smell of the Goddess; but what they worshipped was undoubtedly male, as we could see from the statues nearby. I suppose it is possible for men to make magic by themselves, without the help of women; though in Gaul we would never attempt such foolishness.

When we had seen enough of the wonders of Athens we went to dinner at the best tavern in the city. Nicanor ordered, for he knew what to ask for; but I paid, from army funds. In Greece the food is never so good as in Rome, but the wine is often better.

Nicanor, an excitable youth, was on fire with a new plan

which had just entered his head. He proposed to join the Army of Syria, if we could find him some post where there would be no drilling and he could live in comfort. He explained that his father had sent him abroad only to gain business experience; he had chosen Athens, but any mercantile city would have done as well. The Piraeus branch was run by his clerks, who could get on without him. The Army of Syria promised to be a more important business centre than any of the ancient and bank-rupt cities of Greece; if he could make friends at headquarters he might get valuable orders for the family workshops.

I did not see why we should recommend him to head-quarters, rather than any other merchant who had been useful to us. It was quite as an afterthought that the scatterbrained young man mentioned his important qualifications.

'We mustn't sell you too much leather,' he said casually, 'or you will find all your baggage-animals have been killed for their hides. My father buys his skins from the desert Arabs, and I suppose you will want these Arabs to supply guides and trans-port. If I come with you I shall meet some old friends. I have travelled all over the desert, selling wine and buying camels, as far as the Tigris. I am rusty in the language, but I expect it will come back when I hear it spoken.'

'You know the frontier, and the people who live on it?'

'Of course I know the people who live in the cities beyond Tigris and Euphrates. They are as Greek as I am. No one notices that desert frontier, except sometimes to pay customs-dues if there is no easy way of dodging the collectors. Haven't you heard that the whole east, right up to India, is really Greek? Nearly three hundred years ago our Greek Alexander con-quered it for civilisation, and whether ruled by barbarous Romans or by barbarous Parthians it remains Greek.'

'Then you must come with me to Marcus Crassus,' I said firmly. 'You will be attached to headquarters as guide and interpreter. No one will ask you to drill, and you will live as softly as any soldier on campaign. Afterwards, when we have restored the empire of Alexander, you will have something to boast about to your grandchildren.'

'And at the same time I shall be making money for my

father. Of course I will come with you.

He told us stories of his travels in the desert, which Acco capped with stories of the uncanny wonders of the Druids; until the people of the tavern begged us to leave, for the whole city was asleep. Then we said good night and parted; but while Acco walked back to our lodging I made an excuse to get away (Acco thought I wanted to be sick) and ran to overtake our guest.

'When we spoke of the Triple Goddess this afternoon something came into your mind, though you said nothing openly. I saw it in your eyes. Tell me now, privately, while Acco thinks himself safe. There may be a danger of which I should warn him.'

'When you mentioned the Triple Goddess I thought of Hecate, that's all, Nicanor answered. 'But she is not worshipped officially by the magistrates of the city. You will find her images at forks in the open road, usually three women exactly alike. Yet some older statues show her as an old woman, a desirable bride, and a huntress; just like your Goddess.'

'And who worships her, if the magistrates neglect her?'

'Ignorant old women, and a few young ones who are angry with their lovers. No one of importance.'

I thanked Nicanor, and with a heavy heart rejoined Acco. That night as we undressed for bed I broke the news to him: the Goddess rules in Attica, as she rules in the rest of the earth.

Next day we went up for a last look at Athene in her lovely shrine. She stands there armed, gazing straight ahead from a cold and perfect face, flawless but not desirable. The Athenians call her the Maiden, but in truth she is neither male nor female. A maiden waits to fulfil herself as a bride; Athene is intelligence without flesh. The Romans know her as Minerva, patron of wisdom and learning. Looking on that cold statue I felt she had no part in the loves and hates of men, but in their reasons only.

The same thought must have come to Acco; as we left the temple he said, sneering: 'The finest statue in the world, as any Athenian will tell you. Yet it is nothing but a gold-and-ivory doll. I don't complain that there is no woman in it; they were not trying to make it look like a woman. But there is no divinity

119

either. The divine comprehends emotion; that thing has just
found out that two and two make four, and will never make a
deeper discovery.'

'It's a fine building and a beautiful image inside. No one asks
us to worship her. We can admire, and reverence the man who
made her,' I answered.

'Oh yes, reverence some man. That's what this teaches,
everything round here. They build a mass of expensive temples
on this hilltop, but really they worship nothing but man and
his intelligence.'

Within half an hour we were proved wrong. Not far from the
Propylaea, the fortified gateway of the Acropolis, lay the state
prison. Yesterday Nicanor had pointed it out, for it is famous
as the place where a learned man long ago suffered an unjust
death, and every stranger in Athens asks to see it. It is still in
use as a prison, and we did not like to approach too closely for
fear of offending the guards. As we passed we saw a group of
prisoners exercising in a little yard; several loiterers were
staring, and we thought it safe to join them.

The prisoners looked like prisoners all the world over; dirty
and hungry and anxious to give no trouble to their keepers. All
except one couple. The first was a man all right, as his beard
proved, but he was dressed as a woman. He was very ugly.
Fettered to him was another very ugly man, in male attire.
These two scowled at the guards, who kept their distance and
seemed nervous of angering the strange pair.

A horrid little urchin came up to pester us, as urchins
pester strangers all over Athens. 'Meet my sister, very cheap,
very clean,' he began – and then broke off with a snigger. 'Take
care, barbarians,' he went on in a mocking tone. 'Don't look at
the poison. It might poison you.'

'What do you mean?' asked Acco gravely. 'How can a man
in woman's dress be poison?'

The child continued to gabble in the whining broken Latin
beggar-boys learn in their cradles. 'Poison, bad luck, ugly . . .
all the same thing. Never mind. Next month, whack, skulls
cracked, no more poison. Pharmakoi, ugly, soon dead.' As the
queer couple looked towards us he dropped his head, to avoid

120

meeting their glance. Then he returned to praising the charms of his sister until Acco frowned and he ran away.

Acco never forgot a strange word, I suppose because as an Ovate he had spent years of his life learning meaningless speels by rote. That evening, as we paid the reckoning for our horses, he suddenly shot at the Latin-speaking head ostler: 'Who are the Pharmakoi, and what do you do to them?'

'This year they are a couple of bandits from the Isthmian road,' the man answered readily. Then he saw what Acco was at, and explained more fully. 'It's a very old custom, and there's nothing cruel about it. In fact it does them a kindness, keeping them alive until the festival. You see, they are criminals who deserve death anyway. We never kill men for fun, as they do in some cities. Surely you understand? In a place this size there must be a lot of bad luck. We put it all on the two ugliest criminals in the gaol. One ought by rights to be a woman, but women don't often commit serious crimes, or if they do they are too artful to be caught. So one of them wears woman's dress and pretends to be a woman. Then when the right day comes we take them out of the city, with our bad luck on them. The boys throw stones, and there's our bad luck gone; until next year, of course.'

He saw our interest, and went on making excuses for his city.

'I know you gentlemen are not really Romans. You won't take offence if I tell you that we think some Roman customs beastly. We *never* kill men for fun. Romans tie brigands to a cross until they die slowly; we crack their heads with stones so fast they feel no pain. But there must be two Pharmakoi, one for the men and one for the women. Otherwise we should never be rid of our bad luck.'

Acco thanked him with a piece of silver. When we were out in the street he clasped me by the arm. 'This is what happens to the Great Sacrifice when there are no Druids to perform the rites with due reverence. These people boast that they worship only the Lady of Reason, but in her name they do some very odd things.'

'Is this something that gives pleasure to the Goddess?'

'Of course it is. They do other things as well. Do you know

that the slang name here for a pretty girl is a little bear? That's because their young girls dress up as bears to dance round the image of the Bear Lady. One of the tavern-pimps told me, but I kept it to myself. Yes, the Goddess rules here, in the very stronghold of reason.'

Next morning when we rode north Acco did not turn for one last look at the great shining citadel. Nicanor, who rode with us, was surprised that any foreigners should leave Athens without a backward glance.

At Thessalonica we were once more in the male world, where there is no room for the Goddess. The army was preparing for active service. Besides the legions in their square camp other detachments arrived daily: Greek engineers of the siege-train, Thracian skirmishers whose long hair and broad sabres reminded me of Gallic foot, naked slingers from the islands. Presently the Gallic horse rode in, weary after their tremendous journey from the distant shores of Ocean.

There were more than a thousand of them, all gallant young nobles of high birth, and many of them the oath-bound comrades of Publius Crassus. They had been chosen from a crowd of volunteers, for the expedition was extremely popular. Adventurous young warriors who feared to oppose the Romans at home, and yet thought that fighting for Rome against Gallic rebels looked like treachery, saw it as a way out; in Syria they would be respectable mercenaries, not subjects fighting for a new master.

Presently we took up our march again, still riding into the sunrise. For Acco and me the journey had been broken by our stay in Rome, but our comrades had ridden from Gaul as fast as their horses could carry them; they were awed by the extent of the world and the length of the road. Their talk brought it home to us that we were a very long from the valleys of the Elusates.

They had heard tell, of course, of our Accursed March from the City. Most of them considered it a trick of Roman politics which could not harm free allies who had not been present; and the few doubters were encouraged by Acco's cheerfulness.

'We know what a curse can do, we Gauls who obey the

Druids,' he said when he heard grumbling at our promised ill-luck. 'Armies are blighted by disease, or fortresses hidden by magic mists. When our wise men call down the wrath of the Wargod the army they have cursed does not march a thousand miles unharmed. Who among us has been injured by the curses of old Capito? The gods knew he was making a political speech, and they paid no attention. We are safe enough, as safe as any men who fight for a living.'

Most of our comrades agreed that a curse of real power would have already brought some spectacular result; the others, the really god-fearing, were impressed by the devout practice of the Roman army. Every morning before we set out the Proconsul sacrificed an ox, reverently inspecting the en-trails. The standards of the legions, sacred emblems of the Wargod, twice a day received incense and barley-meal. In this army the gods were served; they should not be hostile.

The savage hills of Thrace now lay on our left, and the sea on our right. We marched in due order, with a cavalry screen and advance-guard, while light-armed skirmishers made good the heights before legions and baggage were committed to a defile. Thus we would march until we encountered the enemy, though we had many hundred of miles to go; for to the east-ward the Roman dominions have no definite border, and though we marched through lands which had submitted to Lucullus or Pompeius we might meet war at any moment.

We continued eastward until we reached the city of Byzan-tium, and then turned to the south, crossing an arm of the sea which seems more like a wide river. Since we left Thessalonica we had traversed a patchwork of cities and kingdoms which were in name free allies of Rome. In fact, they were as obedient to a Roman army as the oldest and most peaceful province. However, now that we were in Asia there might be trouble from Pontus or Armenia, newly won in the last few years. One reason why we took such a roundabout route was to impress the natives, lest while we were engaged with the Parthians there should be trouble in our rear.

Acco and I eased ourselves into one of those comfortable berths which can be acquired, if you are sober and tactful, in most large armies. Our duties lay partly in the quartermaster's department, partly with the Gallic horse. Since Longinus, the quartermaster, and Publius Crassus, the commander of the horse, were both overworked, neither bothered to control us; so long as we gave no trouble and looked busy we could ride with our friends the Gauls and dine in the comfort of headquarters. Whenever we passed a place that seemed interesting we left the ranks to go sightseeing, explaining that we must get in touch with a local merchant. Other staff officers enjoyed the same freedom, though if one of them got scandalously drunk or molested a Roman citizen the high command became aware of his existence and he was returned to regular duty. Our independence depended on continued good behaviour.

As we rode southward through Asia we came to understand that we had never left Greece. The country we rode through was broken and mountainous, cut up by arms of sea which could only be passed by long detours; there were tangled forests and open heaths, as well as great stretches of arable and long slopes of vines. The farms and fields were more extensive than any we had seen, as though here land was cheap and the men too few to work it. But the cities were crowded and rich, and they were utterly Greek.

Nicanor explained this to us. He was as free as we were, or if anything more free; for he travelled at his own expense, though it had been promised that when we reached Antioch he would be put on the strength as a guide. He came with us whenever we went sightseeing, and told us the history of the great cities we visited. His story was that long ago all this land had been conquered by the Greeks; though later, as the empire of Alexander broke up, native rulers from the countryside had imposed themselves on the Greek citizens.

We moved steadily along, the legions covering their twenty miles a day at the unhurrying, inexorable pace of the Roman army on a journey; and as every evening we inspected the sights of another Greek city I began to perceive that they were not really so Greek after all.

The colonnaded temples were built of stained marble, but they were dedicated to gods unknown in Hellas. Citizens loitered in the public square to make speeches and hear them, but in the end they did what their king told them to do. They were too busy earning a living to have time for politics; whereas a true Greek will starve while he debates the government of his city. The biggest make-believe of all was the training of the young men. This athletic and military training is supposed to be the highest peak of Greek culture, the great Greek contribution to civilised life. In every city we visited we might watch the young men throwing spears or wrestling together. Of course they were stark naked, and went out of their way to impress on visitors that they felt no shame for exposing themselves; that also is supposed to be a Greek characteristic, unknown among barbarians. Nicanor said they went too far in shouting amorous invitations at the marching soldiers, for though Greeks approve of love-affairs between men it should be real love and not casual enjoyment. But he excused it on the ground that they were being self-consciously Greek, and perhaps overdoing it in their enthusiasm. He pointed out these groups of young men with great pride, and asked whether we in Gaul had any similar institution.

I said that, of course, our young warriors practised the use of their weapons, though normally they did it at home, not in a group for all to see; since until they were expert they did not want strangers to criticise their swordplay. I then asked where we might see the finished article. Did the garrisons of these cities also exercise publicly in the open?

Nicanor answered airily that few of the cities were garrisoned. Roman troops on the frontier guarded them from invasion, and to keep internal order their rulers preferred to hire barbarian mercenaries; in many cases the walls were never manned, and elderly slave watchmen closed the gates each night. The cities possessed no armed force of their own.

'In other words,' said Acco in disgust, 'these youths prance naked from mere shamelessness. They are not training for war. They do not expect war, and if war comes their rulers will hire strangers to defend them. In Gaul only nobles learn to fence and ride, but every peasant will turn out with axe or scythe if his people need him. I think our serfs possess more of the dignity of free men than these unarmed and timid citizens.'

Acco did not like Asia at all. It was so obviously the domain of the Goddess. In nearly every temple the most sacred image was the Lady in one of her forms, usually the Bride whom the ignorant miscall the Maiden. Sometimes a male god was worshipped, but one could see he was the son or consort of the Goddess. There was no secrecy about it. The Goddess might go by the name of some Greek servant of Skyfather; but a Mother whose whole torso is covered with many breasts is not called Artemis the Maiden Huntress with intent to deceive.

Acco was beginning to think we had outdistanced the vengeance of Pyrene. 'I have greater honour and more riches than if I had stayed at home,' he said to me, as we rode away from a rather horrid little shrine where offerings of blood and pinecones stank before a figure of the Lady of Wild Beasts. 'To the men of our valley Pyrene is only a name, though she wields great power. Here both men and women perform public rites in honour of the Great Mother, but all is so open that she is scarcely feared. The Goddess is older than Skyfather. But since throughout Gaul and the west Skyfather has displaced her, it is reasonable to suppose that he is the stronger. But we are certainly under the protection of Skyfather, as is all the army. Our leader sacrifices to him daily, and the standards we march under are the dwelling of the Wargod. Their protection will preserve us.'

'Perhaps we might count on that,' I answered, to encourage his good spirits. 'Where the Goddess is worshipped in secret she is to be feared, where her altars are public she has no power. In that case we should be safe in Syria, where by all accounts she rules splendidly.'

CHAPTER V

Syria

When at last we entered Syria, after marching all winter through the cities and plains of Asia, the Goddess met us on every side. And here she is worshipped as the Bride, or rather as the Courtesan; young and desirable, she blesses the bed and hides her power as the Mistress of Wild Beasts. We thought the rites we witnessed more disgusting than pious; with us that sort of thing is not done publicly in a holy place (though Gauls do it often enough and find it enjoyable). Acco admitted that a noble warrior ought not to be afraid of a divinity who was rather the butt of coarse jokes than an awesome avenger.

Antioch is in its own way more beautiful than Athens and more impressive than Rome, though it has no buildings to compare with the Capitol or the Acropolis. Its walls climb the steep slopes of Mount Silpius, whose summit is crowned by an almost impregnable citadel. Westward the river Orontes flows through wooded mountains to the sea, and among these hanging slopes lie the groves of Daphne. The troops had heard fascinating tales of what took place in the groves of Daphne, but they were out of bounds to the army; for at last we had genuine military duties to keep us busy.

On the day after we marched into Antioch the whole force paraded in the plain by the river, to witness the formal handing over of the province by the retiring Proconsul, Aulus Gabinius. He was going home in theoretical disgrace, to answer a charge of levying war without the Senate's permission. The charge was true, but Gabinius would not be punished; for he had acted on the instructions of Caesar and Pompeius, or at least with their consent. I gathered from Nicanor, who enjoyed gossiping about eastern politics, that what he had really done was to occupy Egypt without waiting for orders from Rome. Financially this had been profitable, both to Gabinius and the Roman People; but as a result most of his infantry were in Alexandria. When he handed over his charge to the new Proconsul he added only a few cohorts to our forces.

I watched as these men took oath to their new commander, and once again I realised that I was meeting a new kind of Roman soldier. These were not the reckless well-disciplined adventurers who had followed Caesar to the conquest of Gaul, neither were they the slack but willing yokels who had filled the new legions of Crassus. These men were veterans, well trained and difficult to kill; but sly veterans, who drank too much and slept too little. Of course, vice and dishonesty were not actually branded on their foreheads, but if you see soldiers every day for a year or two you get to recognise these signs. I felt that Caesar's men would bring in wounded comrades at risk of their lives, and the raw recruits of Crassus might abandon them to the enemy; but the veterans of Gabinius would think first of going through their money-belts.

After only three days in Antioch we set out for the frontier. Nicanor came with us as scoutmaster; and as he had no set place in the column of march he frequently rode with Acco and myself.

The gay young merchant went to war in a most unmilitary spirit. He was intensely interested, because it was all new to him; but he did not seem to care which side won. He believed that empires are overthrown by political combinations, and that honest fighting with swords is a clumsy way of settling international disputes. According to him, if Gabinius had seized his opportunities there would have been no need for a great Roman army.

'The Parthians are barbarians who rule over Greeks, which is against nature and a most precarious foundation for a state,' he explained, as we plodded through thick dust-clouds towards the Euphrates. 'You Romans are newcomers out here and you don't understand the arts by which eastern kings reign. Our rulers keep great state and look very powerful; but they seldom dare to embark on foreign war for fear of being overthrown by a successful general. If a king is hostile to Rome the sensible thing is to wait until he is murdered by his heir, or anyway murdered by someone; which is bound to happen in a few years. This war is unnecessary. The Parthians stupidly missed their chance to destroy Rome's power in the east, and now your Gabinius has missed his chance of destroying Parthia. So now merchants like my father must see the trade routes closed and all prices rising against them, just because foreigners from the ends of the earth think they can't collect our taxes without first winning a lot of bloody battles.'

'You forget that we know nothing of Syrian affairs,' said Acco. 'Two years ago I had never heard of Antioch, or of Parthia. What are these chances that have been missed?'

'Well, King Mithradates of Pontus nearly chased the Romans out of Asia. If the Parthians had joined him he must have succeeded. Of course then he would have attacked Parthia, and perhaps the Parthians thought a wily Asiatic more dangerous than any Roman Proconsul. But I think they refused to help him because they fear Rome.'

'Will this Mithradates join the Parthians against us?' I asked.

'Oh no, he's been dead for nearly ten years. He committed suicide when his son rebelled and dethroned him. Perhaps he was foolish to allow a son to grow up, but he had already killed several of them and he wanted his dynasty to go on.'

'And Gabinius, what chance has he missed?'

'That was only last year. Another Mithradates, a Parthian prince, rebelled against King Orodes, his brother. He seized the throne but couldn't keep it, and when he was beaten he fled to Gabinius. A Roman army half the size of this could have restored him; instead Gabinius went off to plunder Egypt. Now Mithradates is back in Parthia, fighting his brother. But he's besieged in Seleucia. If we marched there directly we might join either side, and install a king friendly to Rome. In-

9   129

stead I hear we are to spend the summer ravaging the cities of the Euphrates. By next winter the civil war will be ended, one way or the other.'

'You can't conquer a country without fighting,' said Acco sternly. 'It's no good occupying fortresses unless the people know they have been beaten. Anyway, if all these rulers are so insecure, why don't you Greeks win your freedom from them?'

'A Greek tyrant is more expensive than a barbarian who is greedy but stupid,' answered Nicanor with a shrug. 'It's no use telling a Greek that the money isn't there. He knows. For more than two hundred years Egypt has been under Greek rule, and the taxes there are much heavier than in Syria.'

Acco was shocked, and even I thought Nicanor rather lacking in honour. But he was an amusing companion in the ordinary affairs of life. Soon he had us in a good humour again as he described how a desert Arab had sold him the same camel three times over, by altering the brands on its hide.

These camels are queer beasts. At first we thought we ought to learn how to manage them. But no one can look after both horses and camels; for horses, even our Gallic horses who had never before encountered them, will have nothing to do with the nasty creatures; they cannot endure the stink. In the end we decided that our horses probably knew best, for they are honourable beasts. The management of camels is not an occupation for gentlemen.

Once we reached the river Euphrates we marched in full battle order, since that river is the boundary of Parthia. That meant that we saw no more of Nicanor, who stuck close to headquarters while we rode with the van. Our Gallic comrades were very excited at the prospect of action. For the last two years they had marched through the peaceful provinces of Rome; few of them had kept their swords sheathed for so long since they first bore arms. They squabbled with the Arab scouts, whom they accused of driving away the enemy and so cheating gallant Gauls of their prey.

For though we rode in the van of the Roman army, the whole desert on both banks of the river was patrolled by Arab horsemen. The desert is the home of these Arabs, where they

130

wander with their grazing camels. In theory they are all subject either to Rome or to Parthia; though only a well-mounted tax-gatherer can get any profit from them. Merchants hire them to guard their caravans, which is a splendid arrangement for the Arabs – who are the only thieves in the desert.

In that summer every Arab warrior had been taken into pay by Rome or Parthia, or sometimes by both. They scouted zealously among gravel ravines and stony hillocks, continually galloping back to report the movements of strange horsemen – who always turned out to be friendly Arabs of another tribe. If there was a Parthian army over the next crest they might inform us or they might not, depending on which side had paid them last. But we had to rely on their scouting, for we Gauls, the only other horse in the Roman army, could not range over this broken waterless country like the natives. The army marched blind.

I said as much to Publius Crassus, but he replied that it did not matter. 'When the Parthians attack us we shall beat them, and the sooner the better. It doesn't help to know where they are, for their whole army is mounted and our foot can't catch them. We intend to threaten their cities until they either offer battle or run back to their deserts in the far north-east.' After a pause he continued: 'When you fight in these parts you always hire local Arabs; it's the custom. They are not much use as allies and not much danger as foes, but they are cheap and they need the money.'

'Why not pay us extra, and let us do the scouting?' I persisted.

'Because my father needs you on the battlefield. If you went off to patrol the desert half your horses would be destroyed, and you are too valuable to be frittered away in skirmishes. When we fight our battles these Arabs will be afraid to charge, and we shall need steady cavalry to cover the flanks of the foot. Tell your comrades how important they are, and they will feel more cheerful. And remind them that the plunder of Seleucia will be enough to make every man in the army rich for life.'

That is how Romans plan war. One reason why their army has no proper cavalry of its own is that they are always eager

131

for battle, and so well disciplined that an enemy gains no advantage by surprising them. They march straight ahead into hostile country until the defenders are forced to meet them. In this particular army no one was very interested in the inevitable battle; everyone thought and talked of nothing but the fabulous treasure said to be laid up in Seleucia. The battle would come, and the Romans would win it; the subject was not worth discussion.

But that summer there was no battle. The enemy had other foes to cope with, and Marcus Crassus did not lead us boldly into the heart of their land, where they must either fight or submit. We learned from Arab spies that the greater part of the Parthian army was gathered before Seleucia, where two sons of the late king fought for the crown; while the Surenas, a great Parthian war-chief whose force consisted largely of his own sworn comrades, lay on the north-western frontier, to threaten Armenia. So we reached the Euphrates unopposed, and there sat down as though we had all the time in the world, while Syrian engineers constructed a bridge of boats.

When we crossed to the eastern bank it was high summer, and already too hot for cavalry campaigning. Our horses sickened daily; if we had attempted to pass the waterless desert we would all have been on foot by the fourth day.

Instead our commander led us up a tributary of the great river, a small stream which flowed in from the east. Its banks were dotted with little Greek towns which paid tribute to the king of the Parthians; but though they had walls, which might have been defended, they surrendered as soon as our great army appeared. We were not permitted to plunder them, though in each we left a small garrison. It was hard on us Gauls, who after our astounding journey right across the known world found no enemy to fight, and no treasury to plunder.

While the main body was still on the march our Arab allies claimed to have won a great victory. In fact they had encountered only the other Arabs who had been hired to fight for the Parthians. The Parthian chief who governed that frontier, a noble named Sillaces, led off his small force of genuine

Parthian horse without fighting; and his Arab allies had to change sides openly, instead of deserting him on the battlefield as they had planned to do.

Our Roman recruits were eager to record the first victory of the campaign, so that they might be reckoned as veterans who had seen active service; but no one could exaggerate the orderly retirement of Sillaces into a victory. Our soldiers were very pleased when another example of petty treachery gave them an excuse to draw their swords against a helpless foe.

We had dropped a garrison in the town of Zenodotium while the main army continued north-east towards Carrhae, on the headwaters of the stream. I suppose this garrison behaved badly, raping or robbing; for what happened next was unexpected. The people of Zenodotium rose in arms, and after massacring the Roman garrison sent messages of loyalty to the king of the Parthians.

Our army returned in haste to Zenodotium, which defied us behind closed gates. The legionaries were angry, and eager for plunder. They marched straight against the eastern gate, set up a battering-ram, and burst their way in. Marcus Crassus led them himself, on foot, waving a drawn sword; which was creditable in a man of his age and corpulence. But once the gate was down there was no serious fighting.

We cavalry took no part in the action, which was nothing but a skirmish. But it was the first fight the army had seen, and angry legionaries sacked the place very thoroughly, killing most of the inhabitants. In the evening they paraded outside the burning city. The few surviving citizens were auctioned off to the slave-dealers who accompany every Roman army, and after the prize-money had been distributed Marcus Crassus made an eloquent speech about the glory of Rome and the honour of bearing the Eagles so far towards the unknown east. Some of us thought he was making too much of what was really a very minor affair; but the soldiers answered with shouts of: 'Hail to Marcus Crassus Imperator.'

This made it a most important ceremony, as I learned that evening when I visited cavalry headquarters. Publius Crassus had ordered wine to be distributed to all his officers. We went up in a long procession to congratulate him on the honour that had come to his family, while he sat beaming and handing out largesse to his grooms and servants. Imperator I already knew as a word meaning commander of an army; but it seems that no Roman may use it until he has been hailed with the title by his victorious troops on the battlefield. The sack of Zenodotium could hardly be called a battle; but plenty of hostile blood had been shed and it had certainly ended in victory. As Publius exclaimed with glee, his father was now equal to Caesar and Pompeius, the only other living Imperators. Everyone seemed delighted, though I agreed with Cassius Longinus, our quartermaster, who said sardonically: 'Caesar conquered Ariovistus and his Germans. Pompeius conquered Mithradates of Pontus. Crassus has conquered Zenodotium, which until yesterday no one had heard of. If that makes him Imperator, we need another word to describe great generals.'

Then, after leaving garrisons in the cities we had won from the Parthians, the army marched back to Syria and dispersed into winter quarters.

It was still high summer, but much too hot for campaigning. Next year we would take the field really early, as soon as the grass began to grow. In the meantime the army would train, for after our taste of active service we could see that our recruits still had much to learn. The troops were glad to be back in friendly and luxurious Syria, whose citizens are accustomed to keeping on the right side of warlike invaders. It was sensible to split them into smaller bodies for training, and they liked that also. For though to fight under the eye of the commander-in-chief, who can reward brave deeds on the spot, is a very good thing, all veterans agree that it is more pleasant to train out of sight of superior officers.

Only at headquarters was there some discontent; senior officers, discussing the wasted campaign, spoke of stout, deaf, elderly Marcus Crassus as a figure of fun. He was better known as a money-maker than as a warrior, and I heard it whispered that the real object of dispersing the army was to wring contributions from all the wealthy cities of the east. But no soldier dislikes a well-filled war-chest; the rank and file approved of good old Crassus, who fed us well and saw that we had comfortable billets.

All through the appalling heat of late summer Acco and I laboured in the horse-lines. Our comrades would go on managing their chargers as though they were in Gaul, refreshing the panting beasts with cold spring water. In very hot weather cold water brings colic, and horses should drink only from troughs standing in the sun. So Nicanor had told us, and we believed him; but it was hard to persuade our comrades. By the beginning of autumn we were both exhausted. When the weather cooled Publius Crassus granted us leave to visit Antioch for a rest.

After the sack of Zenodotium Nicanor had gone home. But the house of his father, Aristobulus, was one of the best known in the city, and we found it without difficulty. He was pleased to see us, and invited us to stay as his guests. Even Acco, who hated to be under an obligation to a stranger, thought this fair enough; for by our patronage Nicanor had found a well-paid post on the staff.

This was the first time since we entered civilisation that we had lived as guests. In Rome a lodging had been hired for us, and in Greece we had been soldiers on duty. But by now we were accustomed to city manners, and we found it easy to behave like our neighbours. We bathed in hot steam, for hours at a time; we took exercise by running and wrestling in a paved yard, instead of scrambling among the hills; at the dinner-table we played with elaborate food and listened to poetry, instead of first getting drunk and then quarrelling to prove our courage. In one particular only Acco stood firmly by our native custom, and through force of character persuaded me to follow him. In the gymnasium he would not strip naked; wearing trousers we wrestled and fenced with naked citizens, and until they were used to it crowds gathered to stare at the extraordinary sight (naked crowds, naturally, so that they seemed as odd to us as we did to them).

Nicanor was a gay young man, who enjoyed taking us round the taverns; though in the Greek manner we lay about for hours before a small jug of wine, and came home sober. In his

135

native city Nicanor dared not visit low haunts, for his father would have heard of it. We lived very decorously.

Usually we dined at home. That was not exciting; but it was enjoyable all the same, for Aristobulus spoke fluent Latin and had plenty to say. We sat up in proper chairs, and the food was usually a good solid roast; which to us was much more comfortable than reclining on padded couches and nibbling at little morsels drowned in honey and wine.

If there were no other guests we were treated as members of the family, and our host's wife and young children were present. The lady Glauce was stout and dark, and very talkative though not to us; for her only language was Greek, and she talked mostly of servants and the affairs of the kitchen. She was proud of her housekeeping, and related at length her triumphs in the vegetable market. I sat beside her. First I would repeat a few Greek compliments I had learned by heart; after thanking me she would begin on the price of lettuce, while the rest of the family listened enthralled, and I got on with my beef in silence.

There was a boy of ten, Damasippus, a tiresome youth with black curls down to his shoulders and long eyelashes with which he beckoned like a harlot. He already had a lover among the young men of the city, but he was out to capture one of us in addition. He spoke a few words of bad Latin, since he would be a citizen when he grew up; and he constantly offered to take one of us for a long walk alone. We dared not snub him for fear of offending his father, who thought this disgusting behaviour nothing out of the way. He never got either of us alone. We went walking with him when we could not avoid it; but always both together.

The remaining member of the family was the only daughter, Berenice; a quiet little girl of thirteen, dark and rather small for her age, with a serious screwed-up monkey-face set off by great liquid brown eyes. She spoke quite good Latin, for it was hoped to marry her to a real Roman from Italy, to increase the standing of the family.

'I am undoubtedly a citizen,' Aristobulus explained to us with a deprecatory smile, as though there were something absurd in a true Roman complaining of oppression. 'I have a diploma to prove it, bearing the seal of the great Lucullus. But sometimes the publicans come down on the whole province, and then every rich merchant is marched off to the governor's praetorium. My diploma gets me out for nothing, while my colleagues pay heavily for release. But they only arrest me in the first place because they think of me as a Greek; real Latin-speaking Romans are never arrested, and don't pay even their legal share of the taxes. If I can get hold of a son-in-law who speaks nothing but Latin, a real Italian who can't read the Greek alphabet, the officers of the law would not touch me if they saw me rob a caravan in the market square. In the provinces a true Roman can do anything.'

'Would I do for your son-in-law? I don't know the Greek alphabet, or the Latin either. But after this campaign I shall be a citizen.' I said this with a smile at little Berenice, who screwed up her nose to laugh back.

'You lack the true aroma of garlic, my noble Camillus. And the palm of your hand has been roughened by the sword-hilt. The man I am looking for must have soft hands, and a long fingernail to count money with. He will discuss expertly the fencing of gladiators, without knowing how to hold a sword,' answered her father; for of course a young girl could not banter with men.

'He must care nothing for politics, for nowadays politicians die suddenly,' put in Nicanor, carrying on the joke. 'But if he has a cousin a Praetor, or better still a Tribune, we can all laugh at the Law.'

'Well, at headquarters you must see plenty of the right type,' said Acco across the table. 'It's funny. In Gaul we think of all Romans as mighty warriors. Here in the east you see them as crooked financiers.

'That's because we deal so much with Arabs, who are never anything but land-pirates; or with Parthians, who are warriors and nothing else. To us a Roman seems as fond of money as any Greek or Syrian.'

'Are the Parthians such great warriors?' inquired Acco. 'In our army no one takes them seriously.'

'I didn't say they are great warriors,' answered Nicanor, with the quizzical smile which was the signal that he was about to display his celebrated Attic wit. 'I said they were nothing but warriors, which is the exact truth. They don't know how to build or carve or write poetry; they can't even govern themselves except by choosing one man to rule them absolutely. They can fight, but that's all they are fit for. Oh, and of course they breed the most wonderful horses.'

'They can't fight Romans, and they know it,' said the father with decision. 'They proved they were afraid of you when they refused to help old Mithradates of Pontus. I don't believe you will conquer their whole empire, because there's so much of it. But there's no reason why you shouldn't pass next winter in Seleucia.'

'That's very comforting,' I said, rather bored with all this talk of warfare from an unarmed merchant. 'We are warriors by trade and we enjoy a little fighting. But it's always more fun to fight a weak enemy; and I have never yet plundered a real city. Yet if it's going to be so easy it won't be very interesting. Seeing strange places is really my hobby, and I am having my fill of it. By the way, is it true that when training is over the troops will be allowed to visit the groves of Daphne?'

'I'm sorry, but I can tell you nothing about the groves of Daphne. You know how it is. If you live in a place all your life you somehow never have time to see the local sights,' replied Aristobulus. I could tell from his frown that I had opened a subject he did not wish to discuss.

'Of course. That is notorious, even in Gaul,' I answered politely. 'But apart from Daphne there are many famous sights in Antioch. As you know, I like visiting temples. Perhaps you know of someone who would have the leisure to take us round them?'

Rather to our surprise, Berenice spoke up. 'Let me do it, father. You are all so busy, you and Nicanor – don't you remember, you said Nicanor couldn't go off playing at soldiers any more, now you had so many orders to fill. But I know all the temples in the city, and all the legends, and I could translate the inscriptions. It will be good practice for my Latin. And

138

if Damasippus came it would really be quite proper.'

She turned and said something in Greek to her mother, who beamed and nodded. Damasippus languished at Acco with his great brown eyes.

'If you don't mind going about with a child I am sure Berenice can help you,' said her father with pride. 'She's a great one for temples, and knows all the old stories.'

Catching my eye, Acco shrugged his shoulders. It seemed that Daphne was something you did not mention to respectable citizens of Antioch. But in other places even a little girl, who could read Greek inscriptions and put them into Latin, would be better than nothing. He conveyed his thanks to the young lady in a speech of elaborate courtesy. I myself, like every other Gaul, speak more formally than the average Roman; but Acco never for a moment forgot that he was an ambassador of Gallic culture before the ignorant world.

Next time we got Nicanor alone, walking back from the gymnasium, we asked him why Daphne could not be discussed in the family circle.

'Don't you know what goes on there?' he answered. 'It all began more than two hundred years ago, with a temple and groves dedicated to the Pythian Apollo. There's nothing the matter with him; he's a very respectable sort of god, patron of dancing and poetry and such. Unfortunately, when our King Seleucus founded the shrine he decreed that all who worshipped there must be immune from arrest within the sacred precinct. So every rogue in Syria went there and laughed at the law. But when you come to think of it only one kind of rogue can earn a living in the garden of a temple – apart from the priests, of course. The brigands and burglars can live safe enough, but they can't make money. So nowadays the grove of Daphne is the biggest brothel in the world.'

'But every soldier in the army knows that,' said I. 'That's why we're all set on seeing it. I suppose that's also why it's out of bounds to all troops.'

'That isn't what I heard,' Acco interrupted. 'It isn't all the army heard, either. Soldiers like brothels well enough, but they don't have to look for them. Whores find their own way to an army.' He paused as though arranging his thoughts, and continued in a more serious tone. 'We heard – I mean a great many of us heard – that in Daphne you meet more than the girls who are kind for cash down. Are there not women there – ladies of birth – devotees who do what would otherwise be shameful to please Her, so that She may be gracious and bless the crops?'

Nicanor answered with a shrug: In Antioch, when a woman is willing we don't stop to ask why. But are you Romans still taking that kind of worship seriously? You've come to the right country then, for Syria is stiff with it. But only among the natives, you know, Syrians and Phoenicians and that sort of rabble. I believe they go in for it devoutly. As Greeks we think it funny, or disgusting.'

I was afraid that Nicanor's sneer would make Acco think I had been gossiping about his affairs. But he answered sharply: 'All men think it either funny or disgusting. But sooner or later they find out that their wives have been worshipping the Goddess all their lives, without bothering to let the men into the secret. Three years ago I would have laughed if anyone had suggested that my kin would slaughter a young girl to placate a bear, and that's what happened to the girl I had hoped to marry. Do you know how your kitchen-slaves worship, when there are no men about?'

'I see, and I'm sorry I was flippant,' answered Nicanor with charming sympathy. 'The women here, especially the native women, have rites of their own; and in the south I am pretty sure the Goddess is worshipped in the way you fear. Wise Greeks do not inquire into that ritual. But, believe me, all this has nothing to do with Daphne. That's just a bawdy-house which has grown out of a sanctuary of Apollo.'

I thanked him, and said that in that case the place did not interest us. I was telling the truth, for all that we were mercenary soldiers far from home. Romans will sleep with anyone, though they are decently jealous of their wives; but in Gaul we have been taught to believe that continence is part of the self-control of a warrior, who should be able to live without women for years if need be; for on campaign our warriors may not touch even their wives. Since we left home neither Acco nor I had stooped to commerce with a harlot.

All the same, something in the air of Syria breathes of love. The women have a sparkle unknown in the west, and because of it the men guard them the more fiercely. The sky of Antioch is filled with the urgent cooing of doves; dark eyes flash through flowing kerchiefs, and slim wrists under massy bracelets beckon to adventure. The Greek swaggers back from the gymnasium with his hand on the shoulder of a giggling little urchin, but the Syrians are all male or all female.

It was all the stranger to wander through such a garish crowd of lustful bodies under the guidance of a serious and sexless little girl. But Berenice made a good guide for foreigners genuinely interested in the wonders of a great city. She knew Antioch's history, and could repeat all the tales of shape-changing and miraculous intervention which Greek poets tell of their gods. For it seems to me that the Greeks will babble about everything their gods have done, telling it casually even to foreigners; it is only the things men do for the gods, the manner of their worship, that is a mystery revealed only to initiates.

Antioch is a beautiful place, and rich too. But I don't think it has ever been a true city, a community for which citizens will die on the battlefield. It was founded at the command of an absolute king, and now it is happy to be ruled by foreigners who collect the taxes and do any fighting that is needed. As you go round the shrines you feel something missing; this was built by King Antigonus, and that endowed by King Seleucus; you never reach the heart of the place, the spot where the gods of the city will inspire defenders to hold out when hope has gone. Rome breathes that sacrificial defiance from the Capitol, though now she has no enemies within a month's journey; and on the Acropolis you can feel the menace from Persians and Spartans, though the city of the Maiden, after yielding to many foes, no longer defends herself. The great citadel on Mount Silipus was built to house the bodyguard of a foreign king, and the whole city is without honour. I soon grew bored with looking at the monuments of this gaggle of merchants and slaves.

Acco, to my surprise, enjoyed it. But that was because he

enjoyed the company of Berenice. She was an earnest little girl, and he was an earnest young man; both saw the world as a gymnasium for the immortal gods, and devoted much thought to defining the correct attitude of honourable men and women, who must obey and worship these gods without necessarily approving their actions.

Berenice knew something about the Goddess, and spoke freely of what she knew. In Syria, indeed, it would be absurd to keep quiet about her, since she is openly worshipped on the hilltops. But I think Nicanor would have been surprised at his sister's un-Greek enthusiasm. When Acco told her the story of Grane's death and his own misfortune, she refused to see in it anything for regret.

'Sometimes the Goddess demands blood, though not very often,' I heard her explain solemnly to him, sitting at his feet as he rested on a marble bench before a temple. 'But those whom she summons are not called to sorrow. Your Grane was chosen for a high honour, chosen out of all your people. Her spirit did not die with her body. You agree with me there, for you must know from the teaching of your Druids that the spirit persists. She is not in gloomy Hades, the ordinary fate of mortals; she is not even in the Fortunate Islands, with the spirits of great heroes. Her spirit is now one with the Goddess herself. That is the splendid reward of those whose life is spilled for the Lady.'

Acco nodded, seeming to agree. He was, in fact, shocked to hear this child speak so openly of divine secrets, which should be revealed only to chosen seekers; and he did not agree with her, for he had another theory of what had happened to the spirit of Grane. One night he told me he thought it must have entered the body of Berenice.

Our Druids teach that souls after death, or at least some souls, enter into new bodies. In theory the doctrine is secret, but every Gallic warrior has heard of it; and Acco, during his Ovate training, had been told many of the details. By rights the first body should be dead before the second body is born, and Berenice must have been nine or ten when Grane went for her last climb among the high hills. But I suppose an aspirant to

142

the Druid order learns how to argue away difficulties of that kind. Anyway, though the doctrine may have been incorrect, Acco had managed to persuade himself.

I see now that Acco had been very lonely since he left the hills of Pyrene, and it was largely my fault. I tried to be a true comrade to him, and certainly we were very good friends. But Acco all his life needed some one person who would look to him for protection, and I can rub along anywhere. If I had found civilisation too much for me he would have protected me, but I have never felt the need for an elder brother. He also needed sympathy for his deep moral earnestness and somehow I could never take things so seriously as he did. Here was Berenice, earnest, solemn, pious, silly and very young. Naturally she appealed to him. She filled exactly the gap left by Grane.

Perhaps I should not have been so bored if Berenice on our excursions had been escorted by her nurse or maid. Any Syrian woman, even if plump and middle-aged, will flutter her eyelids and giggle, flirting just enough to pass away the time amusingly. But Damasippus jumped at the chance his sister gave him; he insisted on coming with us. Of course, he always tried to pair off with Acco; so did Berenice. I was used to that. Acco was always the favourite for he had something about him, perhaps his own mixture of honesty and kindliness, which made everyone love him. However, good manners compelled one of the children to stay with me, and since I dislike boys who wriggle their bottoms and gaze up appealingly through long eyelashes, I made it my business to thwart Damasippus; seeing to it that he was left with me while Acco and Berenice examined holy images and gossipped with temple servants.

At first Berenice was not interested in Acco as a man; but she was most anxious to win him to her own cult. She held that all good things come from the Goddess, and that Acco, who had already been singled out for her divine attention, was foolish to defy her. It was odd to hear this child, with no experience of the force she described, extolling the merit of allowing nature to control the will.

'You must empty yourself to permit the Goddess to enter,' she said earnestly one day, while we strolled round the biggest temple of Aphrodite 'I sometimes come here alone, with just my maid, and sit before the image to await a command. So far I have heard nothing, though I know of women who have been inspired. They slept in this holy place, after drinking a sacred potion. But the priests won't let me taste it because they say I am too young.'

'And so you are, silly,' said Damasippus. 'When you are older you will have more sense. Then you will leave this Syrian Goddess, and sacrifice to Athene like a true Greek. These noble warriors aren't interested in she-gods. They follow Zeus and Ares. If you like, Acco, we can scramble straight down this hillside to the gymnasium, while Camillus takes my sister home by the paved road.'

'I shall be charmed to come to the gymnasium, if you can find someone big enough to wrestle with me,' Acco answered gravely. 'I am sure Camillus would like to come too. Let us first drop your sister at home.'

'Will you hang up a wreath before the image?' asked Berenice. 'It's a little courtesy most visitors pay, in thanksgiving for the beauty of the temple. It commits you to nothing, and it will please me.'

'My only desire is to please you, madam,' answered Acco, as formally as if he were addressing a great lady. 'But I will not pay tribute to an enemy. That has never been the custom of my house.'

I moved towards the stall where these wreaths were sold. But that sharp-eyed and venomous brat crushed my attempt to smooth things over. 'No one has asked you to offer thanks, Camillus,' he whispered. 'It's your comrade my sister wants to win to the service of her Lady. You and I may worship as we please.'

That was true enough, but there was no need to say it.

More than once Berenice strayed off alone with Acco after we had all left the house together. I did not worry, for I knew that my friend was too honourable to seduce his host's daughter. The only one who suffered by it was that wretched boy, who languished at me because such conduct was second nature to him, but who could not keep his thoughts away from his adored Acco. He would have been the better for a thrashing, though it was not for me to educate him.

Acco enjoyed his cosy little chats about divine affairs. He began to forget Berenice's youth, and to behave as though he were courting her.

My dear friend was much too ingenuous to conceal his feelings. Aristobulus soon noticed that he was growing fond of the child. To my surprise, he did not object. Nicanor explained the family attitude, one afternoon when he and I shared a couch in the hot room of the bath.

'We want my sister to marry into a family who will protect us, a family with influence over the Roman rulers of Syria. We used to think that meant she must marry an Italian with generations of the citizenship behind him; but Acco the Gaul will do very well instead. Publius Crassus thinks well of him, and in due course Publius will inherit his father's power. Oh, I know that's unconstitutional; we new citizens are well up in the rules of the sacred Roman commonwealth. All our magistrates are elected by the people, to hold power for one year only. But the system has broken down; whatever they may think in the Forum, out here we see that clearly. We live under three rulers, of equal power: Caesar the conqueror of Gaul, Pompeius the conqueror of Mithradates, Crassus who could buy them both. But when Crassus has conquered Parthia he will be tyrant of Rome. Whether he calls himself Consul or King, his power will continue to his son. His son's friend may never be a citizen; he will be more than a citizen. Then the business of his father-in-law will prosper, untouched by Roman tax-gatherers.'

That sounded exciting. At headquarters we always spoke of the Roman People as our sovereign, and when living in Rome I had observed that control of the Forum and its elections was the prize for which every leader contended. But now that it had been pointed out to me I agreed that power was passing to the soldiers; and after Crassus had conquered Parthia he would be the most powerful soldier in Rome. I also was an honoured friend of his son, and I also would be a great man.

As autumn deepened into winter even Acco, so slow at noticing his surroundings, became aware that his suit was favoured. One evening as we were going to bed he stood over me to tell me all about it.

'I left Gaul resigned to the idea that I would be the last of my very noble line. But if I marry legally a freeborn lady of Roman family her children will be recognised as my legitimate heirs. There may be sons to ride in my place in the war-band of the Elusates.'

'If the Elusates have a war-band when your sons are grown. The Romans change everything. Our children will never see the world we saw in our childhood.'

'Romans will always have a use for Gallic swords. They have brought us right across the world to fight for them. Our people may obey Rome, who is a good mistress to warriors; they will never sink to the level of these Syrians, who pay tributes so that others shall fight for them.'

'Very well,' I said, to tease him. 'You have decided to seek the hand of a freeborn Roman lady. Who is she? For here in Antioch we meet none but those Syrians whom you so rightly despise.'

'I was too sweeping. They are not all faint-hearted. Our host, for example, has honourably sent his son to serve with the Roman forces. Berenice is a freeborn Roman, sister of a warrior, though her blood may be Greek. I believe her father would approve an alliance with my noble house, she herself seems not unwilling to have me, and I am content to make her the mother of my children. Unless you consider the match grossly unfitting, I wish you to make the formal offer of my hand. Will you be good enough to seek a private interview with Aristobulus?'

'Dear Acco, still clinging to the formal manners of Gaul, as though you were offering for the hand of an Arvernian princess. Here they will consider your wealth and your prospects, not your birth. Why not admit that you love Berenice as a person, not merely as a fitting mother for your children? Among Romans that is a respectable motive for marriage; though they would be less surprised if you confessed yourself hopelessly enchained by Damasippus. By the way, why do you love Berenice?'

146

'Because she is all that Grane was, and more beside. She can read the old stories of the gods, she comprehends this frightening civilised world where I must live, and as a devout servant of the Goddess she may find a way to free me from the curse of divine displeasure.'

'If it's Berenice herself you want, you are right to offer for her. But if you seek an alliance with Aristobulus, remember that he is utterly lacking in honour. If you get his daughter it will be because he expects that one day you will prove useful to him. But if you yourself should need help he will do nothing. He is a merchant, and therefore a friend for fair weather only.'

That was what I felt about my host and all his family. They were pleasant companions, but undependable. They were not dishonest. If they contracted to sell leather they would keep their bargain. My savings, in a sealed bag, lay in their strongroom; whenever I asked I would get back the bag intact. But if the Parthians appeared outside Antioch they would negotiate a peaceful surrender; they would never risk their lives for Rome, or Syria, or Liberty, or anything else. Nicanor had spoken of a wise man of old who taught that all barbarians, including even the Gauls, are slaves by nature. The Greeks of Antioch may not be natural slaves, but they are born taxpayers.

However, Acco was not intending to marry the family. He had fallen in love with the brown eyes and solemn vivacity of little Berenice; and if he wanted her so badly I thought the better of him for offering honourable marriage when he might easily have seduced her.

Two days later I made an opportunity to speak privately with Aristobulus. He agreed to a betrothal; though the marriage must wait until the campaign was finished and the bridegroom rich with Parthian spoil. I did not tell Acco the reason for the delay, but let him think that Berenice must wait until she was fourteen before she could be considered marriageable.

Then Acco developed scruples about the fitness of living under the same roof with his affianced bride. In Gaul it would have been shocking, but then in Gaul there are no houses like the great mansions of Syrian merchants. I pointed out that there were walls and doors and many slaves between the

147

women's quarters and the guest-rooms. But Acco insisted, and Aristobulus was charmed to learn of such an amusing barbarian punctilio. We both moved to a tavern in the lower town, where there was always a noisy party in the next room, cheering the dancing girls; and in the evening we had to get drunk or appear eccentric. I was already so accustomed to civilised life that I found the coarse dissipation of this tavern most boring.

About midwinter the Gallic horse were called out on duty, and we were glad to ride with them; though after two years in the Roman army I knew enough of the arts of a veteran to have remained unnoticed in our lodging had I preferred it. The expedition was a peaceful march, with no prospect of fighting; but the Gauls had been specially chosen for it, as dependable disciplined troops. So in a way it was an honour to march with them.

We were to ride south, through country so hot that midwinter is the best season for travelling. We would call at several walled cities, the capitals of local chieftains who ruled under Roman protection. At each city we would pick up a sum of money the prince had been induced to offer as a voluntary contribution to the cost of the campaign. Then we were to bring the whole sum back to Antioch, guarding it from Parthian raiders and from casual brigandage by the local Arabs.

At a private meeting of Gallic officers Publius Crassus explained our duties.

'Among other places,' he said, 'you will be calling at Jerusalem; and we try to avoid sending Roman troops there. It is a holy city, the home of the god of the Jews, who lives there all the year round in the only temple that belongs to him. A poverty-stricken god, without even a summer villa of his own in the hills. But though he's poor, he's proud. He will not recognise any other gods whatsoever, and he is very angry if strangers bring into his holy city the emblems of some other worship. He hates Romans especially, because they all have images of Mars or the She-wolf embossed somewhere on their armour. His followers, the Jews, hate Romans as he does. If my father sends legionaries to collect the contribution there will almost certainly be a riot. You Gauls have been chosen for the responsible task, because you are reliable troopers who can behave peacefully in a strange city.'

'It is dishonourable to insult the gods of foreigners, unless you are at war with them,' said Acco at once; and we all nodded agreement. Every Gaul accepted Acco's verdict on questions of honour. We others did not always want to be completely honourable all the time, since we were so far from home that our kin would never know of our behaviour; yet when he spoke we must bow to his ruling.

Publius went on to explain what we must do. A few years ago the little country of Judaea had submitted to Pompeius; but the Jews are a warlike race, and Jerusalem is a strong fortress. It would be most inconvenient if they were provoked to rebellion just when we were about to march against the Parthians; and they would rebel without thought of consequence if we insulted their hermit-god.

So we would not enter their holy city. We were to camp outside the gates, quite peacefully; and we would pay for forage and anything else we took. On an appointed day the priests would hand over the money we had come to fetch. If they did not we might ravage neighbouring villages, plundering gently without killing the peasants. Our presence would remind the Jews that Rome had the force to take whatever she demanded; but we were not to provoke resistance if it could be avoided.

'I need not tell you in so many words, gentlemen,' Publius ended, 'what a compliment this is to your discipline and tact. You are sent to carry out a mission thought too delicate for Roman troops. That is because I have assured my father that you are all gentlemen of honour. If you feel tempted to rob defenceless peasants, remember that the reputation of Gaul is in your hands. I am confident you will enhance it.'

Publius Crassus was more than a dashing leader of horse; he knew how to get the best out of every man in his command. As we left headquarters Acco whispered in my ear: 'Do you remember the first Romans we met, at that camp in the Province? They were always telling us to beware of the lash if we were lazy, and of the cross if we tried to mutiny. If there were more leaders like young Plubius we would be as loyal to Rome

149

as our fathers were to their own war-chiefs.'

The column rode proudly south, in excellent order, asking leave with all formality before we took even water for our horses.

As he rode beside me Acco sang, and waved his hand gaily but patronisingly at a garland-hung pillar which topped a hillock beside the road.

'That's another shrine of the Goddess,' he said cheerfully. 'We all know what that pillar signifies, and we all make smutty jokes about it. But it's open and above-board, as frank and prosaic as the latrine outside a tavern door. Here nobody fears the Goddess, though all acknowledge her power. It seems to me that in Syria they know how to worship her, and that in return she is kind to her servants. One day I shall go into one of those shrines and make my peace with her. Berenice has explained to me that the Lady of Wild Beasts is also the kindly Mother, and that I, like everyone else, was born only through her gracious intervention. She took my Grane, by means of her bear; but then she took her bear, using me as her instrument. Now Grane and the bear are both happy in the world of shadows, unless indeed Grane is already returned to earth. When grey Poplar is loaded with Parthian gold I shall return to our cool valley, where the sun shines from a blue sky and pure air brings sleep at nightfall. In Antioch I may grow rich, but only in dust and heat; and after next year I shall be rich anyway, like the rest of the army.'

'That sounds reasonable,' I answered. 'I hope there is really enough plunder to go round. Those legionaries may take all the gold before the cavalry can dismount. But as regards the Goddess I am sure you are right. The gods rule mankind, but there are ways of dealing with them. Every warrior in our squadron knows how to appease Skyfather, and it is not at all surprising that the Syrians should have learned how to appease the Goddess.'

I was not sure of this. If the Syrians can manage the gods it is odd that they are condemned to pay tribute to foreigners; for surely Freedom is the greatest gift that Heaven can bestow. But if the Goddess were really hunting my comrade there was nothing to be done. I was glad to see him cheerful, for all that he might be in great danger.

When we reached the land of the Jews there were no more of those jolly raffish pillars on the hilltops. In all Judaea there is only one temple, at Jerusalem. Other towns and villages possess halls where Jews meet for prayer, but no sacrifice is offered in them and they contain no image. The Jews obey an eccentric, pernickety god, who interferes constantly in the daily life of his worshippers, laying down their diet and forbidding many harmless pleasures. But since this god has only the one altar of sacrifice in the entire world his worship cannot be costly; and perhaps this weighs with the Jews, who are said to be covetous.

The oddest of their customs is to spend one day out of seven in prayer and idleness, refusing to work; there is nothing like that in any other cult. They also hate foreigners and keep secret the name of their god; but those are characteristics they share with other races.

For three days we lay encamped outside the walls of Jerusalem. The gates stood open, but we were forbidden to enter; and remembering the flattering words of Publius Crassus we obeyed our orders. From without it looks a fine city, steep and strong and ready for war. There are few harlots, and the wine is expensive, though good; so our camp was quiet.

The authorities in the city sent us an envoy, a priest named Gnaeus Pompeius; by this time we were used to meeting dozens of new citizens with the same name, from their patron, though sometimes it made for confusion. However, I suppose at home this priest was called by a Jewish name, since he was a thorough-going Jew, wearing Jewish dress and observing all the prohibitions of Jewish ritual. He would not eat with us, though he was willing to drink our wine – from his own cup which he carried in his bosom. It was easy to see that he loathed us, though he carried out his distasteful duty correctly.

Either from a genuine desire to entertain him, or perhaps through a misguided sense of humour, someone told this Jewish priest that among our officers was a seeker after the hidden truths of religion. On our last night before the city Pompeius sought out Acco, to convert him to the extra-

151

ordinary Jewish belief. I was sitting near the same fire, in the open space before the gate; and when I realised that Acco was becoming bored and angry I moved closer, to make a third in the earnest discussion.

'. . . so there can only be one god, the maker of heaven and earth,' the Jew said triumphantly, evidently concluding his chain of reasoning. 'And he must of his nature be male. For otherwise, since there can be only one creator, the creator would be female. That is absurd, for all over the world which we experience with our senses the female is subject to the male. How then in heaven can the female be supreme?'

Acco did not reply. In his eye was a dogged look, and I knew that though he could not think of an answer he was still unconvinced. To save him from the discourtesy of losing his temper with a foreigner who was in a sense his guest, I joined the discussion uninvited.

'I did not hear your proof that there is only one creator. But even if that is true, how does your conclusion follow? In this lower world, the only one known to our senses, life comes forth from the female. Merely by analogy, a female creator is the more likely. But why should heaven follow the pattern of earth? Earth does not follow the pattern of heaven. We have nothing on earth at all like the sun and moon. The creator may be sexless, or both male and female, or perhaps the exemplar of some third sex unknown in this world.'

The Jew grunted, and answered with little courtesy.

'I have already explained to your comrade. If you genuinely seek the truth, ask him. Yet afterwards you will serve your evil spirits unconvinced; for only the Jews, the Chosen People of God, have been granted true insight into the nature of their creator and ruler. Now it grows late, and tomorrow you march. There is no time for further exposition.'

He scrambled to his feet, made a stiff little bow, and strode off to his tent.

Acco, who never forgot the obligations of a host, ran after him to make sure his quarters were in order; and then came back for a last drink before turning in.

'That's a bad envoy, because he shows his hatred of us,' he

152

said quietly as we settled ourselves by the fire. 'But then I gather they all hate all foreigners, so perhaps the high priest in Jerusalem can't find anyone more friendly. He was quite polite, and most interesting, until my dear clumsy bull-headed Camul butted in to deny his most sacred beliefs. A pity. Do you know that these Jews deny the very existence of the Goddess? It's a complicated story, but apparently they hold that she was no more than the first mortal woman in the world, wife of the first man. This woman offended the creator, and the world has been a poor sort of place ever since. That's their theory: that everything bad, and nothing good, comes from a woman.'

'There should be a bawdy answer,' I replied lazily, 'but it's late, and you can make it yourself. Do Jewish beliefs matter, anyway? We are waiting to carry their tribute to Crassus, and they are universally hated and despised. So their special friend, the creator of the world, doesn't seem to help them.'

'Antioch also is subject, where the Goddess is honoured – and Athens of the Maiden – and even Gaul of the Wargod. The Romans, the children of Mars, rule the whole world. But that doesn't prove them right. . . . Just one god, with no female divinity at all. . . . It's a fascinating theory. I wish I could hear it properly argued by Druids.'

'Who rules the bears of Pyrene?' I answered sharply, to shock him out of this ridiculous fancy. 'Why did Grane die? Does Berenice worship an imaginary power?'

'Perhaps Berenice worships nothing. She's a darling, but not very sensible, with all that dreaming. And Grane could have been killed by an ordinary hungry bear. We can't prove that it wasn't an accident.'

'That isn't what you thought when we left the valley of the Goddess. This Jerusalem is an uncanny place, and has given you some dangerous ideas. Probably there's a curse on it. There ought to be, come to think of it, if its inhabitants neglect the Goddess.'

'They may be right, all the same. I liked that Jew. He's proud, for all that his people pay tribute. It's odd to think of this city flourishing without a single shrine to the Goddess. They look fine stalwart men. I wonder how they manage to get

153

born, without the rites of childbirth?'

'That's easy. I expect Jewish women cultivate the Goddess with the utmost devotion, and the men don't notice what goes on under their noses. Jerusalem isn't the only place where that happens.'

'No,' said Acco seriously. 'The Goddess has no shrines in Judaea. You can see that for yourself. I am beginning to change my mind. Perhaps I have been chased across the world by something that cannot harm us.'

'Remember,' I answered, 'we have visited other cities where the Goddess seemed unknown. But whenever we looked close we found her lurking.'

'It doesn't matter. Whether my home is in Antioch or Pyrene, Berenice will do whatever is necessary to win me the favour of heaven,' said Acco with a yawn. 'But in one thing that Jew was right. We ride tomorrow and it is time for sleep.'

As I watched him walk over to our tent I breathed a prayer to the Wargod, for I knew that my friend was in great peril. The Goddess delights to lull her victims before she strikes. Yet Jerusalem is unlike any other place I have ever seen (I did not exactly visit it). The Goddess does not rule there. That gives me courage to imagine that Margu is also beyond her sway, though that stretches from Pyrene to the Euphrates.

Next day the servants of the temple delivered to us several cart-loads of money. We thought it odd that priests should thus dispose of the wealth of their city, but the Jews are ruled by their priests in everything. In the old days priests led the Jewish army, and now that they have submitted to Rome priests collect the tribute.

Pompeius, who supervised the handing over and took a receipt for the money, was reasonably affable. The priests who ruled Jerusalem were grateful that we had remained outside the walls. If our troopers had wandered through the back streets by themselves some of them might have been murdered by fanatics; and then Jerusalem would have been threatened with the fate that befell Zenodotium. But the servants who carried the treasure-chests, and the crowd who watched our departure, were bitterly hostile.

154

Of course we had really been robbing their city, and robbing it of treasure collected to serve their god. Though no swords had been drawn, our expedition was as much a pirate raid as if we had galloped in tossing firebrands at the roofs. The money was not needed to pay the Roman army, which held ample reserves at Antioch; and if our pay had been really in arrears there was no obligation on the Jews to provide it. We could not even pretend that the province was threatened by a sudden emergency, since as far as we could learn there was no Parthian army on the frontier. Marcus Crassus, our Imperator, was blatantly enriching himself by plundering his subjects, under threat of pillage if they did not pay. We knew it, and disliked the task we had been commanded to perform

We were the more uneasy when we recalled that our own nations were under Roman masters. Caesar had taken nothing but corn for his troops and a little silver to pay them. But other governors might come, perhaps men like our present commander. Of course under Rome we had peace in our fields, and for those who liked war there was well-paid fighting abroad. Rome brought us roads and bridges, town halls and city walls; Roman justice was cheap and fair. But all lay at the mercy of a single ruler. If he happened to be a thief his subjects had no redress.

Someone in the ranks raised the old ballad about the Gold of Toulouse, a story inevitably recalled by this robbing of Jerusalem. Years ago a Roman Consul plundered the sanctuary of Toulouse in Gaul, and stole a mighty load of treasure. His theft did him no good. His convoy was surprised by brigands and the treasure lost, and later he and his chief accomplices all came to bad ends. In Gaul it has passed into a proverb: 'to steal the Gold of Toulouse' means to commit a crime and get no good of it. I thought it my duty as an officer to silence the song; but I pretended not to hear when Acco said loudly: 'These Romans have led us across the world to do their stealing for them. There is no Parthian War. We are hired to be robbers, not soldiers.'

As we rode north it was easy to see the boundary of Judaea; in one valley there was no religious building except a hall for prayers, in the next every knoll was crowned with the phallic pillar which is dear to the Goddess. I wish I knew more about the Jews. Their solitary and short-tempered god has not rewarded their devotion; but though they have lost their freedom they have kept their self-respect.

We had come south by the coast road, because that is where all the chief cities of Lebanon and Judaea are to be found. But now, with our tribute, we took the lonelier road which lies among the hills. At the end of the first day's march we camped at the head of a valley, a wild rocky place though it had an olive grove and the usual little shrine with a pillar. A shepherd guarding a miserable flock of sheep and goats sold us some kids for our supper, and we asked him the name of the place. It was Daphne. The troopers laughed and made jokes about breaking bounds, and hunting for girls among the rocks. While they dressed the kids for roasting I flung myself down on one of the least stony slopes I could find. Acco wandered off in the direction of the shrine, which did not surprise me. A little later he came back, a fat dove dangling in his hand. That jerked me to my feet.

'A plump bird for supper,' said Acco cheerfully. He sat down and began to pluck it.

'That's a sacred dove from the grove – that's sacrilege!' I said. But Acco was unmoved.

'May as well be hanged for a dove as a bear. Besides, the Goddess owes me a supper at least, chasing me from Spain to Syria when she doesn't even exist.'

'There's an army regulation against looting sacred property.' It sounded weak and silly but I was too astonished to think of anything better.

'So there is,' said Acco, 'and down there in that waggon is a load of sacred gold our Imperator has looted from the god of the Jews. So I don't think he'll object if I help myself to one of Astarte's chickens.' He went calmly on with his plucking.

I do not myself worship the Goddess; but I cannot say, as Acco could, that I have never knelt before her. For that night, when the rest of the troops were asleep, I stole and killed a kid for her, in her shabby little shrine. I called the roll of all the names by which I had known her – Pyrene, Vesta, the Good

156

Goddess, Hecate of the three ways, Astarte, and Atargaitis who is half-fish, half-woman. I smeared the kid's blood on the pillar, and prayed that it might atone for my friend's sacrilege. But now I know that a warrior cannot plead with the Goddess. I would have done better to have eaten the kid myself.

We reached Antioch without further incident, though we were not permitted to return to our lodgings with Aristobulus. Every day the Gallic horse trained in the meadows at the city gates, and all officers must live with their men. Each morning began with one of those thorough Roman inspections of horses, men and arms; then we practised tactics. Publius Crassus had hired a body of Arab horsemen who brandished little sticks, to represent Parthian bows; we would manoeuvre at full gallop, seeking a chance to charge them in flank. This training was most amusing, and the men enjoyed it. Only in the Roman army would troops practise in this way; in Gaul, if we practised for war at all, we practised shouting our war-cries and swinging our swords, never bothering about the tactics of the enemy.

Publius explained to us that horse-bowmen are tiresome people to deal with, though the army of Lucullus, who had encountered them in Armenia, had always beaten them in the end. 'They may kill a lot of horses, and wound their riders, at the beginning of the day,' he said, addressing us in our ranks. 'There is no way to avoid that, and you must just endure it. You are warriors, and when you volunteered to fight for us you knew that war can be dangerous. When you first meet these horse-bowmen they will halt at long range to shoot their arrows. You will be forbidden to charge, for you will be covering the flanks of the infantry. As I said, you must bear it as cheerfully as you can. An archer on horseback can use only a very short bow, short enough to clear the withers of his horse. Therefore his arrows fly weakly. If they hit you on the shield, or on your body-armour, they will not harm you; if they hit you elsewhere you will be wounded, but probably not killed. Now that is what will happen for about the first hour of the fight.'

After a pause he continued: 'Have you spotted what happens next? If not I shall tell you. The Parthians shoot their last arrows, and then they must either charge or flee. Do you see?

157

Even on horseback no man can carry more than about forty arrows, and a mounted man cannot pick up others from the ground, as do ordinary bowmen. If you stick it out until their quivers are empty they must fight you man to man; and then the Gallic spatha will beat the Persian scimitar.'

We all cheered this comforting speech, and drilled with renewed energy. We knew we were practising for something serious and real, which made it interesting. Some legionaries were compelled to drill for eight hours a day, at futile and time-wasting exercises like the ceremonial salute as the general takes the auspices. They had no idea of what kind of foe they would face, and they drilled slackly, in utter boredom.

Our legions had not wintered well. The men thought themselves veterans, after last summer's bloodless campaign; in fact they still needed training, and they would not train. They had been quartered in luxurious private houses with elaborate heating, so now they caught colds in the head; they had stuffed themselves with rich food all winter, and were short in the wind; months of lounging in slippers had softened their feet. They had made friends with the easy-going townsfolk, who were always asking them why they drilled when there was no enemy near. So the legionaries grumbled that they worked harder than Caesar's men in Gaul, and when we told them they didn't, abused us as braggarts. Until we of the Gallic horse, who knew how a Roman army should train, refused to drink wine with them in the taverns.

Acco saw little of all this. He went about in a dream, telling himself long stories of what he would do when he was married to Berenice and settled as a horse-dealer in Antioch. That is the only way to describe it; he did not make intelligent plans, he told stories to himself. Since we came back from Jerusalem he had not been to see Aristobulus, I suppose because he was afraid of reality interrupting his day-dreams. He had composed his picture, of Berenice managing his household while he worked in partnership with his father-in-law until he had made enough to return to Pyrene; if he visited them he might find that they wanted him to live in Rome, or to continue in the army. He never mentioned the enmity of the Goddess, and

158

eeme d to look forward to a prosperous old age.

Though we saw nothing of Aristobulus or Nicanor, Damasippus often hung about the camp, probably because he could not keep away from such lots and lots of lovely men. The legionaries saw nothing odd in this, though he did not find a lover among them; like most Romans, when they are not trying to be cultured and Greek, they really preferred girls, and in Antioch there were plenty of willing girls for them. Our Gallic horse were shocked, and tried to chase him away.

The poor creature had argued himself into the belief that he was dying of unrequited love for Acco. He would lurk by the hut we shared, waiting for us to come off parade, and then beg to be allowed to clean his beloved's weapons. Acco never found it easy to say 'no' to anyone; but after Damasippus had cleaned a dagger, very badly, Acco offered to teach him fencing instead. But that would be in the crowded gymnasium, not in private; fencing, Damasippus objected, was too rough.

After about ten days he no longer thrust his company on us. But he continued to haunt the camp. We were often aware of him, glowering unhappily on the edge of the firelight, while we chatted before going to bed.

One evening, at the earliest beginning of spring, Acco and I came back to our hut to find a couple of armed legionaries on guard before it; by the badges in their helmets they were of the general's bodyguard, who are also charged in Roman armies with enforcing discipline in camp. There was no special military crime on my conscience, and anyway for something serious they would have sent an officer to make the arrest; we boldly came forward and asked them what they wanted.

The senior soldier thrust a paper under my nose, and Acco stiffened. Any reminder that Romans can read, but not Gauls, put him on his dignity. I relieved the tension, rather neatly, by asking the man whether he could read it to us, or whether I should summon my clerk. In a gruff voice he explained that it was a warrant empowering him to search our quarters, at the complaint of a citizen who feared that his daughter, a freeborn Roman lady, might be concealed there.

We were dumb with astonishment, but there was nothing for

it but to stand by while the legionaries rummaged through the hut and the horse-lines behind it. They found no one, for there was no one to find. Then we saw Nicanor. He came forward, shamefaced, and collapsed in tears, squatting on the edge of Acco's bunk.

'Forgive me, forgive me for suspecting you,' he said through his sobs. 'Berenice has vanished. We feared she might have come here to live with you. She slipped out early this morning alone, without even her maid for companion. We asked everyone we could think of, and learned she'd been seen in the temple of Aphrodite. My father bought a search-warrant from army headquarters, and these soldiers have searched the temple most thoroughly, even the priests' quarters. Berenice is there no longer, wherever she may be. We feared she had come here, with some crazy idea of forcing Acco to marry her before the opening of the campaign.'

'I haven't seen her since we got back from Jerusalem,' Acco answered. 'You should remember that I left your father's house because I thought it unbecoming to live under the same roof as the lady I am to marry.'

'Do you think a man of such delicate feeling would steal an innocent girl from her father, especially when he will have her lawfully within the year?' I added, to make sure that Nicanor took the point Acco was too courteous to put into words.

'Then where can she be?' said Nicanor in great agitation. 'When she wasn't with you she was usually in some temple. Those were her only amusements. Since she isn't either in the temple or the camp I can't imagine what has become of her.'

'Probably raped by one of those gangsters from the new legions,' said the senior soldier. 'Raped and then her throat cut and her body chucked in a ditch.' The veterans of the bodyguard had a very low opinion of the men their commander had recruited in Italy.

'That may be,' Nicanor muttered gloomily. 'Perhaps we shall never find even her body to bury it. But why rape *her*, when there are plenty of willing whores in Antioch? Besides, she's still a child, not a woman at all.'

Acco would not hear of the suggestion. 'Perhaps she has been frightened by soldiers, so frightened that she ran away and hid. If she were dead I would know it, inside me. Her spirit would tell me. I am an Ovate, and I can feel these things.'

After a pause he went on: 'I *can* feel her spirit, and she is not dead. When I fix my mind on her I sense her thoughts flooding into my heart. She is in hiding, hiding from her family and from the world. She wants *me* to find her, not anybody else. Do you hear, Camul? Pick up your sword and come with me to find her.'

It was a long time since Acco had claimed that his Ovate training gave him powers denied to ordinary men. Now he seemed inspired; certainly he imagined himself inspired, which comes to much the same thing.

It was already evening, and we had been all day in the saddle. The men of the bodyguard protested; they had carried out their search as ordered and should now go off duty. But Acco would not rest. When the soldiers left us he marched off with Nicanor and myself to cavalry headquarters. There, just by asking in a menacing voice, he got three days' leave for urgent private affairs, and a written pass to show to any military patrol who might question us. As darkness fell we set off for the city.

'Last seen at the temple of Aphrodite,' Acco muttered. 'I know the one you mean. It is a favourite haunt of hers. It's the only place in Antioch where we know she isn't, because it's been searched; but we may as well begin there. I want to talk to the priest who recognised her this morning.'

'Let's go home first,' said Nicanor. 'She may have come back while I was in the camp.'

At the mansion there was no news of her and the porter explained that his master was too upset to receive guests. Young Damasippus came down to offer us refreshment in the hall, as etiquette demanded. As we drank our wine he burst out with a discovery of his own.

'Aglae, our old nurse, just brought me this. I am the man of the house tonight, in charge of everything. Look. She found it in Berenice's bed, among the coverlets. You see what my sister has been up to? Trying to dream heavenly dreams, just as though she were an initiate!' The beastly little boy sneered in triumph.

'What is it? Antimony for her eyes, I expect,' said Acco, snatching at the little object in his fist.

'No, that came from the temple of Aphrodite,' said Nicanor, holding it up for all to see. It was a small clay pot, shaped and painted to resemble a woman's breast; just one of those quaint little whimsies that make Antioch the most revolting city in the world. The nipple unscrewed as a stopper, and he opened it to show the jar was empty.

'I've seen these before,' he continued. 'The priests give them to chosen worshippers. Inside there is a holy drug in the form of little black pellets. If you take them in a draught of wine last thing at night you are supposed to dream as the Goddess directs you.'

'A love philtre?' I asked under my breath, hoping Acco would not overhear.

'Exactly. They say that if you can slip the pellets into a girl's cup she's yours for the taking. But I have never used it myself. This is important. It's now a matter for the city council. To-morrow I shall show this jar to the magistrates, and the priests of Aphrodite will have to do some explaining.'

'What's this?' asked Acco. 'Berenice was always hoping the Goddess would send her a dream. She has often told me so. But she said she couldn't fall into the right kind of trance, because they only supply these pellets to grown men or matrons of repute.'

'That's right,' Nicanor answered with a grim frown. 'If a priest gave it to a young virgin he was breaking the law. The least that can happen is the closing of the temple, as soon as the magistrates hear of it.'

'Why wait until the council meets tomorrow?' Acco urged. 'That temple never closes; they keep up the worship until dawn. Let's go there straight away and force the truth out of them.'

He strode to the door.

There was a whiff of sticky scent and a flutter of lamp-flames as Damasippus scuttled towards the bed-chambers. His brother was too quick for him. Holding him by the ear,

Nicanor hastened after us. 'Come on, little brother,' I heard
him say, 'you must hear us question the priests. They are
friends of yours, I believe. I have heard that one of them is
more than a friend.'

We hastened through empty streets between the shuttered
mansions of this wealthy quarter, which had long been asleep;
though from the lower town we could hear the distant din of
soldiers carousing. Acco strode purposefully ahead, his hand
on his sword, and an angry set to his shoulders; I kept up with
him, also peering into dark corners for the benefit of any lurking thieves; behind me shuffled Nicanor, in cloak and boots,
and the unwilling Damasippus who wore only his light indoor
tunic and slippers.

A priest in a high felt cap and flowing mantle chanted before
the image of Aphrodite; when Acco stood over him he started,
and hurried aside to light more lamps. He was a middle-aged,
responsible man with an intelligent face. When he saw the
little jar he frowned and paid attention.

He spoke rapidly in Greek with Nicanor; then he went off
and came back with a younger priest, a stalwart young buck in
a gay linen tunic. I was watching closely, and it seemed to me
that the young priest's conscience was clear. He had never
given forbidden drugs to an innocent girl. But he recognised
Damasippus, and the intimate smile he gave him put an idea
into my head.

Plunging my hand into the pretty boy's long curls, I gave his
neck just one shake – not quite hard enough to break it.

'Out with it, before I get angry with you,' I snarled. 'That
priest is your lover. You asked him for the drug and he gave it.'

The priest answered in fluent Latin, before Damasippus
could stammer out his denial.

'Certainly I gave this young man the Seeds of Love. That
may be irregular, since he is not yet an initiate; but it's not
a grave offence. And if his family don't know I am his lover
they know he has lovers. They come of sound Greek stock, and
keep up the old customs. By the way, I also am a Roman
citizen, as you can hear from my speech. So you can't frighten
me with your city council.'

163

'Why did he want the drug? Did he tell you?' Acco asked urgently.

'To give it to a Gallic soldier in the Roman camp, a seeker after truth who yet rebels against the power of the Goddess. He wants this man to dream truly, until he acknowledges the real ruler of the world. I know the story sounds unlikely, but it happens to be true. The lady Berenice also spoke to me of this man, and a few months ago he was a guest in their household.'

Nicanor pulled my hand off Damasippus's throat. 'While he is under my wardship you must not kill my brother. This is a matter to be judged by our father.'

The boy wriggled free. At the entrance he turned on us, his face wet with tears.

'You're all the same, even Nicanor. You won't let me love where I will. I chose Acco the Gaul the moment I set eyes on him. I *chose* him, I tell you! And then *she* stole him, my silly, simpering baby-faced sister. What did she want with a man – what did she know about love! Yes, I gave her the Seeds of Love. I know about love. Acco is blind – is blind – is blind.' He was dancing up and down with fury, tears streaming down his face, and he looked like a weeping monkey. 'Look at me! I am beautiful, a boy in the bloom of my youth, an ephebe, a *Greek* boy! Acco is a barbarian, a brute. I offer him my beautiful body and he seeks a girl, a disgusting girl! I hope he likes her when he gets her. She will have dreamed, and done what the dream told her. Berenice the bride – Acco's bride – everyone's bride – the barbarian's bride – ba, ba, ba, barbarian!'

With that he skipped out into the night, and left us staring helplessly after him, too exhausted for a chase through dark streets.

'There's nothing for it but the city council,' Nicanor said hopelessly. 'Will you rest here until morning? I don't suppose you would care to come back to my father's house?'

Acco answered: 'There are still six hours until dawn, and not a moment to be lost. After her dream Berenice came here, but she didn't stay. Where would she go? Perhaps to some other shrine. To begin with, we shall search every holy place in Antioch.'

164

Nicanor and I followed him, though we were desperately tired. He had a plan, and that made him our leader.

We roused the priests in all the other temples, and then visited the dozens of half-forgotten shrines and sanctuaries which lurk down narrow alleys or cling to the slopes of Mount Silpius. Acco, who was fully armed, did not argue with door-keepers. As he climbed over altars and poked behind holy images Nicanor and I kept guard; but he looked so stark that no temple-servant offered to hinder him.

By dawn we had brushed three times with the city watch, who suspected we might be robbers but feared to arrest Roman soldiers; and had disturbed the rest of a queer collection of holy men – all without result. We were dog-tired, but Acco would not let us rest. When Nicanor admitted that he knew of no more shrines in Antioch Acco made for the river gate.

'We shall work downstream to begin with,' he said calmly. 'We have three days' leave, and it's only twenty miles to the sea. This countryside is covered with little shrines, and I know in my heart that Berenice waits in one of them. Come on, Camul, you can walk quicker than that if you try. Nicanor may sit here if he likes, or send for a litter.'

Nicanor kept up He was only a townsman, but he carried no arms and he had been trained in the gymnasium.

We struggled westward, quartering the rugged river valley where shrines dotted every bluff overhanging the Orontes. By mid-morning we had covered only five miles; and when we reached a long enclosure-wall, its gate guarded by armed men, I insisted on calling a halt.

'That's Daphne,' said Nicanor. 'It is a sanctuary of Apollo. Berenice never bothered about Apollo. No decent woman goes there and besides it's out of bounds to troops. Let me hire litters from the tavern by the gate, and we can go searching beyond the Grove.'

'This is the Raven,' answered Acco, tapping the sword on his thigh. 'No place is out of bounds to the man who carries her. Those watchmen may keep out Roman troops, but they will not stop a warrior of the Elusates.'

I don't know why Acco insisted on entering Daphne; I suppose because Nicanor advised against it, but there may have been something in his boast that an Ovate sees things hidden from ordinary men. Anyway, he walked straight up to the gate. The sentries, who were temple-guards, not real soldiers, stood aside for us. Passing through a narrow wicket, we came out on a broad stretch of grass.

A furlong away stood the temple of Apollo which in theory was the centre of the whole sanctuary; a decent neat temple, but nothing out of the way. Its door hung open, and a thread of smoke rose from a tripod by the threshold; but none of the many paths that crossed the lawn led to its steps. On either side of the temple, and behind it, a grove of oaks, interspersed with laurels, filled the horizon.

The lawn was neat and smooth, and almost empty. As we stood hesitating a few seedy touts appeared from nowhere, muttering furtively in Greek which I could not follow. But the look of us, and of the swords we carried, showed these pimps that we were not the kind of customer they wanted. Nicanor brushed them away, and we followed as he hurried down a path leading to the wood.

Within the grove the trees rose straight, without undergrowth. It seemed that we could look a long way, but in fact the boles soon blocked our view; and dotted about were close screens of laurel. This was a secret place, for all its feeling of openness. Our path wandered among the trees, so that we could not look forward or back.

In the first clump of laurels lurked a little pillared hut of painted plaster. As we passed it a young negress came out. She was naked except for a few scarlet ostrich-feathers she had stuck on herself here and there. Round the next corner another hut sheltered a Syrian girl. She was dressed up in vine-leaves and fawn-skin. Then came a group of Egyptians, wearing heavy black wigs and nothing else. In this sanctuary every taste was catered for.

These whores didn't trouble us. I suppose they had all the customers they needed; so they just let us see we would be welcome, along with the rest, and left us alone. The path wandered and turned, and we must have walked for half an hour through this delightful garden with its disgusting inhabitants.

Nicanor, very exhausted, went slower and slower. Presently Acco took the lead, striding as though he knew the goal he must reach. With eyes half-shut and mouth half-open he lurched and stumbled, unaware of his surroundings; but all the time he pushed on. It was like the end of a long hunt in the old happy days of our boyhood.

By now we had passed the best pitches, near the entrance. Instead of little painted houses the women called from miserable wicker booths, and they were battered and ugly. The path narrowed, and seemed less trodden. Acco still pushed on.

And then we came out in a little glade where three paths met. In the centre was a rough pile of boulders, about waist-high; and on it a crude figure made by plastering clay on a wooden frame. It seemed to have been done hurriedly, the sort of thing a child might make. But its significance was clear enough: three vaguely human figures joined at the back, each looking down one of the paths. In front of the piled base fluttered a low canvas shelter, and at the sound of our footsteps there emerged from it, on all fours, a tattered thing – it was some horrified minutes before we knew it for a young, a very young, girl. Her face was scratched and filthy, and her hair a bush of tangles; she wore nothing but a sheepskin wrapped below her childish breasts; under dusty ankles her rose-tinted toenails were rimmed with dirt.

She spoke in a thick, weary voice, half to herself. We could no longer hope that it was not Berenice.

'Ah, my darling Acco! Then it was true, my dream was true! I knew it, I never doubted, never really doubted. Only sometimes – you have been a long time – sometimes I wondered. But of course I never really doubted, for the Goddess never deceives. First the dream, then the ecstasy. Then I must do what was enjoined, and then the reward. That is what they told me in the temple – and it is all true! I have done what was enjoined, I have built her image – here, do you see, I made that, really made it myself, I put it up at the three-went way, and waited for those who come down the ways; that was enjoined

167

too, you know. But you must know, for now you yourself have come down the way. Oh, give thanks, give thanks to the Goddess, the Mother, the Bride, the adorable Goddess!'

She sprang up and flung one arm round the feet of the ugly doll; the other she bent back in what I suppose the poor child thought was a gesture of invitation. Her voice rose in a wailing chant.

'Come Acco, my lover, this is my reward and yours. We shall share the ecstasy together and the whole earth and the sky shall share it and there will be vintage and harvest –' All at once she stopped wailing and finished in a brisk, practical voice: 'Camillus must wait for his turn, unless he likes to find someone else in the grove. And Nicanor must go away because he is my brother and it is not fit.'

Nicanor and I stood motionless, too astounded to answer. But Acco went and stood over the kneeling girl, erect, his hand on his sword. When he spoke he held his head high, addressing the shapeless image rather than Berenice.

'Do you suffer this because you have offended heaven and must be punished, or because you think this worship is good in itself?'

She answered simply, like a child sure of having done well.

'It is good, and I am glad to take my part in it. I am here to make the corn grow and the vines ripen. Someone must do it. If it wasn't done all Syria would starve. The Triple Goddess, Maid-Bride-Queen, chose me from all the women of Antioch. In my dream it was quite clear.'

'Do you think you may have been mistaken, that your dream came from drugs alone, not from the Goddess? Would you like to leave, now that you know what it is like to worship in Daphne? If you wish, you may come with me to Gaul, where no one will know what has happened. Do not fear the guards at the gate. The Raven here, and Camul's Mare, will see you past them.'

'Thank you,' she answered mechanically, a little girl remembering her party manners. 'But I am here to do what I must do. I have been specially chosen, and that is a great honour.' Then she smiled, and Someone older than Berenice seemed to be smiling through her lips. 'Acco, come to me. Come and worship the Bride – and with you I too shall have pleasure.'

'That is impossible, lady. I grant you your Goddess has power, but worship her in act or thought I never have and never shall. Since you are here of your own free will I shall leave you to your religious observances.'

He made a rigid right-about turn, as though on parade, and marched stiffly back by the way we had come. Nicanor and I stumbled after him.

Not a word was spoken until we were outside Daphne. The guards insisted that we leave singly, fearing that one of us was being carried off by the others against his will. Their duty is to ensure that Daphne remains an asylum; not to keep men out, but to protect those whom the magistrates wish to remove. We had no spirit to argue with them, and submitted quietly.

At the tavern across the road, while we waited for hired litters, Nicanor spoke at last. 'Renegade Roman soldiers murdered my sister Berenice. We found her body and buried it, secretly but with all due rites. That is what I shall tell my father, and the council of Antioch. You have been my guests. You must tell the same story.'

'We shall tell the same story,' I answered. 'We shall tell it once, to the city council; and then never speak the name of Berenice again. Do you agree, Acco?'

'Eh, what's that? I agree, of course. Anything you suggest. I am sure you know best. Could we order some breakfast while they find bearers for the litters? Do you know, I feel quite hungry.'

We returned with our thoughts, each alone in the seclusion of a one-man litter. Nicanor stopped at his father's house, but we went on to the camp. As we entered our hut Acco said to me quietly:

'The Goddess is a subtle enemy. She hunts more than my life, she hunts also my honour. But I remain her foe. I shall never serve her.'

As he pulled back the covers of his bed he added in a musing voice: 'Poor Berenice.'

169

Then he instantly fell asleep. I stayed awake longer, for I could not rid my mind of the picture of Acco as I had seen him at that other Daphne, with the dead dove in his hand.

I never heard Acco speak of Berenice again.

CHAPTER VI

The Desert Road

We had two days' leave remaining, and after that the whole army was given a holiday in honour of the spring festival; so poor Acco could stay in our hut to recover from his shock. He was dazed, as though from a physical blow. But on the fourth day he dressed and came out with me for a stroll in the plain by the river. I was relieved to see he was no longer in an agony of grief.

The truth is that he had never loved Berenice herself. An experienced warrior could not make a companion of a half-grown girl whose chief interest was in religion; she was gawky and ungraceful, and so desperately serious. What Acco had loved was the memory of Grane and of his own youth; he saw that youth reflected in Berenice, but any other mirror would have done as well.

Besides, he was angry, and anger allays sorrow. He thought more of his injuries inflicted by the Goddess than of the plight of her latest victim. As we walked by the river-side, feeling warm sunshine on our shoulders, he did not speak of what must be happening in the Grove of Daphne.

But once again the Goddess thrust her presence on us. We turned our backs on the great city whose gates we would not enter; but those gates stood open, and a throng of women passed the camp on their way to the river. In these parts the spring festival is named after Adonis, a handsome youth killed in the bloom of his beauty. The women mourn him with elaborate ritual, a ritual which shows him to be, in fact, the necessary but doomed consort of the Goddess; though some Greeks, in their preoccupation with male beauty, think of him only as a desirable boy. The women came down to the river to fill trays with a layer of mud; in this they would plant quick-growing seeds, which sprout and wither within a few days. As they withered the women would mourn for Adonis. There is nothing secret in this ritual, no mystery; and you may interpret it for yourselves.

'Perhaps the Goddess makes the corn grow, and perhaps it would grow without her,' said Acco, as we watched a prosperous matron direct her maids in the filling of a handsome copper dish. 'My masters the Druids pay her no honour, yet Gaul seldom goes hungry. She demands blood, and the better she is served the stronger she becomes. I shall never serve her. You, Camul, must never serve her. Perhaps as her worship diminishes so will her strength. She is entirely evil.'

'Is it necessary to say that out loud, while her votaries prepare their greatest festival of the year?' I asked. 'We have come to a land where she rules more openly than in the west, and we are about to ride on a dangerous campaign. Need we remind her that we are her foes?'

'I am her foe, not you. She will not forget me just because I keep silent. Honour compels me to defy her openly.'

'Then there's no room for persuasion. Your honour must, of course, come first. All the same, if we are to fight worthily against the Parthians we must turn our thoughts to war. Let's get away from these silly mud-pies and look over our horses.'

Acco's obsession was never out of his mind; but he was a trained soldier who could keep his thoughts in compartments. As we walked through the horse-lines he talked of war and stable-management as though he had no other problems in the world.

It was late in April, and the army was nearly ready to set out. All seven legions were concentrated at Antioch, thirty thousand foot; and we had more cavalry than the average Roman army, about six thousand in all. But of these only a thousand were Gauls, trained long-service volunteers who had followed Publius Crassus for the last three years, men so integrated into the Roman army that we might ourselves be reckoned Roman soldiers. The rest were Arabs serving under their own leaders. They followed the Arab method of fighting, which is nearly all show. These men ride magnificently, and their charge can look very menacing; but they never push it home. They will not risk death for a soldier's wage, though in their private quarrels they are brave enough.

Since there were no trustworthy horse to be hired locally a great responsibility fell on us Gauls. Romans refuse to take cavalry seriously, and in action we were only supposed to line up on each wing because that had been the custom in civilised battles since as long as anyone could remember. But an army always needs mounted messengers. If our general wanted to send a despatch only Gallic horse could be trusted to deliver it, instead of selling it to the nearest enemy agent. Whatever the war, Syria is always full of enemy agents.

Our Gauls could not carry out their important duties unless they were well mounted; and Acco and I were responsible for the condition of their mounts. But in a Roman army keeping horses fit is largely a matter of conscientious supervision. So long as we inspected the horse-lines every day, and made the men ride exercise, all went well. Forage, physic, and bandages were always forthcoming when we asked for them, and the farriers were expert in their craft.

In the Roman service, headquarters supplies the necessities of life. Cassius Longinus, our chief quartermaster, was a sardonic, bad-tempered man, unpopular with his underlings; but he understood his business, and worked hard. He himself took a commission on all goods supplied, or so it was generally believed; but he allowed no one else to steal, and his department worked smoothly.

Marcus Crassus, the Imperator, had made his name as a financier, though many years ago he had conquered an army of rebel slaves in Italy. He was proud of the great expedition now entrusted to him, and instead of making a profit out of its supplies he bought us extras with his own money. The whole force was exceptionally well-found. Even Romans remarked on it; to Gauls and Greeks, in fact to all the auxiliaries, it was a novel experience to find plentiful food, warm clothing, medical atten-

173

tion and dry billets all provided without anyone having to look for them. So long as we drilled and took our turn of guard duty there was no other work to waste our time.

We Gauls have no cavalry tactics, except to gallop up to the foe and hit them over the head with a sword. But the Romans follow numerous theories, in which we had been thoroughly trained during our long ride. They lay great stress on keeping all the horse in line, to guard the flanks of the foot; and they hold it a serious crime to charge before the order has been given. We were now accustomed to riding knee to knee, and to remaining halted until told to advance; when taking ground we never galloped, for fear the men should get out of hand and charge on their own. At drill we kept silence in the ranks, to hear the orders of our commander; though in my opinion it is absurd to expect Gallic nobles to remain silent when they hear the enemy's war-cries. On the parade-ground we moved like veteran Romans, so that a stranger might have taken us for brothers of the legionaries.

Our equipment by this time was mostly Roman. Acco and I had kept our Gallic weapons, as we had kept the horses we brought to the army. But the Romans, who like uniformity in the appearance of their troops, were generous in replacing damaged swords or worn-out clothing. When our men discovered that they could get regulation cloaks and issue swords for the asking, many of them sold their handsome Gallic outfits or gave them to their sweethearts. On our last parade before the march, at the end of April, our ranks looked like Romans on horseback. Nearly all had plain Roman steel caps, Roman cuirasses, and short two-edged Roman swords. Only the officers kept to the weapons and dress of their ancestors, gay feathered helmets, bronze-hilted longswords, fluttering cloaks and bright enamelled shields; but all were distinguished from Romans by their thick trousers. Or we would have been distinguished, if some mounted Roman officers had not adopted our dress. Apparently their ancestral custom was to ride in the linen drawers they wear for fighting on foot. No wonder the Romans have never taken kindly to mounted warfare.

Acco and I took pride in our exotic appearance. We still

dressed completely as Gallic nobles of high rank, though our trousers and shoes had, of course, been made locally as copies of worn-out originals. We attracted attention, which is the object of Gallic war-dress; though Roman veterans hold that on the battlefield a man should look like all his neighbours unless he wants to receive more than his share of arrows. Because we caught the eye, and because we also held responsible rank, we were assigned to the ceremonial escort of young Publius; and occasionally to the escort of the Imperator himself, if he wished to make an unusually splendid show.

It was while acting as escort that we saw our first Parthian warriors. When the army was concentrating in Antioch an embassy from the King of the Parthians appeared before the camp.

There was really nothing to be discussed. Even if the Parthian king offered to live in peace with the Roman People, we would still advance into their land; we were determined to plunder Seleucia. The Imperator therefore decided to receive the envoys in public audience, where the Syrians could see and hear all that passed and be suitably impressed by the power and majesty of Rome. High words were bound to come from such an encounter, and the war would move more briskly.

Outside the main gate of the camp a platform was set up, and on it a throne for the Imperator: the sacred chair inlaid with ivory that was an emblem of his rank. The platform was shaded by a purple awning, supported on slender gilt poles terminating in spearheads. A sanded path led to it; and gleaming white railings, decked with purple streamers, kept the crowd at a respectful distance. All this was run up in a few hours by carpenters from the theatre of Antioch, who are skilled in the construction of such gimcrack settings. I heard some legionaries mutter that all this splendour was meretricious and un-Roman; but we were far from Rome.

At the back of the platform were massed the Eagles of seven legions. Before the Eagles stood a group of senior officers, both staff and bodyguard to the Imperator. They wore cuirasses made of many thicknesses of glued linen, moulded to form flat stomachs and brawny chests which hardly fitted the wrinkled wary faces above. All the same, these were warriors – of the

Roman breed; many were too grand or too cunning to fight sword in hand in the front rank, but all had braved the axe of the executioner or the dagger of the assassin during long years of a successful political career.

The centre and focus of this array of polished steel, winking gold, and nodding horsehair, was the sacred curule chair, where a figure at once flabby and scrawny sat with uneasy dignity. Marcus Crassus, our Imperator, was not looking his best. As a fashionable Roman he had felt obliged to sample all the curious delights of Syria, and at the same time he had been very busy with administration and diplomacy. His face bore the strained expression of the deaf, and his wrinkled neck sagged with age; his belly protruded, and the sunburned thighs above the chased and gilded greaves seemed unhealthily fat. Besides its main crest of purple horsehair his helmet bore two auxiliary crests jutting out over his ears; its peak was formed of dolphins in high relief, and the cheek-guards bore naked winged boys. Between the herculean breasts of his cuirass a jewelled gorgon-mask fended off the Evil Eye, and the hilt of his sword was so encrusted with pearls that no hand could hold it firmly in battle. The general effect was at once revolting and pitiful; you felt that an unhappy old man, who could yet do good service as a councillor, had been persuaded against his better judgement to hide himself behind this parody of warlike vigour.

Below the lofty platform a score of picked Gauls sat on well-trained motionless chargers. Of course I was one of them, since my armour and horse-furniture were second only to Acco's in the whole army. I was placed rather to one side, where I could see the Imperator out of the corner of my eye while still keeping my head to the front; and I could hear everything. We well-mounted, well-dressed, well-armed Gauls saved the dignity of the scene. I have often noticed that Romans, who look well in plain woollens or plain armour, cannot wear gold or gems without appearing hopelessly vulgar; I suppose because they have usually stolen their wealth. But we wore the adornments of our hereditary rank, heirlooms which denoted the splendour of our ancestry; because it had been designed for men like us, and because we wore it proudly knowing that it was ours by right, our costume made us noble where the Romans seemed ostentatious.

Outside the painted wooden railings were massed the citizens of Antioch and a crowd of soldiers off duty. There were no large formed bodies of Roman foot, for it had been decided that anything like a show of force would be unfitting for the reception of an envoy. Besides, no foreigner needs to be *shown* the Roman army; the fame of its deeds is spread all over the world.

The proceedings began with the entry of a Greek herald, bearing his staff of office. After commanding silence he delivered an oration in the Greek tongue, which I could not understand. I gathered that he was introducing the Parthian envoy, and describing his rank; the word Surenas cropped up more than once, and a stir travelled through the stiff ranks of the Roman guard as we realised that we were about to meet the most famous warrior in Parthia.

Then I felt Starlight twitch and quiver with excitement; he broke out into a sweat, and I could sense fear in the other Gallic horses. But not one broke rank, after more than two years of Roman training. Towards us, along the sanded path, came the footsteps of a great beast. Without turning my head I swivelled my eyes to the left.

No wonder my horse was astonished and frightened! When the envoy advanced fully into my field of vision I in my turn shuddered in amazement.

The horse he rode seemed more like some heroic statue from a Greek temple than an ordinary beast of flesh and blood. He was a full eighteen hands high, probably more; yet his legs were on the whole short for that might body. Much of his barrel was hidden by a fringed and tasselled saddlecloth, but behind it his huge quarters heaved with a steady motion suggestive of great power in reserve. His neck also was veiled by a silken housing, under which it loomed thicker than a bull's. He had been trained to raise his forelegs and bring them down firmly; indeed his vast weight made such action natural. If that was a horse, then what I rode was some different animal.

When I could tear my gaze from this astonishing beast I looked at the rider. He seemed a young, slight figure; though he wore so much armour that it was hard to make out his body. A long leather coat, covered with overlapping metal scales, rose from his shoulders to form a hood under the helmet. This coat divided at the waist, and then fell to his calves; I could see that below it his thighs were naked, though his feet and ankles were protected by high mailed boots. That was a point to be remembered; Parthian warriors wore a great deal of armour, and the place to strike at was the thigh.

The mail hood was laced close round the rider's neck, and his brow was covered by a lofty helmet. Little of his face could be seen, but what appeared was beardless and youthful. A broad baldric on his shoulder supported a massive double-edged sword in a leather scabbard, and on his left arm was a round leather shield. In his right hand, guarded by a mail gauntlet, he bore a heavy lance, as big as a young tree; from it fluttered a yellow silk pennon, ending in a fork like the tongue of a snake. This young man must be one of the chiefs of the Parthians; for his equipment, and that stupendous horse, were worth a fortune.

Behind him rode three lesser men, in short tunics and padded trousers. Their horses were of the ordinary size, and they themselves were armed with light sabres; at their saddles hung on one side a large quiver, on the other a curved bow in a case. These were the horse-bowmen whose tactics we had been trained to meet. With their bows cased they looked like any other light horse, and I returned my attention to their leader.

The Greek-speaking herald ceased his oration as the mighty horse halted close under the edge of the platform. Its rider could easily converse with the Imperator on his lofty chair, for this horse was truly of more than mortal height. With a final flourish the herald made his bow, and in the breathless silence which followed the Surenas spoke.

A man who rode such a horse was capable of anything, but even so it was surprising to hear him address the Imperator in Latin, with a very fair accent.

'I bear a message from my ruler, the King of the Parthians, to the commander of the Roman army in Syria. Forgive my foreign tongue any errors in the forms of ceremonious speech.

Are you Marcus Licinius Crassus, Proconsul of the Roman People in Syria?'

When our leader had nodded his assent the young man went on: 'I am the Surenas, chief of my noble clan and cousin to the King, who has empowered me to speak in his name. The magistrates of Antioch know me, and will identify me if you desire it.'

'I grant that you are the Surenas, cousin to the King of the Parthians and empowered to speak in his name. I am ready to hear your petition,' said our general stiffly.

That sounded like the beginning of an interesting exchange. I had feared that we might be compelled to sit grimly at attention while two statesmen haggled endlessly over a treaty of peace.

'I do not bring a petition,' the Surenas announced firmly. 'The King my cousin commands me to ask two questions. First, when will he receive the land in Armenia that was promised many years ago, in the days when Pompeius made war on Mithradates of Pontus? Parthia might have joined Pontus against Rome. We did not, because of this promise. The promise has not been kept.'

'It will not be kept,' Crassus answered cheerfully, while the Surenas paused in a dignified attitude, one hand stretched forth above his horse's ears. 'If you care to listen I shall explain why. The land was not promised to your present King Mithradates, but to the King of the Parthians then ruling; his death has dissolved the obligation. Secondly, though Pompeius is a very great man and my colleague in the government, he had no authority to promise rewards in the name of the Roman People. Thirdly, the land was not his to dispose of, for it belongs to our ally, the King of Armenia. Do you want any more reasons?'

'That question is answered,' said the envoy, sitting straight in his scarlet saddle. 'Here is the second. The King of the Parthians, my cousin, has concluded a treaty with the Roman People. The river Euphrates is recognised as his boundary. In this condition of firm peace he is astonished to learn of your arrival with a great army. He wishes to know whether it is Rome, the Roman People, who make war on him; or whether you lead this expedition for your own private profit.'

'It will be profitable, certainly,' Crassus answered with a grin. 'My friends here look forward to dividing the plunder of Seleucia. But I am under the orders of the Roman People, a warlike race who have grown tired of your peace. Now your questions are answered and your mission fulfilled. Later, if you seek further negotions, you may wait on me in Seleucia.'

Drawing off his gauntlet the splendid young horseman shifted his lance to his bridle hand. He thrust out his bare palm, in the gesture which to horsemen all the world over means Halt. 'Do not march on Seleucia,' he cried fiercely. 'Stay in your own dominions. You go to your death. Hair will cover this naked palm before I meet you in Seleucia.'

His great horse turned on its hind legs, pawing the air. The four envoys rode back along the sanded path without a glance at the platform. As they reached the edge of the enclosure they halted and faced about. With astonishing speed the three archers drew their bows and fitted arrows to the string. All together the arrows sped whirring into the sky; while they still rose, twinkling in the sun, the riders were spurring to the east. They must have been out of earshot before the Imperator pulled himself together and ordered the general salute, the correct compliment for a departing embassy. It was a very pretty exhibition of swift, disciplined horsemanship, and it had some effect on the temper of our men. I myself was chiefly interested to see that the great horse could turn as quickly as its companions, and keep up with them at the gallop. In spite of its size the giant stallion was handy and fast.

That evening there was an extra issue of wine, to celebrate the opening of the campaign. Probably our commander wished also to revive our spirits, for there was no doubt who had scored during the interview that afternoon. We were, in fact, preparing to invade Parthia without just cause, merely because in Seleucia there were sacks full of gold and we thought we could take them for ourselves. Throughout the winter we had heard so much about our sacred duty to protect civilisation from the barbarians of the east that we had begun to see ourselves as selfless heroes. It was unpleasant to be reminded, unanswerably, that we were no better than the thieving Arabs of the desert.

That evening Acco and I were commanded to headquarters. We hung about outside the tent, for the Imperator was entertaining most of the leading citizens of Antioch and we feared to encounter Aristobulus. Publius saw us through the open doorway. With the tact that made him a good leader of Gallic troops he came out to talk with us in the court, strolling under a black sky burning with stars.

He was in high spirits. 'This is it, at last,' he greeted us. 'Tomorrow we ride for the Euphrates, and then through the desert straight for Seleucia. No more messing about in front of little walled towns, no more dallying in hope that the enemy will come to fight us near our base. My father has taken the plunge. If the Parthians bar our way we shall fight a decisive battle, and the sooner the better; if they are afraid to meet us we shall plunder the heart of their land. We shan't bother about our own communications. After we have won the Arabs will respect our convoys, and until then it doesn't matter. We shall carry enough food to see us through the Tigris. But of course from the day we cross the Euphrates our horses will be losing condition; they will be travelling over sand and rocks, short of water and with never a bite of grazing. When they leave the river they must be as fit as you can make them. Now have you any questions?'

'Dozens of them,' said I, for I knew that once the march began Publius would be too busy to talk to us. 'In the first place, what about that horse the Surenas rode this morning? I have never seen anything like it. Are there many of them? Must we fight them in the desert? Why do we go through the desert, anyway? I thought the usual road from Antioch to Seleucia was north-about, by the southern hills of Armenia, where there is grazing and water in plenty. Where is the Parthian army? Do we expect to meet it at the beginning of the campaigh? Is there really no water at all in this famous desert? If there isn't, what do the Arabs drink?'

'None of that matters,' Acco put in. 'We are paid to fight for Rome, and whether we fight in desert or mountains makes no difference at all. But that horse the envoy rode – I should like to know where he came from, and where I could get one like him.'

'Splendid, wasn't he?' Publius answered casually. 'I have never seen one before, but I have heard of them. He must be a Nisaean. They are a sacred herd, dedicated to the Sun. They live in a valley far to the east. The old Kings of Persia used them only to draw the sacred chariot of the Sun that went with them to war. (But the Greeks beat them, so the Sun is not always in his chariot.) They used to be bigger than common horses, and the Parthians have bred them bigger still. They look impressive, certainly; but they must have their disadvantages, like everything else. Probably they are slow and clumsy.'

'Not the one we saw,' I said hastily. 'I was watching him, and he turned as neatly as any Arab pony. He kept up with the others, too, when they galloped away.'

'Well, if he's better than anything in the Roman army, the sooner we win our battle and capture the whole herd the better for us,' Publius answered with a shrug of unconcern. 'There are not very many of them, only enough for the nobles. The common archers ride shaggy little beasts, descended from the ponies their ancestors brought from the Sea of Grass when they first broke into tilled lands. After Acco has chosen the best of the big horses there may be only enough left for me and a few more cavalry officers. So don't go ordering heavy mail until you have the horse to carry it. You may never get him.'

'This is not a joking matter, sir,' I persisted. 'The men who follow us will charge anything within reason. They are brave warriors, willing to earn their Roman pay. But a squadron of those mighty horses would scatter them.'

'They won't encounter them by squadrons. I tell you they are rarities,' our commander said shortly. 'You have been taught the correct tactics for dealing with horse-bowmen, and if you stick to them nothing can go wrong.'

'I apologise, sir,' I said, seeing him annoyed at our importunity. 'That horse was a novelty, and we are horsemen and horse-breeders. Of course, a few giant horses will not influence a war in which armies are counted by myriads. What about the campaign as a whole? We supposed we were to march by the highlands of Armenia, the main road. Why do we go straight across the desert, and where is the King of the Parthians and his army?'

'Ah, that's the point. My father has good information. Naturally, since these Syrian Greeks would sell their own mothers for a handful of copper. We know exactly where the King of the Parthians lies encamped, and presumably he knows all about *us*. He still hankers after that slice of Armenia that was promised to his predecessor. His main army is mustered far to the north. They expect us to march north also, to manoeuvre among the fertile foothills. By dashing straight across the desert we take them by surprise. If we are quick enough we may enter Seleucia without a battle, while the Parthians are toiling south to meet us.'

'They can't march south,' I said, beaming; partly because I was pleased with the plan, partly to encourage the affable mood of my commander. 'They won't dare to leave their Armenian frontier unguarded.'

'That's it exactly.' Publius patted me on the shoulder. 'In a land filled with spies we can't hope to surprise them by a secret march. But we can still surprise them by taking an unexpected route. It means hard marching, through very bad country. That's why I sent for you. You must keep the horses on their feet for about ten days of most unpleasant going. Then we reach the Tigris, and all will be well.'

'But these desert Arabs, what do they drink?' Acco asked once more.

'There is little water,' Publius said indifferently. 'But the shallow pools will be no use to a great army. We shall not waste time hunting for them. We must carry all the water we can, and then perhaps go thirsty for a day or so. It won't be more than we can endure. My father has it all planned, and he is famous as the best organiser in Rome.'

'I see, sir. You put it very clearly. Camillus and I will keep the horses fit for as long as possible. And when the battle comes at last you can count on your Gauls.'

I saw that Acco was eager to end the interview. He was not usually so deferential, even to his oath-bound leader. I asked no more questions, and we took our leave.

Back in our dismantled quarters, as we sat perched on canvas bundles which tomorrow would go in the baggage-carts, Acco

183

turned to me in great excitement.

'Thirst!' he said. 'Publius wouldn't say it, even to us; but the reason why our march across the desert will surprise the Parthians is because they think any army that takes that route will die of thirst. You are in danger of death from thirst, Camul. But I'm not, at least if there is any truth in what I was taught as a boy.'

For a minute I was at a loss; and then I remembered the parting gift of the old Druid.

'You mean the Druid ring? Have you kept it? Do you think it will help?'

'I have it here,' he said, drawing the battered scrap of copper from his bosom. 'Tomorrow I shall wear it on my finger. How much do you believe in it? Shall I really avoid thirst, when the rest of you are panting? Don't you see how important this is? We know, to our cost, the great power of the Goddess. But Druids have no dealings with her womanish beastliness. Whatever this ring does will be done by the power of Skyfather, protector of Druids and Ovates and of all true Gallic warriors. We are men, servants of the immortal gods. Who cares for the Goddess?'

'And suppose you feel thirsty, with the rest of us?'

'Then I shall know that the world is meaningless, and that we are all at the mercy of that horrible bitch, the mistress of wild beasts who makes her servants behave as wild beasts. In that case I may as well die, and thirst is a way of dying like any other.'

'H'm, it isn't often you get a chance of putting a magic amulet to the test. If it works we can trust in Skyfather; though if it doesn't the Druids will find some plausible excuse.'

That was what really worried me. You hardly ever hear of a useless amulet. If it fails to avert evil, someone always has an explanation. The man who carries it made some mistake in his ritual, or the spell has been weakened by stronger magic. Yet no one puts all his trust in a lucky charm. My father believed that a bead of blue glass sewn on his belt would protect him from the kicks of horses; but he gave their heels a wide berth. It is well known that a gold ring in the ear averts drowning, but earringed sailors still fear shipwreck. I expected that Acco would find his amulet undependable, and that later some Druid would explain that in Daphne the Goddess had stolen its virtue.

When we began our march there was no work for the Druid ring. The Imperator was determined to bring his army to the desert in the pink of condition, and he had devoted all his great business talents to arranging depots of supplies on our route to the Euphrates. On the first day we marched barely six miles before camping, and the officers were ordered to note any deficiences among their troops; so that anything lacking could be fetched from our base at Antioch before we had gone too far. This is the custom of the camel caravans which regularly cross the desert. The idea is that a march of two hours will show up any weakness in the transport, but that such a short journey will not harm a galled or badly-loaded beast. It is a good plan for caravans, since merchants suffer loss if even one load must be abandoned. It is not quite such a good routine for an army, since an army on the march is always in a hurry.

We ought to have hurried, since we were trying to reach Seleucia before the King of the Parthians could get back from the Armenian border. Our troops had marched from Rome to Asia without trouble, and they should now have been capable of marching anywhere. In fact, on that first day we could not have gone any farther. The winter's rest among the cities of Syria had been very bad for our discipline.

The infantry were out of training. They had been carefully drilled, and they had done plenty of route-marches. But route-marches, even under the burden of full equipment, are never the same as carrying all you need for a campaign, especially in an army which has already gathered plunder.

I cannot see myself why high feeding and luxurious quarters should render a warrior unfit for battle; I was in excellent trim, and so were the other Gauls in our contingent. But both Romans and Greeks believe that soft living makes soft soldiers, and perhaps the history of Syria bears them out. The Greeks who marched from Macedonia to India must have been mighty warriors; two centuries of Syrian luxury have rendered their descendants incapable of self-defence. Our soldiers were fat and

185

rested, and I think they felt brave. But they were certainly lazy.

Most of them had found girl-friends whom they were reluctant to leave. They were used to hard work for a few hours at a time, but at the beginning they were bound to miss the wine and amusement they had enjoyed every evening. It was not so much the hardship of that short march as the knowledge that the fatigue would go on for months that made them surly and unwilling.

Whatever the reason, the bad performance of the army on that first day was beyond dispute. All the officers were disappointed at it. By every stream men left the ranks to drink; when waggons broke down or overturned, as they will at the outset of a campaign, it was hard to collect a working-party and the men chosen stood about trying the effect of will-power instead of pushing and heaving. The detachment from the bodyguard who brought up the rear had by evening collected a numerous and sulky band of legionaries who had been found squatting by the roadside with their drawers down, by their own account too sick to keep up with the Eagles. At nightfall the bank and ditch round the camp would not have stopped a lame ox, far less a Parthian skirmisher; the men were dismissed to their suppers all the same, because otherwise they would have buried their entrenching tools under cover of darkness.

The Gallic horse behaved excellently, though that may have been because little was demanded of us. We had ridden first in the column, behind a screen of Arab scouts; so we escaped the worst of the dust and did not even have to keep a look-out against surprise. At the appointed halting-place we found plenty of fodder waiting for us, and a convenient watering-point; and of course cavalry are never asked to help with the fortification of the camp. That evening I inspected horses for lameness or saddle-sores, and saw the men comfortably settled round their supper fires. When all was in order the Romans were still blundering about their trench, and I decided to call at headquarters to find out what the high command thought of affairs. All day Acco had ridden beside me. But he had hardly spoken and he was not in the mood for a conference. I left him and went alone.

Headquarters was crowded. When things seem to be going wrong subordinates like to meet and gossip; it reassures them to be told by their friends that today's bad record was really the fault of someone higher up. The praetorium itself was the usual big tent of linen and canvas, and at the far end of it the Imperator sat in conference with his legates; but under the brilliant stars in the courtyard servants passed drinks and sweetmeats to any officer who cared to attend.

The chiefs of the Arab auxiliaries were there in full force, saving the price of supper by gobbling up the light refreshments. They were not the kind of men to appeal to a noble of Gaul; but I thought that since we must work together it was time I made their acquaintance. A group of them squatted round a large tray, easily to be distinguished by their curved daggers and womanish shawls. I went over and introduced myself, asking if any of them could speak Latin.

King Abgar himself answered me. He motioned me to squat beside him; but that posture cames awkwardly to a long-legged Gaul, and instead I knelt on the ground. Abgar was something of a savage, but I scrupled to sit when a genuine King squatted.

The king wore too much jewellery, and it seemed odd that a warrior should paint artificial eyebrows on his face; but he was a fine-drawn athlete, who looked as though he could take care of himself on the battlefield. He had been chatting with his followers in their own language, but now he ignored them to speak to me in Latin.

'You are the leader of the Gallic horse? When we meet Parthian scouts I shall look to you to support my patrols.'

'I do not lead the Gallic horse,' I hastened to explain. 'Our leader is the legate Publius Crassus, son of the Imperator. I am not even the highest Gallic officer, for a comrade from my own people, Acco of the Elusates, is better born. But when Publius must be absent he sometimes entrusts the horse to my command.'

'Ah yes, your young comrade leads by right of birth. I understand. But the Romans sometimes prefer your judgement. And isn't it true that your comrade lies under a curse?'

'My comrade is at enmity with the Goddess, and has been

her foe since he left his native valley. But he is a faithful servant of Skyfather and of the gods who protect warriors. He carries a most sacred charm, the gift of one of our holy men. No one can say he is under a curse. On the contrary, he is specially favoured by the gods.'

'The gods? Yes, I see. But not the Goddess? It is hard to win the favour of both. I myself am a warrior, serving a god. However, this is not the time to discuss theology. I only mean that at present you bear your comrade's responsibility in addition to your own.'

I smiled politely, for that was true; and in any case good manners call for politeness to allied kings. At first I had felt annoyed that Acco's misfortunes should be common gossip in the army, but a moment's reflection showed me that this might not be common gossip. Arab kings know everything that is happening round them; unless they keep absolutely up-to-date they do not keep alive.

'They tell me that you and your horsemen have ridden here from a very distant land,' the king continued. 'In your own home, had you ever heard of the Parthians? I thought not. But of course you have been engaged by the Romans to fight any foe they may point out, so it doesn't really matter. Now my countrymen have been raided by the Parthians for generations. We shall fight desperately. In fact we shall try to fight as stubbornly as those allies who serve Rome only for pay.'

'As you say, my lord, most of us fight only for pay,' I answered. 'Even so, we shall try to give value for money. And for some of us there is a more binding obligation. My comrade Acco, for example, has taken Publius Crassus to be his oath-bound war-leader. In Gaul such an oath binds to the death.'

'The virtues of northern warriors are known even in the soft south. I was only wondering whether perhaps you might feel the need for a guide through the intricacies of local politics. The cousin who preceded me in the rule of my people was himself clumsy in these matters. He made such a tangle of his affairs that I was compelled to replace him, purely out of a regard for the public good. Now you and your followers, ignorant of the local language, cannot know what goes on round you. You

188

would be unwise to follow your orders quite blindly. I was wondering, only wondering, whether you would appreciate the guidance of a veteran statesman with local experience. Let us suppose all the horse of this army have to make some proposal, to protect their own interests. It would be a great advantage if we could fix on some spokesman to represent the cavalry as a whole.'

'This is a most generous offer, my lord,' I said, rising to my feet. 'I shall always be deeply grateful for your advice. As you say, we are far from home, among strangers whose language we cannot understand. I shall come at once to your headquarters, whenever you deign to summon me. But now I must point out that I came here to report to Publius Crassus, legate in command of the horse. The Imperator is ending his council of war, and with your leave I should like to seek my commander.'

The king did not detain me. He had nothing to lose, except his reputation; and he already knew what that was worth among warriors.

The legates were in fact leaving the Imperator's tent. Publius halted when I thrust myself in his path.

'What's this? Urgent news? Have you made contact with the enemy?' he asked with a smile, his hand on my shoulder.

'Nothing urgent, my lord,' I answered quietly 'King Abgar is planning to change sides, and he has just suggested to me that the Gauls might do worse than change with him, when the time comes.'

'Oh, that,' he said with a shrug. 'Of course Abgar would like to change sides. They tell me the Parthians won't offer a bribe, because they don't think him worth buying. What shall we do with him? If he has impugned your honour I can have him crucified. Otherwise we may as well leave him alone. He won't desert us while we are winning, and we are going to win. All he wants is a bribe from each side, and in addition his share of the plunder of Seleucia. It is the custom to hire Arab horse, and Abgar is no worse than the others.'

'Then let him be, my lord. He took great care not to insult me. Perhaps it would be wise to put his baggage in the middle of the army, under a good Roman guard; so that if he deserts he must leave his wealth in our keeping.'

'That has been attended to. We also have three of his wives, in cages on camel-back. Cassius suggested holding his eldest son as a hostage, but my father pointed out that Arab rulers are rather pleased than otherwise to see the heir to the throne somewhere where he can't hasten his own succession. Abgar is useful and we don't trust him. Now forget the rogue, and talk about soldiering. What do you think of our legions? Are they slack on the march from disaffection, or because they are frightened? Or are they just very lazy?'

'Only lazy, I think, my lord. Certainly not frightened. Some of them may hold their own political opinions; but after all they all volunteered to follow the Imperator.'

'Yes, they have no reason to grumble. I don't like it, all the same. My father has enemies in Rome, and he may have enemies in this army. Today's marching would have seemed impossible in the old days, when we followed Caesar.'

'Oh, Caesar, that was different,' I said without thinking, and then blushed at my bad manners. Of course, there could be no comparison between Caesar, the tough forty-year-old rake who outmarched, outfought, and outdrank the ruggedest veteran in his legions, and the pitiful old wreck of a City politician who was leading us to plunder. But that was not the way to speak to his son.

'Yes, Caesar is different,' Publius answered with a sigh. 'You and I have ridden behind him, and there's no use in us denying it.' Then he smiled and spoke more cheerfully. 'Caesar has a fine army, but he treats it very rough. Not many of his soldiers will be alive ten years from now. My father will bring his legions safely home, and when they are farming on their pensions they will vote for *me*. That's not so glorious, but it's a sound investment for the future. Anyway, there's nothing to worry about. I expect they will shake down after a few more marches. Seven legions of Roman foot! There's nothing in the east can stop us if we choose to march to India!'

'That's the spirit, my boy,' said a croaking voice behind me. 'Silly old men in the City may try to bring down bad luck on us, but it takes a load of bad luck to stop seven legions!'

I stiffened to attention. The Imperator was my paymaster and my lawful commander, to whom I owed a reasonable respect, but this evening he looked less like a leader of gallant Gallic nobles than ever. Although the night was warm his neck was muffled in a woollen scarf, and round his protruding belly was wrapped a long red sash with a heavy bullion fringe; his legs were covered by linen bandages, as support for his tired muscles; on his gouty feet were the lightest of slippers. He was unarmed and bareheaded, and as he leaned on a staff he cocked his face sideways to favour his deaf ear.

'Nobody loves me, but they can't keep me down,' he continued. 'That stupid Tribune tried to curse me, and half Rome would be pleased if I left my head in the desert. The Parthians hate me, of course; so do the Greeks of Syria, and our gallant allies the Arabs. I suppose Caesar and Pompeius hate me also, though at present they aren't free to show it. Even my own legions think I work them too hard, as though six miles a day were a forced march. The gods themselves ought to hate me, if there's anything in the old rigmaroles of King Numa. But I keep a sword in my tent, though at my age I don't always carry it. I'll show 'em. I'll go where I like, and take what I like. I am a Patrician of Rome, of the sacred race to whom dominion over the earth was promised long ago. I'm a Consul too, with full imperium and the right ot inspect the auspices. Everything sacred in Rome should be working for me. No matter how I am cursed, even the Infernal Gods can't harm a leader who enjoys that protection. I'll show 'em, and you boys will help me.'

'Of course, father,' said Publius quietly, while I stood rigid with my eyes to the front. 'We shall do whatever you command, and when we return victorious the College of Augurs will prove that from the start we enjoyed favourable omens. They will have to, or lose their jobs. Now it's time you were resting. As soon as you have dismissed Camillus here, who gets up early in the morning, I shall come back with you to your tent.'

As I returned to my quarters my thoughts remained with my unhappy commander-in-chief. Evidently he could not forget, even for a moment, his Accursed March from the City. I had supposed that, like so many Roman nobles, he was an atheist

191

who complied formally with the religion of the state. Instead, he was a haunted man. At the back of his mind he was expecting defeat, or he would not be talking like a leader who encourages his troops to a forlorn hope. King Abgar was more foresighted than I had supposed.

I found Acco sitting, as usual, on the edge of his bed. He forced a grin as I entered the tent, and nodded at the wine flask. 'Any news?' he asked casually, without meaning it.

'No news,' I answered in the same tone. 'That is, nothing about the enemy or the campaign. Two little bits of background information may interest you. One, our Arabs hope the Gauls will come with them when they desert. Two, the Imperator expects to be beaten.'

That roused him. 'What, Marcus Crassus expects to be beaten? How can seven Roman legions be beaten? Of course they are under a curse, but what of it? That doesn't bring death it only means that you go on living. I ought to know.'

His head sank back between his hands, and again he stared at the ground.

'Come on,' I said briskly. 'You carry a famous sword. When someone hits you it is your duty to hit back, even if the someone is the Goddess. Apart from that, the Romans pay you to lead troops. Unless you do your duty you rob them. Today we made the first march of the campaign, and everyone was disgustingly slack. I did half your work, and the other half wasn't done at all. Tomorrow you must command, or ask Publius to send you back to the ranks as a trooper.'

He sat up and shook his head from side to side, like a warrior whose helm has been dented by a heavy blow.

'You are right. I am more than a paid mercenary. I follow Publius Crassus as my sworn lord. Of course I shall do my duty, against all the gods and goddesses in Heaven. It's a pity so many of them are against us. Even the eccentric god of the Jews must hate us for robbing his treasury. Originally he came from this desert, and he has power here.'

'That's the spirit! As the Imperator said to me, we'll show 'em. A thousand Gauls, and seven legions of Romans! If we meet any trouble we'll just storm Heaven and rule there in place of those envious gods. There's nothing more to be done tonight, but tomorrow we must get to work.'

Next day the army marched the normal twenty miles. But the men continued surly and unwilling. Someone had put it about that the Parthians intended to invade Syria, and that we might have remained in the comfort of our friendly billets throughout the summer, to fight a battle on our own ground in the autumn. After that we could plunder Seleucia without the fatigue of a desert march. I suppose this was the bright idea of Parthian agents among the Syrians; but the agents may have been working for Pompeius or the Senatorial opposition in Rome. Our foreign foes were not the only men who wanted Marcus Crassus to blot his reputation.

One evening at the beginning of May we camped on the eastern bank of the Euphrates, to prepare for a crossing at daybreak. After supper there was a final conference of senior officers, before we plunged into hostile territory. Besides the three legates, Publius, Vargunteius, and Octavius, the tribunes of the legions attended; and King Abgar and I went along to represent the cavalry.

I had never seen the Imperator so deaf. He turned his head jerkily from one officer to another, as though he suspected we were whispering against him. He was in a thoroughly bad temper, and would not listen to any of our proposals.

Vargunteius suggested building up a store of water, buried in big jars, a long day's march inside the desert. It is a method known to the Arabs, who maintain that the water keeps well enough if sheltered from the sun. But Arabs do not move about in armies of thirty thousand men; when King Abgar estimated that it would take two months to lay the store the Imperator grew very angry.

The legate Octavius wanted us to march north-east, to keep in touch with the hills to the north. He explained that we might still march on the flat, but that farther north it would be possible for detachments to fetch water into camp. That seemed to the rest of us a silly idea. To gain the advantage of surprise we must use the shortest desert route; if we did no more than skirt the desert the King of the Parthians might intercept us after a single day's forced march.

I realised, as I sat listening, that not one of these Roman officers really liked the plan we had agreed to follow. Even the Imperator had called this conference only because he hoped to learn of some alternative scheme before the army was committed. What in Antioch had seemed a dashing stratagem, which might win Seleucia without a battle, was much less inviting now that we were on the borders of the desert. But even when we had talked over every suggestion we could think of nothing better. Tomorrow the army might march due north to link up with our Armenian allies; but that would so obviously be a change of plan at the last moment that it would harm the reputation of our leader, besides bringing us up against the main Parthian army. There was nothing for it but to continue as we begun.

Next morning the troops very nearly refused to cross the river. We had a bridge of boats, and a ferry for the baggage, besides a deep and rather dangerous ford for the cavalry; so the crossing ought to have been speedy. The Gallic horse, with the Arabs of King Abgar, crossed first by the ford and formed up on the eastern bank. We knew there were no enemies for many miles, but that is just the time when careless armies get ambushed; and none of our veterans complained at the long stand-to.

After the bridge had been swung out to the farther bank a great clamour and confusion arose as the leading legion began to cross. From my post I could see what was happening, but rumours spread quickly through the whole army; the most popular story, among many, was that the Eagle of the first legion had tried to turn back westward of its own accord. That would be about the worst omen that anyone could imagine, if it was a genuine supernatural event. But it could so easily have been faked by the Eagle-bearer that to me it did not sound very convincing.

That Eagle-bearer should have been flogged to death as a traitor; or else promoted for his courage in opposing the will of Mars – and posted to a remote garrison where his story would find few listeners. The Imperator took no action at all, and this dangerous and disheartening story spread through the army.

We all crossed in the end, except for a small garrison left to guard the ford. Some soldiers openly envied this garrison, safe from the enmity of the gods; others boasted of the part they had played in the disturbance round the Eagle, and threatened that voters now on military service would in future find stronger ways of conveying their wishes to Marcus Crassus, the politician who owed all to the voters. The Imperator ignored this grumbling, making his deafness an excuse for hearing nothing. It would have been wiser to execute a few malcontents before leading an unwilling army on such an invasion.

Even after crossing the Euphrates we were still in known country, where water could be found. Our next two marches took us up the little tributary which had been the theatre of last summer's campaign. There were still Roman garrisons in the towns, and they were very pleased at our arrival. But our march had been slower than expected. It was already May, and the sun blazed down.

On the 4th of May we rode into Carrhae, the farthest of our garrisons and the limit of last year's advance. The Gallic horse camped outside the east gate, while Arab scouts ranged the empty desert over which we must march tomorrow.

It was our last evening in peaceful quarters, and the Imperator ordered a generous distribution of wine and comforts. The chiefs of the Gallic horse supped with Publius Crassus, and everyone seemed in very good spirits. But soon after the meal, before we had begun the serious drinking, Publius was summoned to another conference with his father. We all strolled back to our bivouacs in the comparative coolness of midnight.

I walked with Acco by the flimsy walls of the little town. At supper he had been alert and genial, talking freely with his neighbours; he seemed to be cured of his black fit, and I timidly mentioned this improvement in his spirits.

'I forgot to tell you,' he said cheerfully. 'I have come to terms with Heaven, and no one haunts me. Of course the Goddess still pursues me, but she is the foe of all warriors. She can harm me, but she cannot make me afraid. The gods of the Druids, Skyfather and the Wargod, are on my side. Today I

195

wore the ring you know of; I wore it all the time we rode under that brutal sun. I carried an empty flask and never went near the water-skins. Do you know, all day I never once felt thirsty!'

'So the ring works? Well, he was a powerful Druid who gave it to you. I am not surprised.'

'Yes. But you see what that means? There are gods on my side. I am not especially cursed by all the company of Heaven. I have only the Goddess to fear, and tomorrow we shall have left even the fringe of her land. This is an army of men, who worship the Wargod; and we go into the desert where no gods live, except perhaps that queer god of the Jews. Until we storm the walls of Seleucia my ring will keep me strong enough for battle, and the Raven will guard my head. We are grown men and warriors, far from the wiles of women. If I saw a bear tomorrow I would chase it with my empty hands.'

'That is very good news. At Seleucia we shall charge together as we charged in the old days, when Caesar led us on the Rhine. By the way, what you see behind that rock is not a bear, though he looks like one. He is a groom in the service of King Abgar, and since we left the supper-party he has been trying to attract my attention. But I know his message, and I shan't bother to hear it. The old king want us to promise to desert when he does. I don't want to have a definite break with him, so I won't see his messenger.'

We were both happy and at ease.

CHAPTER VII

The Parthians

In the morning we plunged into the desert. We marched with full military precautions, the legions in close column and our slender baggage in the midst. The Gallic horse, in close order, rode as advance-guard. Every man carried a large flask, and with the baggage were mules and camels laden with water-skins. It was calculated that we had with us enough water to last the men three days; there would be one good drink for the animals on the evening of the second day; and on the third night, with luck, we should reach the Tigris.

Each Gaul had taken oath not to open his flask until he had seen a comrade drink. That was the best I could do, and it might help them to obey orders; though nothing would stop them giving water to their horses if they saw the beasts suffering. I thought Roman discipline would hold the legionaries, but to my surprise they began to swig their ration before they had been marching two hours. I found an excuse to ride down the line to the rear-guard, to judge how the foot were bearing up. They were badly out of hand, singing rude songs in mockery of the Imperator and waving their flasks defiantly at the centurions. Marcus Crassus, as I passed headquarters, was swearing fiercely at the Tribunes; but he only threatened, instead of punishing. If the first man to drink had been flogged until he died the army might have come to its senses.

At the tail of the column had been posted a handful of Gallic horse; not to guard the rear in a military sense but to make sure no straggler was abandoned in the desert. I found them worried over what to do with three legionaries whom they had picked up, drunk and incapable, by the roadside. My men could not carry them, nor could they dismount without a risk that they would be left behind themselves.

These Romans could only have got drunk by stealing the reserve of wine intended for the sick; and anyway they seemed to me pretty useless as soldiers. I told my Gauls to deliver their heads to the officer commanding the cohort marked on their shields; they might leave the rest of them in the desert, as too heavy to carry. I had no authority to execute Roman citizens, but I was sick with anger at seeing this great army fall to pieces; and I knew that if there was trouble my men would back me in saying we had caught them trying to desert to the enemy.

Then we came on a man who had cut his foot against a sharp stone, so that he genuinely could not keep up with the column. I feared that if I left them to it my men would take the same easy way out with blameless stragglers, so I had to remain in the rear. I sent forward a steady trooper with this man on his saddle-bow, to be delivered to the officer in charge of the mule-train. Altogether, it was a most harassing march.

In the afternoon, as we sweltered in a cloud of penetrating dust through which burned a relentless sun, Acco suddenly loomed ahead of me. He had his sword drawn, and drove before him an Arab horseman; but there were already plenty of odd sights in that sweating, plodding army, and no one had inquired what he was about.

'This man says he has a private message for you from King Abgar. He also proposed that I should join him in deserting to the Parthians. Because he insists that he must speak to you I brought him along instead of handing him over to the body-guard.'

'It's not a private message,' I said, 'it is addressed to all the Gallic horse. That's so, isn't it? King Abgar thinks that if we would join him we might take the Roman pay-chest with us when we desert.'

'I serve my lord at risk of my life,' the Arab said in broken Latin. 'That is honourable service. Do not kill me. King Abgar will not join the Parthians. When darkness falls he will lead his

198

men home. If you come with us we can harry the fugitives after the battle. If not we must hide in our tents, for the desert will be filled with great armies who care nothing for our puny javelins.'

'Be off with you then,' said Acco with a shrug. 'We are hired to fight, and we keep our bargains. If you Arabs fear both Romans and Parthians you had best keep to your tents. And don't hire yourselves out as soldiers,' he shouted in a sudden access of rage, hitting the shrinking messenger across the face. 'Go, and avoid the company of your betters.'

As the man galloped off Acco turned to me with a grin. 'What a fine ring,' he chuckled. 'Even after that outburst I still don't feel thirsty.'

I sent off a messenger to inform Publius Crassus that the Arabs were about to leave us. Looking back now, I don't think it was treachery; it was nothing but fright. I also told Crassus that the Arabs believed the Parthian army was within a day's march. But of course Arabs will believe anything, especially when they are frightened.

That night the army encamped in the usual square. But the sand of the desert was too light to be piled into an entrenchment, and many legionaries had thrown away the stakes they are supposed to carry to form the palisade. It was not the usual Roman camp.

It had been intended that our horses should have only a mouthful of water that night, and a full drink on the following evening. But if the Parthians were near there would be hard work for horses next day, and I sought out Publius to get his authority for an extra issue of water.

Publius already knew of King Abgar's evasion. 'The Arab horse are far away, and a good riddance,' he said to me. 'They have forfeited a month's pay, due to them when we reach the Tigris; so I suppose they are genuinely frightened. That means they believe the report they sent in at midday. Here it is.'

He began to read from a written paper. It was not the breathless report of an excited scout, but a careful digest composed at headquarters.

'The King of the Parthians remains on the Armenian border,' he began. 'No detachments have left his army. But the Surenas, a young noble charged with the defence of the Tigris, has mustered on his own authority ten thousand mounted archers. These will be second-line troops, old men or boys, and badly horsed. He has further collected some heavy lancers, mounted on the great horses of Nisaea. Reports make these a thousand strong, though it is hard to believe so many first-rate horses would be left at home when the King rode north. They cannot be more than a thousand, making the whole force eleven thousand. They are within a day's march of us, and contact may be expected tomorrow. Their Arab auxiliaries are expected to desert today, to avoid the impending battle. The Parthians have no foot, but they are accompanied by a long train of camels. Message ends.'

'So that's all right,' I said, much relieved. 'We may fight tomorrow, but since we outnumber them by three to one it won't be much of a battle. Perhaps this Surenas is hoping to start negotiations, so that after we have sacked Seleucia we shall make him our puppet King of the Parthians.'

'With the Arabs out of it on both sides their horse outnumbers ours by eleven to one,' answered Publius. 'You will water your beasts tonight. For tomorrow we must trust to finding a spring. This campaign has been a muddle from the start. Even if we are not delayed we won't reach the Tigris for two more days, and we may all of us be on foot by then.'

'Very good, sir,' I said formally. 'I shall at once arrange for the watering. Do you wish me to send out patrols, to feel for the enemy?'

'There's no point in tiring our beasts before the battle. Just keep a good look-out, and be ready to mount quickly if there is a night alarm. Their mounted archers will be roaming all over the desert. We shall march in close order straight for the nearest point on the river, disregarding the enemy unless they attack us.

'Yes, sir. Are there any instructions from the Imperator?'

'No. My father will not change his plan. Indecision would have a bad effect on the men; and anyway, unless we turn back to Carrhae there is nothing else we can do. We can't wait here to beat off an attack behind entrenchments, or manoeuvre all over the waterless desert. Within two days we must reach water.'

'I understand, sir. The horse will be ready to move off at first light.'

For most of the night Acco and I were on our feet, looking over horses and equipment. Neither of us liked the state of affairs, chiefly because it was so un-Roman. Romans usually win their wars by careful planning and good administration, as much as by the courage of their soldiers. In the Roman army you are normally sure of your next meal, and of a bivouac where you may relax in confidence, knowing that trustworthy sentries watch over you. Yet here we were committed to a plan that German raiders would have considered rash. We *must* march in a given direction, and the enemy knew it; we *must* reach our destination in three or four days at the most. If they could hinder us, merely slowing down the rate of our advance, the Parthians could destroy the army.

But our Gauls were in high spirits. In last summer's campaign there had been no cavalry charges; this would be their first battle since they left home, more than two years ago. As they sharpened their swords they crooned war-cries, pleased that soon they would be winning glory so far from home.

At earliest dawn we stood to our horses, while the Roman foot struck camp. Most of the native followers had vanished in the dark, but they still had their regular Italian drivers of the baggage train; in the end these got the mules and camels loaded. That meant a late start. About mid-morning Publius Crassus took over the parade and ordered us to move off.

We sent out patrols a furlong or so from the main column, so that we should have a little warning before an attack. We did not try to scout the whole neighbourhood, as Arabs do; Gauls would soon have gone astray in that featureless plain of gravel-ridges and drifts of soft sand.

Since there was no particular track the foot marched in two broad columns side by side; between them straggled the baggage animals, in very poor order; for they lacked the proper complement of drivers. Even in this broad formation our seven legions made a line more than two miles long. In the midst rode the Imperator with a few mounted messengers, the only horsemen in the army other than our Gauls.

A thousand strong, the line of cavalry overlapped the heads of the double columns. Publius rode a few lengths in front, where he could see the whole array; Acco and I were half a length behind, one on each side of him. Acco was in a gay mood, flashing his magic ring and reminding me from time to time that he did not feel a bit thirsty.

We had been going for about an hour when we saw the first Parthians A group of several hundred horse-bowmen sat quietly on the brow of a ridge, awaiting our approach. Birds wheeling in the sky indicated that there were more troops behind the ridge.

Our Gauls cheered and waved their swords; though the foot, already tired by the bad going, still plodded in silence. Publius held us to a walk until we were less than a furlong away, and then halted us to dress the line. At that moment a little band of armoured lancers rode over the crest and cantered towards us.

There were only a dozen of them, but all were mounted on Nisaean horses. The pennons on their lances merged into a solid clump, so that what approached seemed one figure, as tall as a house. They cantered towards our motionless line, and then all halted together, less than a javelin-cast away. One man walked his enormous horse forward until we could see the little gold bell at the end of its forelock, and the silken tassels dangling from the housing. He alone carried no lance, and his head was bare. As the horse halted in a statuesque pose, neck bent and hocks well out, we recognised the Surenas. He was young and beardless, his face as elaborately painted as a dancing-boy's; his long hair hung in corkscrew curls, and from a narrow coronet of gold a great ruby dangled on his forehead. He was cased in gilded mail; from his shoulders fluttered a short cloak, purple to match the housing of his steed. He looked a young and happy god of war, or rather a god of victory.

He was barely out of reach of our swords. I held my breath, waiting for a muttered command and a flight of arrows that must riddle that flaunting white throat. Then I understood that he was perfectly safe. Though we marched against ten thousand archers, there was not one bow in the whole Roman army.

The Surenas flung out his empty right hand, palm forward in the command to halt. There were still no hairs on that palm, and I remembered his boast outside Antioch. As his horse swung round to gallop away a distant clamour broke out in our rear.

That was the first Parthian attack. Some squadrons of horse-bowmen had sneaked up unobserved while everyone was watching the defiance in front. The legionaries of our rear-guard faced about, their shields overlapping. The horse-bowmen did not charge; after emptying their quivers they trotted back out of sight. Rumour ran up the line, as speedily as always at the opening of a battle, that only one of our men had been killed and half a dozen wounded. That was comforting in its way; but not a single Parthian had been even frightened.

Our infantry were deploying from double column to hollow square, and until they were properly in their new formation the horse could do nothing but stand fast. Publius, cool and alert, told us to dismount to spare our beasts.

It was an odd beginning for a desperate battle, to stand by our hungry horses as they nosed the sterile gravel. The sun was high, and we all sweated. The stink of a thousand horses crowded close was remarkable, but the quite different stink from seven legions of foot who had no water for washing was in its way more unpleasant. Turning to me, Acco spoke in a casual ruminative tone:

'You know, when we joined the Romans I thought I was enlisting under the standard of civilisation. Caesar's army did things that had never been done in Gaul. That bridge over the Rhine . . . and the way they paid for their food . . . and the camps they built, all those thousands of men working together without any quarrels. . . . Gaul is the better for their presence, and it seemed right to help them. But this army we are in now is a seedy collection of cut-throats. Think of that young Parthian riding bareheaded to defy us, and then think of old Marcus Crassus, the businessman. His soldiers shirk their duty, and I'm not surprised. Who would die for that deaf old bully, panting for other men's gold? It's time I left this service. I have no regrets, though I hope young Publius, my oath-bound lord, gets safely home. Perhaps one day you may return to Gaul. If you do, take back the Raven for my cousin's sword-belt. He will be the next head of my house, since I am childless. And tell them I was faithful to my paymaster, even though I did not care for his behaviour.'

Acco spoke in such a matter-of-fact tone that at first I did not understand him. It is not unusual for a warrior to be granted foreknowledge of his death. But usually such men are exalted and made strange by it; they do not remember to tighten a loose cheekstrap, as Acco was doing while grey Poplar drooped his head.

'What do you mean?' I asked in surprise. 'Today there will be some skirmishing, between seven legions of Romans and a few Parthian squadrons. Men will be killed, though not very many. Why should you in particular expect death?'

Acco flourished his hand until the copper ring caught the sun.

'Do you recall the properties of this amulet?' he asked. 'Whoever wears it cannot feel thirst – so long as he lives. However the battle goes, tonight every living Roman will be horribly thirsty.'

He looked round the bare gravel plain.

'A gloomy place, and I shall never leave it. But the sun shines, and birds sing. There is brighter light than in Gaul. And here nothing makes love or is brought to birth. This is a battlefield of men. I have ridden right away from the Goddess even though at last her bear is avenged. . . . Hold Poplar while I see if that man really wants to make water and nothing more; though I don't think we have shirkers in the cavalry.'

He strode away, whistling cheerfully.

Then the infantry reached us, and we filed through intervals in their ranks to take position within the great square. Publius ordered us still to lead our horses, for now the heat was very great and they were weakening after a day without forage. It was no longer so easy to learn what was going on, when all we could see was a row of Roman heads.

Publius himself remained mounted, and I pushed my way close to him. By now the whole army was advancing, very slowly and with frequent halts. Our square took up a lot of room, and some part of it was nearly always crossing difficult

204

ground; the rest must slow down or leave them behind.

In this disjointed fashion we advanced against the Parthian bowmen, who all this time had been holding their position on the ridge. I could see nothing, but I could hear Publius talking, half to himself.

'Here come the first arrows. Those bows don't range far, a horseman's never does. But they shoot very fast. How long at this rate before they empty their quivers? Oh, good. There's a cohort advancing at the double. We'll see if these horsemen will fight at close quarters. No, they're off. The ridge is clear, with our cohort waiting for us. This isn't really a battle, nothing more than a long skirmish. How many days to the Tigris, if we keep at this speed?'

Slowly we surmounted the ridge. At the top I had a brief glimpse to the front, over the heads of our men descending the slope. Before us stretched a wide and shallow valley, with an awkward dry gully at its lowest point. Then the ground rose again to another ridge, perhaps half a mile away. There stood the main Parthian army.

There may have been seven or eight thousand horse-bowmen sitting quietly in loose order. Their front made an extended half-moon straight ahead of us, and they were waiting until we came within range. They seemed quite calm. We heard no war-cries and saw no weapons brandished; whatever happened our dismounted swordsmen could not harm them. Their quiet confidence was most unnerving.

As our van struggled across the gully the enemy advanced to long arrow-range, giving ground again as our foot tried to get to close quarters. The dry stream-bed was a difficult obstacle; we got our horses over with a scrable, but the baggage animals had to be pushed and pulled. At the height of the confusion other Parthians approached our rear, who must turn about to march backwards. These Parthians rode very close, but they did not actually charge.

Their short light arrows seldom killed, but already our wounded were becoming a problem. We could not leave them where they fell. The only solution was to place them on the baggage animals – but that meant throwing away something we needed very badly, or we would not have brought it so far across the desert. There could be no question of jettisoning water-skins, but we had to abandon reserve weapons and the last of the officer's baggage.

When at last the whole army had clambered over the gully we began to plod up the next slope. I had my eyes on the ground, and most of my weight leaning on Starlight, when I was forced to an abrupt halt as the men before me surged backwards. For a minute the whole army stood swaying in its own dust-cloud, until I heard trumpets and shouted commands.

Publius himself loomed over me, calling for the Gauls to get mounted and file to the front. In the saddle I was able to see the obstacle that had halted the Roman advance.

Ahead of us the horse-bowmen had withdrawn well out of range, splitting into two wings to disclose a solid block of stationary lancers. There were certainly a thousand of them, Parthian nobles clad in mail and mounted on great Nisaean warhorses. They held their lances upright while their horses stood still. But our foot would not advance against them – and I was not surprised.

After leading us through gaps in our front line Publius formed us carefully in two ranks. Then, still facing us, he began the speech before battle which is a convention of Roman tactics; though it is not a Gallic custom. On this occasion it did no good; in fact it did harm, for the longer we looked at that motionless line of enormous animals the more frightened we felt.

'Nobles of Gaul,' he cried in an exultant shout, 'to us has fallen a great honour. That little band of lancers is all that stands between us and the plunder of Seleucia; and we, out of the whole army, have been chosen to overthrow them. Never before have Gallic warriors fought in these eastern lands; even the names of your glorious ancestors are here unknown. Today you will make them famous. When I give the signal, follow me to glory and splendid booty.'

He urged his horse into our ranks, and spoke to me privately, in an undertone. 'Camillus, bring in the second rank immediately behind the first. We shan't bother with fancy tactics, reserves and delayed shock. We must break those fellows at the first impact, or the whole army will be stuck. If it comes to a standing mêlée the legions can join in, and then we can't be beaten. But we must go in hard to start with. See there is no flinching in the second line. Acco, you will ride on the left to keep that end of the line from edging clear of the enemy.'

'No, my lord,' said Acco stoutly. 'You are my oath-bound war-leader, and when you charge I guard your bridle-hand. Gallic nobles will not flinch. But don't keep us waiting. Those Nisaean horses grow bigger every minute.'

'Very well. We three will ride together in the centre. My father is watching, and he rewards courage more splendidly than any barbarian can imagine. Make for the purple pennon of the Surenas. If we knock him over the battle is won.'

All this suggested to me that we were taking a desperate chance, which Publius himself hardly expected to succeed. Romans despise as barbarous a direct attack on the enemy leader; if Publius was trying it now he must have despaired of finding a better plan. A moment later we were galloping, and there was no time for thought.

My eyes were fixed on that line of huge beasts. I saw their outline change as the lances came down into rest; then they charged, downhill, to meet us.

I was leading the second rank, as close to the first as I could get without striking into the horse in front; near me our men kept up, but on both flanks there was a little understandable reluctance. When we met the foe our formation was a wedge, with Publius and Acco at the point and myself directly behind them.

There is no telling with Gauls. Since the Romans have conquered us I suppose they are the better warriors; but sometimes some Gallic nobles will fight with more than human courage. Publius led us, but we followed Acco – the son of the Wargod, his blue cloak flying behind him, the Raven gleaming above his head, the war-cry of his noble house dinning in our ears. Our wedge broke into the line of huge Nisaean horses.

Then our charge was spent, and we were hacking about at a standstill. I was directly behind our leaders, my sword clean;

though a Parthian lance, coming from nowhere, had scored a furrow right across my shield. I could not reach the enemy while Acco and Publius rode before me.

At first the Parthians were hampered by their great poles of lances. Then they dropped them to draw the biggest broadswords I have ever seen. Our Gallic swords were more nimble, and our unmailed bodies swifter; some Parthians tumbled from their saddles, though their heavy mail preserved their lives. The first man I saw killed was Publius himself, who was badly equipped for such a fray. Like other Roman officers of high rank, he carried no shield; and his short Roman sword had little reach. A great Nisaean charger shouldered his horse nearly off its feet, and as he lurched in the saddle a broadsword clove his linen corselet to the waist. He and his horse went down together.

We might have been children fighting against grown men. Those Nisaeans must weigh twice as much as an ordinary horse, and the riders were in heavier mail than any western soldier can carry. We were pushed backwards and hustled off our feet; many of our men were overthrown and trampled flat without ever being wounded.

For a moment Acco alone guarded my front; then he rammed little grey Poplar against the mighty beast which had overthrown Publius. There was one man he had to kill, at any cost; I saw him drop reins and sword as he grasped his adversary round the waist. In his hand was the little ivory-hilted dagger Publius had given him long ago in Gaul; as he strove to stick it under the skirts of the Parthian's mail he was lifted clean out of his saddle. I am sure he killed his man; but in the same instant another Parthian broadsword bit into his backbone. That was the last I saw of him. I had made no effort to save him, for I knew that he could not survive the fight in which his oath-bound lord was slain. Honour forbids it.

But I had never sworn. I served the Romans for pay, and I thought our charge had been enough to earn our wages. Straight ahead of me rode two Parthian nobles and behind them I could see the empty desert; for the point of our wedge had pierced almost through the enemy's ranks. Remembering the weak spot in Parthian armour, I dropped my hilt low and thrust upwards at the thigh of the man on my right; my shield fended off the broadsword on my left, and when I raked outward with my spurs the two great chargers edged away. Starlight was so terrified that I could not have stopped him even if I tried; but as I galloped free I told myself that the only man to penetrate the Parthian line had done enough for honour.

There was still a cloud of horse-bowmen between me and the Roman legions, but my horse was galloping at full stretch and I came at them from an unexpected direction. They shot arrows after me, but most of them flew wide. I had almost reached the Roman line when a long shot lodged in Starlight's foreleg; as his other leg blundered into the shaft he turned head over heels as though he had tripped over a rope.

I hit the ground hard, and rolled over and over. The Mare shot out of my hand, and my shield-straps broke. A moment later, completely unarmed, I was staring stupidly at the arrows thudding into Starlight's ribs; then I scuttled on all fours to the line of linked Roman shields only a few paces away. I nearly reached it unscathed. At the very last moment an arrow nicked the calf of my leg, but I went the faster for it.

Perhaps it was as well that I arrived in that dishevelled condition. If I had galloped up waving a drawn sword the Romans might have killed me first and recognised me after. As it was they hauled me to my feet inside the square. A legionary was binding my wound with wool from my tattered sleeve when the nearest centurion came up to question me.

I told him at once that I had news for the Imperator, and he sent me hobbling off to headquarters. I could walk more easily than I had expected; Parthian arrows are very sharp, and this one had made a neat slit in my calf without damaging either muscle or vein.

The Imperator sat on a pack-saddle, where a little rise in the ground enabled him to see most of the stationary square of Roman infantry. I could hardly make out his expression, for his face was thickly coated with dust and sand; that happens when you sweat and there is no water for washing. He kept his bloodshot eyes almost closed against the glare, and he moved his head very slowly like the tired old man he was. But his mind was alert.

As I drew myself up to salute the legate Octavius brushed past me. He spoke urgently: 'My lord, you must see this immediately. It's bad news, though I am sure not unexpected. A few minutes ago a Parthian threw this into our front rank.'

He pulled out something from under his cloak and displayed, as reverently as one can handle such an unpleasant object, the severed head of Publius Crassus.

The old Imperator heaved himself to his feet, gasping and swallowing. 'Thank you, Octavius. If there is a fire going anywhere will you burn my son's head on it? That may count as proper burial, and give rest to his spirit. What is the conventional thing one says in these circumstances? I remember. "I never supposed that my son was immortal." It goes better in Greek. . . . Well, the battle still rages, and I must direct it. You may return to your post.'

Then he turned to me. 'Do you also bring bad news? You look like a Gaul. Were you in the Gallic charge? Did you see my son killed?'

'Yes, my lord. I was close behind him. He rode in front of all his men, and broke the Parthian ranks. He died from one blow of a broadsword, without pain. A good death, such as any warrior would desire.'

'Yes, a good death. But it came too soon. He was a leader whom men would have followed against even Caesar or Pompeius. He would have been Consul and Imperator. . . . That's enough about my family affairs. What happened to the Gallic horse?'

'They are dead, my lord, behind your son. I made a gap and charged right through, but no one followed. One or two stragglers may get away, but your cavalry has been destroyed.'

'A thousand horse, and all destroyed? But those Nisaean chargers are more than flesh and blood can face. How many are there of these heavy lancers? Do you think they will charge the legions?'

'We were not outnumbered, though the great horses outfought us. They cannot be more than a thousand – less, now that they have fought with Gauls. Steady foot ought to beat off even those great horses.'

'Then the horse-bowmen are still our main adversaries. Their quivers must be nearly empty. Soon we shall get the square moving, and continue towards the Tigris until every Parthian arrow has been shot away. It may work out. Who knows? Perhaps we shall soon see Seleucia.'

As he turned away he spoke to me again, over his shoulder. 'You are hurt, and I suppose tired and shaken. But there is room in the ranks for every willing fighter.'

He spoke most graciously, as though to an equal. I was so encouraged by his courtesy that I limped off to the nearest cohort, where they quickly found me the sword and shield of a wounded man.

They posted me in the third rank of the second line, so that there were five ranks between me and the enemy; that was all to the good, for I still felt very shaken. But even the men in the front rank stood quiet, their swords sheathed, hiding behind their shields. So far, no legionary had struck a blow, though the rain of arrows continued.

The Parthian horse-bowmen hovered a javelin-cast away; but the Romans had already thrown the two javelins every man carries, and we had no more. There was nothing to be done but to stand in our ranks, where the enemy could do us little harm behind our shields. I wondered what we would drink when night fell.

Beside me stood an elderly man in a shabby civilian tunic, though like me he was armed with a borrowed sword and shield. A rope headstall was tucked in his belt, and I placed him as one of the retired veterans who often take service as transport drivers. He was hot and tired and dirty, but not a bit flustered; his calm radiated a little glow of confidence in our dejected ranks.

'Hallo,' he said cheerfully, 'wasn't your horse fast enough to escape from the bodyguard? We must be short of reserves, if they are shoving stray Arabs into the ranks. Oh, I apologise. You're a Gaul. You people can fight, as I know very well. Here we shall have a fine view of the battle, when it starts. It ought to begin in about half an hour. I remember these horse-bowmen. Years ago I marched all through Armenia behind Lucullus. There was a leader! We ought to have stuck by him when he called on us to march against the Senate. Then I would be captain of the guard to the Tyrant of Rome, instead of a broken old muleteer with both my beasts dead in action. But about these horse-bowmen: any minute now they ought to finish their quivers. Then they must either charge or run away. Whichever they do we march to the Tigris, and if we don't drink tonight we shall wallow in the river by tomorrow. So just take things easy, and save your strength. So long as you keep your shield up they can't hit you.'

That was what they had told us when we trained during the winter; in an hour or so a horse-bowman must shoot away all his arrows, and then the infantry can chase him. It seemed very simple.

Meanwhile, centurions were trying to get this side of the square to move to a flank. This was the southern face of the formation, and the Tigris lay to the east; so we must turn to our left. But that would mean presenting our unshielded right shoulders to the foe; the men were reluctant, and moved slowly.

I had lost enough blood to make me very thirsty, though now the bleeding had stopped. I was also very tired. But it seemed that our ordeal must soon end; every Parthian arrow fell within our ranks, so that the enemy could not pick them up to use again.

Then from the eastern face of the square came a confused uproar, and the jostling in the ranks that showed something had gone wrong. Orders were passed, with trumpet-blasts and a great deal of shouting. The nearest centurion bellowed that we were to turn about and march westward.

This order was obeyed at once, for it placed our shields to-wards the enemy. We were worried; in battle nothing is more frightening than a sudden change of plan, which indicates that the high command are trying to counter an unforseen danger. But Roman legions obey orders and never break their ranks. We moved smartly.

All this time we had been breathing a disgusting mixture of sand, dust, sweat, and the stink of blood, while the thick cloud stirred by our feet made it hard to see farther than a furlong. Now I noticed a fresh ingredient in the stench, something animal but foreign, something I had never smelled in Gaul. The veteran beside me identified it at once.

'Where are those camels?' he suddenly asked. 'They say some Arabs ride camels in war, but I never heard of Parthians doing it.'

Close at hand we could hear the ugly bubbling cry of camels. A dead mule lay in my path, and I stood on it to see over the heads of the front ranks. Camels mingled with the horse-bowmen who still shot at us; mounted Parthians led them, and each of the ungainly beasts was festooned with bundles of arrows. As I watched, three horse-bowmen reached over to replenish their quivers.

'They won't run short of arrows,' I said to my companion. 'What can we do?'

'Make for the nearest walled town, and then go home to Italy,' he grunted in answer. 'We can't beat them, especially now that we have no cavalry. But they won't do us much harm unless we break.'

From that moment I accepted the fact of our defeat. Until the camels came I had not really bothered about the outcome of the battle. That was something for the high command, who fed us daily and paid us punctually; if they were rebuffed today they would find a way round tomorrow. Now I knew we had lost the war. But I still did not suspect that I myself was in any danger, in the second line of a Roman legion, one of seven Roman legions marching together.

Presently Parthian lancers, and a few horse-bowmen, began charging into our rear. Whenever this happened the whole square had to halt while the rear faced about; but they never broke in.

My leg throbbed as the wound stiffened, and at every step I felt more lame. I looked towards the centre of the square, where baggage mules were carrying wounded men. But we had very few mules, and all were heavily burdened. The setting sun

213

flayed our peeling faces, and every time I stumbled I groaned aloud in agony. There was nothing to do but keep on.

The next thing I remember is the legate Octavius riding up on a three-legged mule. He seemed quite composed. He was telling the whole army our new plan, which was to march through the night until we reached Carrhae, where there were strong walls and plenty of water. Inside the town we would be safe.

Probably I had a touch of fever. The veteran from the transport helped me over some rough patches, and then he was no longer beside me. I hope, for his sake, an arrow found his heart; that was the best ending to that nightmare march. One other incident sticks in my memory. A centurion with a broken leg lay in my path, waving his money-belt and offering all sorts of rewards to anyone who would carry him; no one had the energy even to cut his throat and take his savings. That was the first time I knew for certain that we were abandoning our wounded.

At sunset the Parthian attack ceased, though small detachments of men still hung about our flanks. I suppose they had camels carrying water-skins somewhere in the background. Our last reserve of water had been plundered by disorderly stragglers, and none reached the troops who still marched in rank. I kept my rather inglorious position in the scoend line of my cohort, which was as much as I had been ordered to do. Since Starlight had been killed in the morning I had not fought the enemy, but neither had I failed in my duty.

About dawn we staggered through the gate of Carrhae, and fell asleep in the streets before our officers could dismiss us. Townsmen and soldiers of the garrison brought us bread and wonderful skins full of water; behind closed gates, where no arrow could reach us, we slept.

For three days we loitered behind the walls of Carrhae. Though we had lost heavily in the desert we were still more than twenty thousand strong; we outnumbered the Parthians two to one. But the army was afraid.

On the second day trumpeters came round proclaiming that every man must report to his unit or be executed for desertion.

I now found it difficult to walk, though my leg was healing as well as could be expected. It seemed likely that I was the only survivor of the Gallic horse, and that therefore wherever I sat was their station; but to be on the safe side I hobbled, leaning on a stick, to general headquarters.

There I found a groom who had been servant to Publius Crassus. He advised me to report to the legate Octavius, who was in charge of the muster rolls. Two other Gauls had made their way into Carrhae, on foot; but one was since dead of wounds and fever, and the other had lost his right hand; so I was the only survivor still more or less fit for duty.

During the long march from Italy I had once or twice met Octavius at cavalry headquarters. When I limped into his office he remembered me as a friend of poor Publius, and waved me to a stool. Then he sat back and grinned sardonically.

'What can I do for you, Camillus, leader and second-in-command and rank and file of the Gallic auxiliaries? As far as I know you are the only cavalryman in the army, but I can't offer you a horse. We have only three, to mount the Imperator and the two surviving legates. Would you like your pay and discharge? Take one of those chests by the wall. You will have to carry it home by yourself. Or I can attach you to the body-guard, where we send all the odds and ends who still keep turning up.'

'That will suit me, my lord,' I answered, nettled by his sneer. 'I am a soldier by trade, and I see no reason why I should go home in the middle of a war. Also I happened to witness the gallant death of Publius Crassus. Perhaps the Imperator would like to hear the full story.'

'Excellent. The Imperator is lodged two doors away. Report to him immediately. Tell him about his son, and make sure you put in all the details of his gallantry. . . . The old skinflint may wake up and take notice. Anything would be better for him than sitting glooming at the floor,' he added savagely, half to himself.

Octavius was disillusioned, but quite accurate. The Imperator sat staring at the floor, while outside his door senior officers waited anxiously for orders. He had me in to tell my story, in which I gave a full account of the Parthian champions Publius had slain before he fell. When I had finished the Imperator got to his feet quite briskly, considering his age, and walked about the room as he talked to me. Or rather he talked, and I occasionally put in a word to remind him that he had a listener; but really he was talking to his own conscience.

'It's a check, but we can't be beaten. It's ridiculous even to think of it. Seven legions of Romans, led by the conqueror of Spartacus. I have been too lenient. Our winter quarters were too comfortable, and now the men are lazy. But they are still sound at heart. They must be; their ancestors beat Hannibal. They will be angry at this setback, and next time they will fight the harder. I've given my son, too, on the field of honour. And took the news of his death in the grand manner. We are worthy Licinians, both the living and the dead; our ancestors must be proud of us. Tomorrow we shall fight again – and win. I have done nothing disgraceful. The men were disheartened by thirst. We must try some other way. I wonder what Publius will suggest? Oh, but of course he's dead. Let me see, you Gaul – you also had a friend who gave you advice. I suppose he's dead, like my son. Wasn't there some story that the gods were angry with him?'

'My friend Acco was killed on the body of your son, my lord. It was necessary, for they were oath-bound comrades. Every Gallic warrior hopes to die gloriously in battle when it is time for him to die. I am sorry that my friend's time was so short, but in his death there is nothing for regret.'

'Nor in my son's, you mean. It's a silly waste, all the same. Had he lived, he would have ruled in Rome. Why do we get no help from the gods? The Roman People have empowered me to take the auspices as their representative. Do you think that silly cursing we got as we left Rome has harmed us?'

'We were devoted to the gods of death, my lord. So is every living man on earth. Who knows what curses have been laid on the Parthians?'

'But your Acco had a special curse of his own. Could my son have been killed just because he was his comrade?'

'No, my lord. The Goddess hunted Acco, but in the end he

216

escaped her. He was taken by the Wargod, taken to feast in the Hall of Heroes until it is time for him to be born again on earth. Or so our Druids teach. He is free of the Goddess, for ever.'

'And my son also is with the Wargod? If he is not asleep, never to waken.'

'With the Wargod, my lord, and bearing on his breast the scar of a Parthian broadsword, to prove that his wounds were in front.'

'That's comforting, if I could believe it. Well, we must all die, and an arrow can strike even a brave man in the back. How will *my* life escape my body?' He glanced down at his bulging linen corselet. 'But of course I shall come home safe, and so will my army. Tomorrow we shall march, and overcome the Parthians. This time we must keep near water. . . . There's no one I can consult. . . . If Publius were here. . . . Send in the legates. We must draw up tomorrow's orders.'

That was the first I had heard about marching tomorrow, and I think the Imperator himself only came to his decision as he spoke to me. When the news was published the troops were surprised and dismayed, for all had assumed that we would retire on the fortresses of Syria. The Imperator alone was eager for another great battle.

But march we must, for we had eaten all the food in Carrhae. The Parthians were so close that wherever we went we must fight them at the outset. Put that way, the men saw that it was as reasonable to continue the invasion as to retreat. But they were not anxious for more fighting.

Even among the bodyguard, when I joined it, I heard grumbling. The Imperator was blamed for having led us into a trap, though no one could say exactly where he had gone wrong. It was agreed that we could not plunder Seleucia until we defeated the Parthian army, and that our seven legions should make us strong enough to conquer any barbarian realm. In that case the only explanation of our defeat was that the Parthians were the better men, and no Roman could admit that.

I knew that in truth the Parthians were better, though I kept my opinion to myself. I had seen that gay young Surenas, with

217

his painted face and his curled locks, exulting at the prospect of leading his household against odds, to defend his people while their king was fighting on another frontier. Such a careless, fearless hero must prevail over grasping bloody-minded robbers who had marched into his land solely because they thought themselves strong enough to plunder it. And our leader was even more repulsive than his followers: a vain, stupid, selfish old man, with the gluttonous acquisitiveness of a hog, for all that he was also endowed with the unthinking courage of a boar. We would be beaten; I knew it. So long as there was a Roman army I must keep troth with my paymasters; so much my ancestors would demand. But if the Roman army were utterly destroyed I might justifiably look to my own safety.

Because the Imperator had frittered away three days in useless mourning for his son we marched from Carrhae without food in our wallets. We left not a loaf of bread in the place, and unless we drove off the Parthians the garrison must surrender within a few days. But the water-skins were full, and three day's march would bring us to the streams of the Armenian foothills. We would not die of thirst.

Of course we were nothing like the army which ten days ago had crossed the Euphrates. We had no baggage, and no horses; even the Imperator plodded on foot. The troops had lost confidence in themselves, and in their leader.

I carried a long staff, to which I tied my water-skin and wallet. With that to lean on I could march with the bodyguard; though I had made up my mind to do as little fighting as possible, to preserve my strength. I was placed in the third rank of the third line, as far from the enemy as a fighting-man could be; but it seemed probable that the reserves must be engaged to repulse the first Parthian charge, for the spirits of the men were very low.

I heard soldiers recalling the Accursed March, and talking old, stale Roman politics about the misdeeds of Marcus Crassus; how he thought of nothing but money, and offended respectable Senators who held by ancestral ways. They went on to regret that they had not volunteered for the Army of Gaul, where Caesar led the way to glory, or the Army of Spain, which lived in peaceful comfort. The real reason why they were in the Army of Syria was that they were not good enough for the other legions; but of course I did not say so.

Outside the city gate we formed the usual hollow square, though with no baggage in the middle because we had none. Then we set a course due north, to where the mountains of Armenia showed faintly through the heat-haze. The Imperator marched with the northern face of the square, his bodyguard round him. When we had gone two miles the Parthians closed in.

They were fewer than in the first battle, but much bolder. The horse-bowmen charged home with the sword as often as they hovered to shoot. They attacked in close order on a narrow front, and then galloped off to attack somewhere else. We could not move cohorts to counter them, for our weary supports could not be continually running from one part of the square to another. We must keep our formation at all costs, and save our energy for marching.

Naturally, the rearguard was most often attacked, for that delayed the whole army – and compelled us to abandon our wounded. The enemy gave us no quarter, continually waving trophies before us: the heads of Romans who had fallen into their hands, or other, even more depressing, bits of them. So far they had not attacked our van.

Presently Octavius ran forward to the Imperator (since we were all on foot, and on the move, officers could only consult together with great labour and difficulty). I heard him complain that we were marching too fast, and that the troops at the rear, busy repelling Parthian charges, could not keep up. The Imperator heard him crossly, poking his head as though deafer than ever; but presently he ordered a halt.

His order was not obeyed, even by the bodyguard. Every man knew that once we had reached the mountains we might dig in on a well-watered hilltop and beat off any number of Parthian charges; there were the hills in front of us, fading into the haze. As we lurched forward men began to shout curses on the money-grubbing old politician who had dragged them to

219

perish in the wilderness merely to fill his treasure-chests. Even the Imperator walked on, waving his drawn sword and cursing back at the cowards who would not defend themselves against a paltry band of light-armed horse.

At that moment Parthian lancers, on their great Nisaean horses, charged the north-west corner of the square. That made us halt, and so saved the cohorts in the rear. Leaning on my staff I watched the fighting. I was too tired to walk over and help.

After some hundreds of Romans had been killed the Parthians were beaten off. We continued our march. But now our losses grew very heavy. Men continually fell out, exhausted by thirst and fatigue, sitting on the sand to wait for death. By midday we had abandoned perhaps a third of the army.

Soon after midday the attacks ceased. The Parthians dismounted in plain view, two furlongs off; I suppose to eat their dinner. Watching them over our shoulders, we struggled on. Octavius, who still controlled the relics of the rearguard, sent another message to say we were going too fast.

The Imperator himself seized an Eagle, and planted its staff in the ground. The Eagle-bearer and a few centurions halted to guard it, and the idea of halting spread to other men nearby; this was not obedience to orders, merely that the exhausted troops were glad of a rest.

I was one of the last to sit down, for I was fearful of bending my wounded leg. Over the heads of the seated front ranks I saw a solitary Parthian, riding towards us and waving a withered branch. I called to the Imperator: 'See, my lord. The enemy seek a parley.'

'So they do,' he answered, as though not at all surprised. 'I wonder why? Perhaps they also are tired and thirsty. I may as well go and talk to them. I still lead about fifteen thousand men, and if they offer us safe passage to the Euphrates both parties should be satisfied. Pass the word for Octavius. Before I go I must speak to him.'

When we set out we had three legates. Publius had been killed before my eyes, and Vargunteius had disappeared during this last morning.

When Octavius arrived the Imperator beckoned him aside. Then he stared at his apathetic bodyguard. 'I want three volunteers, for my escort when I meet the Parthian commander. Are there no volunteers? Then I'll take you and you and you.'

I was the third man he picked out. We had not reached the stage when a single man could defy such a direct command. As I stepped over to stand beside him I tightened my swordbelt and hung my shield correctly on my arm.

With his hand on Octavius's shoulder the old Imperator tottered out of the square, Out of earshot of the ranks he spoke. I think he meant to whisper, but he was deaf and very excited; I could hear all he said.

'If they offer quarter I must accept it. There's no other way to save the lives of these worthless cowards who disgrace the name of Rome. Of course I myself shall never return to the City. But you may be able to get away, with the steadiest of the veterans. Tell them in Rome, if ever you get there, that the army was destroyed by my incompetence. Don't tell them the bitter truth. Don't let them know that I was compelled to surrender because my men were too afraid to go on fighting.'

He stumped off towards the waiting Parthian, with his escort of three at his heels. Halfway across the open space my two companions turned to scuttle back to the Roman square. I don't blame them for feeling frightened. We all felt frightened. But I was sure we would all be dead within a few hours, and I did not want my last action to be a panic-stricken flight before the eyes of thousands of warriors. I stumbled along behind my leader.

The Surenas himself rode out to meet us, with half a dozen lancers. As his great horse towered over us he reined in, and spoke pleasantly in Latin. 'You can tell your men that when they have laid down their arms their lives will be spared. But first you must hand over your own sword, here, between the armies, where all can see you.'

The Imperator, that fat old businessman, was tired and cross and very dirty. As he walked to the parley he had been weeping, and the obstinate expression that came over his tear stained face seemed that of a sulky urchin, not a grown man.

221

His hand went slowly to his sword-hilt.

Then he squared his shoulders, and drew a deep breath. His eyes snapped, and his answer sounded in the ringing tones of a warrior.

'I am Marcus Licinius Crassus, Patrician, Senator, Consular, Imperator. The Roman People have commanded me to make war on the Parthians, and I shall obey that command as long as I live. You are a Parthian. Guard yourself.'

As his sword flashed out he lunged at the Surenas, who of course was far outside his reach. Then a lance ripped into his belly and his guts fell out in great coils. I was hampered by having to get rid of my staff before I could reach for my sword; it was not yet free of the scabbard when the Nisaean charger shouldered into me and sent me sprawling. The young hero loomed above me, reining his horse that strove to trample my ribs.

'You are no Roman,' he said from his great height. 'You followed your leader to the end, after your comrades had forsaken him. If you still wish to live, you may. But first you must hand over that sword.'

I handed it over, and with it my freedom. Life goes on.

That afternoon the Parthians killed the Army of Syria, though Octavius got away with a handful of resolute swordsmen, and a lucky thousand or so were spared. Some of them are here in the Sea of Grass. Occasionally we talk over the campaign, but not very often. The subject depresses us.

At least I am safe from the Goddess, who can have no place in this masculine world of horses and bloodshed. Acco is safe from her also; the sand of the desert will have given him burial, if men did not. But in Pyrene the Goddess still reigns unchecked. I may be better off than you would suppose.

NEL BESTSELLERS

Crime

T017 648	HAVE HIS CARCASE	*Dorothy L. Sayers*	60p
T020 983	UNNATURAL DEATH	*Dorothy L. Sayers*	45p
T017 095	LORD PETER VIEWS THE BODY	*Dorothy L. Sayers*	50p
T019 608	HANGMANS HOLIDAY	*Dorothy L. Sayers*	40p
T021 548	GAUDY NIGHT	*Dorothy L. Sayers*	60p
T019 799	THE NINE TAILORS	*Dorothy L. Sayers*	40p
T012 484	FIVE RED HERRINGS	*Dorothy L. Sayers*	40p

Fiction

T017 087	BEYOND THIS PLACE	*A. J. Cronin*	50p
T018 539	A SONG OF SIXPENCE	*A. J. Cronin*	50p
T018 202	THE GREEN YEARS	*A. J. Cronin*	50p
T016 544	THE CITADEL	*A. J. Cronin*	75p
T016 919	THE SPANISH GARDENER	*A. J. Cronin*	40p
T020 967	BISHOP IN CHECK	*Adam Hall*	35p
T015 467	PAWN IN JEOPARDY	*Adam Hall*	30p
T021 270	THE RATS	*James Herbert*	40p
T018 156	SAMSON DUKE	*Seymour Kern*	40p
T017 737	COLOSSUS	*Stephen Marlowe*	90p
T019 152	A PORTION FOR FOXES	*Jane McIlvaine McClary*	75p
T015 130	THE MONEY MAKER	*John J. McNamara Jr.*	50p
T014 932	YOU NICE BASTARD	*G. F. Newman*	50p
T022 536	THE HARRAD EXPERIMENT	*Robert H. Rimmer*	50p
T019 381	THE DREAM MERCHANTS	*Harold Robbins*	90p
T022 986	THE CARPETBAGGERS	*Harold Robbins*	£1
T016 560	WHERE LOVE HAS GONE	*Harold Robbins*	75p
T019 829	THE ADVENTURERS	*Harold Robbins*	95p
T020 215	THE INHERITORS	*Harold Robbins*	80p
T020 347	STILETTO	*Harold Robbins.*	40p
T015 289	NEVER LEAVE ME	*Harold Robbins*	40p
T020 339	NEVER LOVE A STRANGER	*Harold Robbins*	80p
T011 798	A STONE FOR DANNY FISHER	*Harold Robbins*	60p
T015 874	79 PARK AVENUE	*Harold Robbins*	60p
T011 461	THE BETSY	*Harold Robbins*	75p
T020 894	RICH MAN, POOR MAN	*Irwin Shaw*	90p
T018 148	THE PLOT	*Irving Wallace*	90p
T020 436	THE NAKED COUNTRY	*Morris West*	30p

Historical

T018 229	THE CUNNING OF THE DOVE	*Alfred Duggan*	50p
T017 958	FOUNDLING FATHERS	*Alfred Duggan*	50p
T010 279	MASK OF APOLLO	*Mary Renault*	50p
T015 580	THE CHARIOTEER	*Mary Renault*	50p
T019 055	BURKE AND HARE – THE TRUE STORY	*Hugh Douglas*	40p
T020 169	FOX 9. CUT AND THRUST	*Adam Hardy*	30p
T017 044	SWORD OF VENGEANCE	*Alexander Karol*	30p

Science Fiction

T014 576	THE INTERPRETER	*Brian Aldiss*	30p
T015 017	EQUATOR	*Brian Aldiss*	30p
T014 347	SPACE RANGER	*Isaac Asimov*	30p
T015 491	PIRATES OF THE ASTEROIDS	*Isaac Asimov*	30p
T019 780	THROUGH A GLASS CLEARLY	*Isaac Asimov*	30p
T020 673	MOONS OF JUPITER	*Isaac Asimov*	35p

T011 631	MASTER MIND OF MARS	*Edgar Rice Burroughs*	30p
T015 564	LOST ON VENUS	*Edgar Rice Burroughs*	35p
T010 333	REVOLT IN 2100	*Robert Heinlein*	40p
T021 602	THE MAN WHO SOLD THE MOON	*Robert Heinlein*	40p
T016 900	STRANGER IN A STRANGE LAND	*Robert Heinlein*	75p
T022 862	DUNE	*Frank Herbert*	80p
T012 298	DUNE MESSIAH	*Frank Herbert*	40p
T015 211	THE GREEN BRAIN	*Frank Herbert*	30p

War

T013 367	DEVIL'S GUARD	*Robert Elford*	50p
T020 584	THE GOOD SHEPHERD	*C. S. Forester*	40p
T011 755	TRAWLERS GO TO WAR	*Lund & Ludlam*	40p
T012 999	P.Q.17 – CONVOY TO HELL	*Lund & Ludlam*	30p
T014 215	THE GIANT KILLERS	*Kenneth Poolman*	40p
T022 528	THE LAST VOYAGE OF GRAF SPEE	*Michael Powell*	35p

Western

T016 994	No. 1 EDGE – THE LONER	*George G. Gilman*	30p
T016 986	No. 2 EDGE – TEN THOUSAND DOLLAR AMERICAN	*George G. Gilman*	30p
T017 613	No. 3 EDGE – APACHE DEATH	*George G. Gilman*	30p
T017 001	No. 4 EDGE – KILLER'S BREED	*George G. Gilman*	30p
T016 536	No. 5 EDGE – BLOOD ON SILVER	*George G. Gilman*	30p
T017 621	No. 6 EDGE – THE BLUE, THE GREY AND THE RED	*George G. Gilman*	30p
T014 479	No. 7 EDGE – CALIFORNIA KILLING	*George G. Gilman*	30p
T015 254	No. 8 EDGE – SEVEN OUT OF HELL	*George G. Gilman*	30p
T015 475	No. 9 EDGE – BLOODY SUMMER	*George G. Gilman*	30p
T015 769	No. 10 EDGE – VENGEANCE IS BLACK	*George G. Gilman*	30p
T017 184	No. 11 EDGE – SIOUX UPRISING	*George G. Gilman*	30p
T017 893	No. 12 EDGE – THE BIGGEST BOUNTY	*George G. Gilman*	30p
T018 253	No. 13 EDGE – A TOWN CALLED HATE	*George G. Gilman*	30p
T020 754	No. 14 EDGE – THE BIG GOLD	*George G. Gilman*	30p

General

T021 009	SEX MANNERS FOR MEN	*Robert Chartham*	35p
T019 403	SEX MANNERS FOR ADVANCED LOVERS	*Robert Chartham*	30p
W002 835	SEX AND THE OVER FORTIES	*Robert Chartham*	30p
T010 732	THE SENSUOUS COUPLE	*Dr. 'C'*	25p

Mad

S004 892	MAD MORALITY	40p
S005 172	MY FRIEND GOD	40p
S005 069	MAD FOR BETTER OR VERSE	30p

NEL, P.O. BOX 11, FALMOUTH, TR10 9EN, CORNWALL

Please send cheque or postal order. Allow 10p to cover postage and packing on one book plus 5p for each additional book.

Name ....

Address..

....

Title ....
(NOVEMBER)